THE
LAMPLIGHTERS

✶

THE
LAMPLIGHTERS

✶

EMMA STONEX

VIKING

VIKING
An imprint of Penguin Random House LLC
penguinrandomhouse.com

First published in hardcover in Great Britain by Picador,
an imprint of Pan Macmillan, London, in 2021.
First United States edition published by Viking, 2021.

Library of Congress Cataloging-in-Publication Data

Names: Stonex, Emma, 1983– author.
Title: The lamplighters / Emma Stonex.
Description: New York : Viking, [2021]
Identifiers: LCCN 2020040708 (print) | LCCN 2020040709 (ebook) |
ISBN 9781984882158 (hardcover) | ISBN 9781984882165 (ebook)
Subjects: GSAFD: Suspense fiction.
Classification: LCC PR6119.T6845 L36 2021 (print) | LCC PR6119.T6845 (ebook) |
DDC 823/.92—dc23
LC record available at https://lccn.loc.gov/2020040708
LC ebook record available at https://lccn.loc.gov/2020040709

Printed in the United States of America
1   3   5   7   9   10   8   6   4   2

DESIGNED BY MEIGHAN CAVANAUGH

This is a work of fiction based on actual events.

For IFTS and KMS

We stood a moment still tongue-tied,
And each with black foreboding eyed
The door ere we should fling it wide
To leave the sunlight for the gloom . . .

—Wilfrid Wilson Gibson, "Flannan Isle"

Two different men; I've been two men so long now.

—Tony Parker, *Lighthouse*

AUTHOR'S NOTE

In December 1900, three lighthouse keepers disappeared from a remote rock light on the island of Eilean Mòr in the Outer Hebrides. Their names were Thomas Marshall, James Ducat, and Donald Mac-Arthur. *The Lamplighters* is inspired by, and written in respectful memory of, this event, but is a work of fiction and therefore bears no resemblance to these men's lives or their characters.

I

·

1972

1

RELIEF

When Jory opens the curtains, the day is light and gray, the radio playing a half-known song. He listens to the news, about a girl who's gone missing from a bus stop up north, and drinks from a mug of brown tea. Poor mother's beside herself—well, she would be. Short hair, short skirt, big eyes, that's how he pictures the girl, shivering in the cold, and an empty bus stop where someone should have stood, waving or drowning, and the bus pulls up and away, never the wiser, and the pavement shines on in the black rain.

The sea is quiet, with the glass-like quality that comes after bad weather. Jory unlatches the window and the fresh air is very nearly solid, an edible thing, clinking between the trawler cottages like an ice cube in a drink. There's nothing like the smell of the sea, nothing close: briny, clean, like vinegar kept in the fridge. Today it's soundless. Jory knows loud seas and silent seas, heaving seas and mirror seas, seas where your boat feels like the last blink of humankind on a roll so determined and angry that you believe in what you don't believe in, such as the sea being that halfway thing between heaven and hell, or whatever lies up there and whatever lurks down deep. A fisherman told him once about the sea having two faces. You have to take the both, he said, the good and the bad, and never turn your back on either one of them.

Today, after a long time, the sea is on their side. They'll do it today.

✶

He's in charge of whether the boat goes out there or not. Even if the wind's good at nine it doesn't mean it'll be good by ten, and whatever he's got in the harbor, say he's got four-feet-high waves in the harbor, he can guess they'll be forty feet round the tower. Whatever it is ashore, it'll be ten times as much round the light.

The new delivery is twentyish, with yellow hair and thick glasses. They make his eyes look small, twitchy; he reminds Jory of something kept in a cage, living in sawdust. He's standing there on the jetty in his cord bell-bottoms, frayed ends darkened by the slopping sea. Early morning it's quiet on the quay, a dog walker and a milk crate unloading. The frigid pause between Christmas and New Year.

Jory and his crew haul in the boy's supplies, Trident red cartons containing two months' clothes and food, fresh meat, fruit, proper milk not powdered, a newspaper, box of tea, Golden Virginia, and rope them down, covering the containers in tarpaulin. The keepers will be pleased: they'll have been on tinned stew the past four weeks and whatever was on the *Mail*'s front page the day the last relief went out.

In the shallows, the water burps seaweed, slurping and sucking round the sides of the boat. The boy climbs in, his plimsolls wet, groping the sides like a blind man. Under one arm he carries a parcel of belongings tied up with string—books, cassette recorder, tapes, whatever he'll use to pass the time. He's a student, most likely: Trident gets a lot of students these days. He'll be writing music, that'll be his thing. Up in the lantern thinking this is the life. They all need an activity to do, especially on the towers—can't spend your whole time running up and down the stairs. Jory knew a keeper way back when, a fine craftsman who put ships in bottles; he'd spend his whole stay doing them and they were beautiful things by the end of it. And then they got televisions put in and this keeper threw it all away, literally chucked his whole kit out the window into the sea and from then on sat watching the box every free moment he got.

"Have you been doing this long?" the boy asks. Jory says yeah, longer than you've been alive. "Didn't think we'd make it," he says. "I've been waiting since Tuesday. They put me in digs in the village and very nice it was too, but not so nice as I'd want to stay there much longer. Every day I was looking out and thinking, Will we ever get off? Talk about a bloody storm. Have to say I don't know how it'll be out there when we get another. They told me you've never seen a storm till you've seen it from the sea, and it feels like the tower's going to collapse right from underneath you and wash away."

The new ones always want to talk. It's nerves, Jory thinks, about the crossing and if the wind might change, about the landing, about the men on the light, whether he'll fit in with them, what the one in charge is like. It isn't this boy's light yet; probably it won't ever be. Supernumeraries come and go, land light this time, rock the next, shuttled round the country like a pinball. Jory's seen scores of them, keen to start and taken up in the romantic bit of it, but it isn't as romantic as that. Three men alone on a lighthouse in the middle of the sea. There's nothing special about it, nothing at all, just three men and a lot of water. It takes a certain sort to withstand being locked up. Loneliness. Isolation. Monotony. Nothing for miles except sea and sea and sea. No friends. No women. Just the other two, day in, day out, unable to get away from them, it could drive you stark mad.

It's usual to wait days for the changeover, weeks even. Once he had a keeper stuck out there on a lost relief for four months straight.

"You'll get used to the weather," he says to the boy.

"I hope so."

"And you won't be half as ticked off as the poor sod who's due ashore."

In a bevy at the stern his relief crew look despondently out to sea, smoking and grunting conversation, their damp fingers soaking their cigarettes. They could be painted into a dour seascape, brushed roughly with thick oils. "What're we waiting for?" one of them shouts. "D'you want the tide to turn before we're off?" They've got the engineer with them too, out to fix the radio. Normally, on relief day, they'd have been in touch with the light five times already, but the storm took out the transmission.

Jory covers the last of the boxes and starts the motor and then they're away, the boat rocking and bobbing like a bath toy over the wavelets. A flock of gulls quarrel on a cockle-speckled rock; a blue trawler chugs idly into land. As the shoreline dwindles the water grows brisker, green waves leaping, crests that spume and dissolve. Farther out the colors bleed darkly, the sea turning to khaki and the sky to ominous slate. Water butts and slops against the prow; strings of sea foam surge and disperse. Jory chews a roll-up that's been flattened in his pocket but is still just about smokable, eyes on the horizon, smoke in his mouth. His ears ache in the cold. Overhead a white bird wheels in a vast, drab sky.

He can decipher the Maiden in the haze, a lone spike, dignified, remote. She's fifteen nautical miles out. Keepers prefer that, he knows, not to be so close to land that you can see it from the set-off and be reminded of home.

The boy sits with his back to her—a funny way to start, Jory thinks, with your back to the thing you're going to. He worries at a scratch on his thumb. His face looks soft and ill, uninitiated. But every seaman has to find his legs.

"You been on a tower before, sonny?"

"I was out at Trevose. Then down at Saint Catherine's."

"But never a tower."

"No, never a tower."

"Got to have the stomach for it," says Jory. "Have to get along with people too, no matter what they're like."

"Oh, I'll be fine about that."

" 'Course you will. Your PK's a good sort, that makes a difference."

"What about the others?"

"Was told to watch out for the Super. But being your age roughly, no doubt you'll get along fine."

"What about him?"

Jory smiles at the boy's expression. "No need to look like that. Service is full of stories, not all of them true."

The sea heaves and churns beneath them, blackly rolling, slapping, and slinging; the breeze backs up, skittering across the water, making it pimple and scatter. A buffet of spray explodes at the bow and the waves grow heavy and secretively deep. When Jory was a boy and they used to catch the boat from Lymington to Yarmouth, he would peer over the railings on deck and marvel at how the sea did this quietly, without you really noticing, how the shelf dropped and the land was lost, where if you fell in, it would be a hundred feet down. There would be garfish and smooth hounds: weird, bloated, glimmering shapes with soft, exploring tentacles and eyes like cloudy marbles.

The lighthouse draws near, a line becoming a post, a post becoming a finger.

"There she is. The Maiden Rock."

By now they can see the sea stain around her base, the scar of violent weather accumulated by decades of rule. Though he's done it many times, getting close to the Queen of the Lighthouses always makes Jory feel a certain way—scolded, insignificant, maybe slightly afraid. A fifty-meter column of heroic Victorian engineering, the Maiden looms palely magnificent against the horizon, a stoic bastion of seafarers' safety.

"She was one of the first," says Jory. "Eighteen ninety-three. Twice wrecked before they finally lit her wick. The saying goes she makes a sound when the weather hits hard, like a woman crying, where the wind gets in between the rocks."

Details creep out of the gray—the lighthouse windows, the concrete ring of the set-off, and the narrow trail of iron rungs leading up to the access door, known as the dog steps. The Maiden stands above the boy's shoulder, summoning.

"Can they see us?"

"By now."

But as Jory says it, he's searching for the figure he'd expect to see waiting down there on the set-off, the Principal Keeper in his navy uniform and peaked white cap or the Assistant waving them in. They'll have been watching the water since sunrise.

He eyes the cauldron around the base of the lighthouse with caution, deciding the best approach, if he'll put the boat ahead or astern, if he'll anchor her down or let her stay loose. Freezing water splurges across a sunken warren of rocks; when the sea fills up, the rocks disappear; when it drops, they emerge like black, glistening molars. Of all the towers it's the Bishop, the Wolf, and the Maiden that are hardest to land, and if he had to pick, he'd say the Maiden took it. Sailors' legend had it she was built on the jaws of a fossilized sea monster. Dozens died in her construction, and the reef has killed many an off-course mariner. She doesn't like outsiders; she doesn't welcome people.

But he's still waiting to see a keeper or two. They're not getting this boy away unless there's someone on the end of the landing gear. At that point with the drop and surge he'll be ten feet down one minute and ten up the next, and if he loses sight of it, his rope's snapping and his man's taking a cold bath. It's a hairy business, but that's the towers all over. To a land man the sea is a constant enough thing, but Jory knows it isn't constant: it's fickle and unpredictable, and it'll get you if you let it.

"Where are they?"

He hardly hears his mate's yell against the gush of water.

Jory signals they'll go around. The boy looks green. The engineer too. Jory ought to reassure them, but he isn't quite reassured himself. In all the years he's come to the Maiden, he's never taken the boat around the back of the tower.

The scale of the lighthouse rears up at them, sheer granite. Jory cranes his head to the entrance door, sixty feet above water, solid gunmetal and defiantly closed.

His crew holler; they call for the keepers and blow a shrill whistle. Farther up, higher still, the tower tapers into the sky, and the sky, in return, glances down at their little vessel, thrown about in confusion. There's that bird again, the one that followed them out. Wheeling,

wheeling, calling a message they don't understand. The boy leans over the side of the boat and loses his breakfast to the sea.

They rise, they fall; they wait and wait.

Jory looks up at the tower, hulked out of its own shadow, and all he can hear are the waves, the crash and spit of foam, the slurp and wash of the rocks, and all he can think of is the missing girl on the radio that he heard about that morning, and the bus stop, the empty bus stop, and the driving, relentless rain.

2

STRANGE AFFAIR AT A LIGHTHOUSE

The Times, Sunday, December 31, 1972

Trident House has been informed of the disappearance of three of its keepers from the Maiden Rock Lighthouse, fifteen miles southwest of Land's End. The men have been named as Principal Keeper Arthur Black, Assistant Keeper William "Bill" Walker, and Supernumerary Assistant Keeper Vincent Bourne. The discovery was made by a local boatman and his crew yesterday morning when attempting to deliver a relieving keeper and bring Mr. Walker to shore.

As yet there is no indication of the missing men's whereabouts and no official statement has been made. An investigation has begun.

NINE FLOORS

The landing takes hours. A dozen men scale the dog steps with a taste on their tongues like salt and fear, their ears raw and their hands bloody and frozen.

When they reach the door, it is locked from the inside. A slab of steel built to resist crashing seas and hurricane winds must now be broken by brawn and bars.

Afterward, one of the men gets the shakes, the bad white shakes, which is partly exhaustion and partly the worm of disquiet that has clung to him since Jory Martin's relief boat went unmet, since Trident House told them, "Get out there."

Three of them enter the tower. Inside, it is dark, and there is a musty, lived-in smell, symptomatic of the sea stations with their battened-shut windows. There's not a lot to see in the storeroom; bulky shapes masked by the gloom, coils of rope, a life belt, a dinghy suspended upside down. Nothing is disturbed.

The keepers' oilskins hang in the shadows like hooked fish. Their names are called through a manhole in the ceiling, sent spiraling up the staircase:

Arthur. Bill. Vincent . . . Vince, are you there? . . . Bill?

It's eerie how their living voices cut through silence, the silence robust, indecently loud. The men don't expect a response. Trident told them this was search and rescue, but it is a mission for bodies. Any thoughts they had about the keepers escaping are gone. The door was locked. They're here, somewhere, inside.

Bring them off quietly, Trident said. Do it discreetly. Find a boatman who'll keep it under his cap; don't make a fuss; don't make a scene; nobody needs to know. And make sure the light's all right, for God's sake somebody make sure about that.

Three men climb, one after another. The wall on the next level is lined with detonators and charges for the fog gun. There is no sign of a struggle. Each man thinks of his home, his wife, his children if he has any, the warmth of the fire, and a touch at his back: "Long day, love?" The tower isn't a place that knows families. It knows three keepers only: three keepers who are concealed here somewhere, dead. Where will they find the bodies? What state will those bodies be in?

They ascend to the third floor, to the paraffin tanks, then the fourth, where the oil for the burner is kept. One calls again, as much to ward off that taunting quiet as for any other reason. There is no indication of a getaway, no sign of flight, nothing to suggest the keepers have gone anywhere at all.

From the oil store, they mount the staircase, a cast-iron coil that runs around the inner wall all the way up to the lantern. Its banister gleams. They're an abnormal breed, lighthouse keepers, obsessed by the intricacies of domestic detail, polishing, tidying, buffing; a lighthouse is the cleanest place you'll ever set foot. The men check the brass for prints and find none: keepers never touch the rails on account of this diligence. Though if one had been in a hurry, if one had fallen or grasped, if one had forgotten himself due to a terrible thing . . . But nothing is out of the ordinary.

The men's tread sounds the death drum, dogged and deep. Already they long for the safety of the tug and the promise of land.

To the kitchen they come. Twelve feet across and a socking weight tube set down the middle. Three cupboards are mounted on the wall, inside which are tins of food, precisely stacked: baked beans, broad beans, rice, soup, OXO cubes, luncheon meat, corned beef, pickles. On the counter sits an unopened jar of frankfurters, tightly packed like tissue in a science lab. By the window there's a sink, red tap for rainwater, silver for fresh, and a washing-up bowl left to dry on its side. A wizened onion remains in the cavity between the inner and outer walls, on the racks the keepers use as a larder. Over the sink hangs a mirrored cabinet that doubles as their bathroom: the men find toothbrushes, combs, a bottle of Old Spice, and one of Tabac. Next to that a dresser containing cutlery, plates, and cups, everything organized and put away with the expected level of care. The clock on the wall has stopped at eight forty-five.

"What's this——?" says the man with the mustache.

The table is laid for a meal uneaten. Two places, not three—a knife and fork each, a plate waiting for food. Two empty cups. Salt and pepper. A tube of mustard and an ashtray, cleaned. The counter is Formica, a half-moon, and fits snugly round the weight tube; there's a bench tucked under and two chairs, one with the foam spilling out and the other positioned askew as if the person sitting in it had risen quickly.

Another man, the one with the comb-over, checks the Rayburn in case there's something warming, but the temperature's fallen and anyway it's empty. Through the window they can hear the sea, sighing against the rocks below.

"I have no idea," he says, and it is less an answer than an admission of general, fearful ignorance.

The men glance to the ceiling.

Nowhere to hide on a lighthouse, that's the thing. In every room from bottom to top, it's two strides to the weight tube and two to the other side.

Up they go to the bedroom. Three banana bunks curved round the shape of the wall, each with its curtain open. The beds are fastidiously made, with sheets drawn tight, pillows and camel-colored blankets scratchy to the touch. Above are two shorter bunks for visitors and a ladder for climbing. Under the stairs, a storage hollow with its curtain pulled. The comb-over draws it, breath held, but all he finds is a cowhide jacket and two hanging shirts.

Seven floors up and they're a hundred feet above sea level. In the living room there's a television set and three worn Ercol armchairs. On the floor by the biggest, they're guessing it's the Principal Keeper's, is a cup with an inch of cold tea in the bottom. Behind the tube is the flue coming up from downstairs. Perhaps the PK could come down to them now; he's been up in the lantern cleaning the mantle. The others are there too, out on the gallery. Sorry they didn't hear.

The wall clock here reads the same, stopped time. Quarter to nine.

Double doors access the service room on the eighth. Feasibly, the dead men could have been here—the cavity would have stopped the smell escaping. But, as they have come to expect, it is deserted. They are running out of tower. Only the light left. Nine floors found and nine floors empty. Up to the top and there she is, the Maiden lantern, a giant gas mantle encased by lenses fragile as birds' wings.

"That's it. They're gone."

Feathery clouds advance on the horizon. The breeze freshens, switching direction, flicking ridges of white onto the jumping waves. It's as if those keepers were never here in the first place. That, or they climbed to the top and simply flew away.

II

·

1992

4

THE RIDDLE

Independent, Monday, May 4, 1992

AUTHOR PLOTS TO SOLVE
MAIDEN ROCK MYSTERY

Adventure novelist Dan Sharp is out to discover the truth behind one of the greatest maritime mysteries of our age. Sharp, the author of naval action bestsellers *Eye of the Storm*, *Quiet Water*, and *Dreadnought Down*, grew up by the sea and has long been inspired by the unsolved vanishing. Diving into factual writing for the first time, he explains: "The story of the Maiden Rock has captivated me since my childhood. I want to shed new light on the matter by speaking to the people at the heart of it."

Twenty years ago, in the winter of 1972, three lighthouse keepers disappeared from a Cornish sea tower, miles from Land's End. In their wake, they left behind a series of clues: an entrance door locked from the inside, two clocks stopped at the same time, and a table laid for a meal uneaten. The Principal Keeper's weather log described a storm circling the tower—but the skies, inexplicably, had been clear.

What strange fate befell these doomed men? Sharp intends to find out. He adds: "This riddle has everything a fiction writer looks for—drama, mystery, peril on the seas. Only it's real. I believe every puzzle can be solved: it's a question of looking in the right places. For my money, someone out there knows more than we realize."

5

HELEN

So this is it, she thought as she watched him park his car a little way down the street, a Morris Minor in racing green with its exhaust hanging off the back like a cocked tobacco pipe. Helen wondered why he drove such a thing. He must be rich, if the claims on his books were to be believed: number one bestselling author and all that.

She spotted him immediately, even though he hadn't given her a description over the telephone. Perhaps she should have asked for one, because you couldn't be too careful about letting strangers into your home. It had to be him, though. He wore a navy-blue peacoat and a fixed, scholarly frown, as if he spent hours hunched over manuscripts that never quite gave him the time of day. He was younger than she had imagined, not yet forty.

"Get off," Helen said absentmindedly, the dog's whiskers brushing her palm. "I'll take you out after." She would go up to the woods, walk her in the dank, wet mulch. It calmed her to think about that: that there would be an after.

The writer carried a canvas bag, which she pictured full of receipts and cigarette lighters; she could see him living in a house with the beds unmade and cats asleep on the counters. He'd have had Weet-abix for breakfast, something that came out of a torn box, but he'd run out of milk so a squirt of water from the tap. A fag while he thought about the Maiden Rock and scribbled down the questions he wanted to ask.

All these years later, she still did it. Made an assessment on sight, before any of the rest, the yardstick against which she held every new person. Had they lost someone, as she had? Did they understand what that felt like? Were they on her side of the window or the other, im-possibly distant one? She didn't suppose it mattered if he had or he hadn't: he was a writer; he could imagine it.

Though on that point Helen was skeptical: his ability to imagine what could not be imagined. She thought of it as falling. Weightless. Disbelieving. Waiting to be caught but nobody ever did, for years and years and on it went and down she fell and there were no resolutions, no clarity or closure. That had become a fashionable word these days—*closure*—for people whose relationships failed or who got fired from their jobs, and she thought how those were relatively straight-forward things to move on from; they didn't push you over the ledge and let you drop. So it was to lose a person to the wind. No trace, no reason, no clue. What could Dan Sharp, whose game was battleships and weaponry and men who drank themselves dumb in the dock-yards, imagine of that?

She yearned to reciprocate with others of her kind: to identify them and be identified in return. She would be able to tell their loss in their faces, not an obvious thing, some bitterness or resignation, those ghouls she had tried for so long to throw off. She'd say, "You know, don't you: *you know*," and it was anyone's guess what they'd offer in return, but if there wasn't that to come of it, some upside in the matter of kindness and understanding, then what was it for?

In the meantime, the ghouls continued to slip between her clothes in the wardrobe, making her shiver when she got dressed in the morning, or she discovered them crouching in corners, picking the skin off their thumbs. She had no certainty, said the therapists (it was awhile since she had visited them), and certainty was at least a millimeter one could get one's nails around.

Here he was, then, opening the gate. He fumbled closing it behind him because the latch was rusted. "Scarborough Fair" played on the kitchen radio; it made Helen woozy, the melancholy of it, all that about sea foam and cambric shirts and true love sourer than sweet. Wild thoughts entered her head, from time to time, about Arthur and the others, but on the whole, she'd learned to keep them at bay. What secrets a lighthouse could tell. The men's were buried underwater, like hers.

Helen remembered her husband in pieces, parched scales that blew about like leaves coming in through the kitchen door. Sometimes she would catch hold of one and be able to look at it properly, but mostly she watched those leaves blowing about her ankles and wondered how on earth she'd find the energy to sweep them up.

Nothing changed, in the aftermath of loss. Songs kept getting written. Books kept getting read. Wars didn't stop. You saw a couple arguing by the trolleys at Tesco before getting in the car and slamming the door. Life renewed itself, over and over, without sympathy. Time surged on in its usual rhythms, those comings and goings, beginnings and ends, sensible progressions that fixed things in place, without a thought to the whistling in the woods on the outskirts of town. It began as a whistle, expelled from dry lips. Over the years it sharpened to a bright, continual note.

That note sounded now, with the ringing of the doorbell. Helen put her hands in the pockets of her cardigan and rolled the lint between her fingers. She liked how it felt, rolling it there right under her nail, a painful thing that wasn't quite painful.

6

HELEN

Come in. Do come in. I'm sorry it's a mess. It's kind of you to say it isn't, but really it is. Can I make you tea, coffee? Tea, lovely—milk and sugar? Of course, everyone has milk and sugar these days. My grandma used to take hers black with a slice of lemon; they don't do that much anymore. Cake? I'm afraid it isn't homemade.

So, you're an author, how fascinating. I've never met an author before. It's one of those things everyone says they could do, isn't it, writing a book. I did think about it myself but I'm not a writer—I can think of what I want to write but it's difficult to get that across to other people and I suppose that's the difference. After Arthur died everybody said it would be a good thing, to put my feelings down on paper so they were out of my head. You must believe that, in being creative yourself, to have something creative to do makes you feel like a more rounded person? Anyway, I never did write anything. I'm not sure what I would have written that I'd want a stranger to read.

Twenty years, my goodness, it's hard to believe. May I ask why it is you've chosen our story? If you're hoping my husband's like the macho men in your books and I'm going to give you a tale about missions and shipwrecks or whatever it is, you'll have to think again.

Yes, it's intriguing, if you believe the hearsay. For me, being on the inside, and being so close to it, I don't think of it like that; but you shouldn't feel bad about that, no, you shouldn't. I'm fine to talk about Arthur; it keeps him with me that way. If I tried to pretend it hadn't happened, I'd have hit trouble a long time ago. You have to admit what happens in your life.

I've heard it all, over the years. Arthur was abducted by aliens. He was murdered by pirates. He was blackmailed by smugglers. He killed the others, or they killed him, and then each other and then themselves—over a woman or a debt, or a washed-up treasure chest. They were haunted by ghosts or kidnapped by the government. Threatened by spies or gobbled by sea serpents. They went lunatic, one or all of them. They had secret lives no one knew about, riches buried on South American plantations you could only find by a cross on a map. They sailed off to Timbuktu and liked it so much they never came back. . . . When that Lord Lucan disappeared two years down the line, there were those who said he'd gone to meet Arthur and the others on a desert island, presumably with the poor beggars who flew through the Bermuda Triangle. I mean, honestly! I'm sure you'd prefer that, but I'm afraid it's all ridiculous. We're not in your world now, we're in mine; and this isn't a thriller, it's my life.

Is five minutes OK? As in the minutes of a clock, if you think of the cake as a clock, that's how big the piece is I'm cutting. Pass your plate, then; there we go. I must say I've never got the hang of baking. It seems the thing for women, though I don't know why. Arthur was better at these things than me. Did you know they learned to bake bread as part of their training? You learn all sorts being a lighthouse keeper.

Of all the towers, I think the Bishop has the best name. It sounds very stately to me. It makes me think of that chess piece, quiet and dignified. Arthur was extremely good at chess; I never played him on that account because we both like to win, and I wasn't used to ceding to him or him to me. As a keeper he had to be enthusiastic about cards and games because there's so much time to spare. It's a bonding thing as well, a game of cribbage or a hand of gin rummy. And the tea! If a keeper's skilled at any one thing, it's drinking tea. They'd get through thirty cups a day. On a lot of stations, the only rule was, if you're in the kitchen, you make the tea.

Lighthouse people are ordinary. You'll find that out and I hope it doesn't disappoint you. People on the outside think of it as a clandestine sort of occupation, seeing as we're quite closed off in the way we lead our lives. They think being married to a lighthouse keeper must be glamorous, because of the mystery of it, but it isn't. If I had to sum it up, I'd say you've got to be prepared for long periods of time apart and short, intense periods of time together. The intense periods are like a couple of distant friends reuniting, which can be exciting but challenging as well. You've had things your way for eight weeks and then a man comes into your home and suddenly he's the master of the house and you have to play second fiddle. It could be very unsettling. It's not a conventional marriage. Ours certainly wasn't.

Do I miss the sea? No, not at all. I couldn't wait to move away from it after what happened. That's why I came here, to the city. I never cared for the sea. Where we used to live in keepers' cottages we were surrounded, it was all you could see from the windows, everywhere you turned. Sometimes you felt you could be living in a fishbowl. When there was a storm and we got some lightning that was quite spectacular, and the sunsets were pretty too, but on the whole it's a gray thing, the sea, big and gray and not much happens on it. Although it's more green than gray, I would say, like sage, or eau de Nil. Did you know that "eau de Nil" means "water of the Nile"? I always thought it meant "water of Nothing," which is how the sea makes me feel, in a way, so I still think of it like that. Water of Nothing.

It doesn't make any more sense to me this morning than on the day Arthur disappeared. It does get easier, though. Time gives you a bit of distance where you can look back at whatever's happened to you and not feel all the feelings you once had; those feelings have calmed down and they're not at the forefront of your mind in the way they are at the beginning. It's odd because on some days it doesn't seem so strange, what they found on that tower—and I think, well, a heavy sea must have washed up and drowned them. Then on others it strikes me as so outlandish that it takes my breath away. There are too many details I can't shake off, like the locked door and the stopped clocks, they nag at me, and if I start thinking about it at night, I have to be strict with myself and get rid of those thoughts. Otherwise I'd never sleep, and I'll remember the view of the sea from our cottage window, and it seems so huge and empty and uncaring that I have to turn the radio on for company.

I think what transpired is what I just told you: that the sea came up suddenly and caught them unaware. Occam's razor, it's called. The law that says the simplest solution is usually right. If you've got a mystery, don't go complicating it beyond the sum of its parts.

Arthur drowning is the only realistic explanation there is. If you don't agree, then you're making your way down all sorts of fanciful roads such as ghostly things and conspiracy theories and all the nonsense I just told you people believe. People will believe anything, and given the choice they prefer lies to the truth because lies are usually more interesting. Like I said, the sea isn't interesting, not when you're looking at it every day. But it was the sea that took them. There isn't a doubt in my mind.

The thing you need to know about a tower lighthouse—have you ever been on a tower?—is that it comes directly up out of the sea. It's not a rock station where you're on an island and there's a bit of land around you where you can walk or have a vegetable plot or keep some sheep or whatever it is you want to do; and it's not a land light, where you're on the mainland so you stay close to your family, and when you're not on duty you can drive into the village and go about your life as normal so long as you're fulfilling your responsibilities when your watch comes about. A tower light's just stuck out there in the sea, so there isn't anywhere for the keepers to be except inside the lighthouse or out on the set-off. You could go running around the set-off if you wanted some exercise, but you'd get dizzy very fast doing that.

Oh, right, sorry: the set-off's the platform underneath the entrance door, it wraps all the way round like a big doughnut. The set-off's about twenty or thirty feet above the water, which sounds like a lot, but if you're out there and a wave comes up and catches you, then you're gone. I've heard about keepers fishing from it, or bird-watching, or passing the time of day reading a book. I'm sure Arthur used to do that because he was always one for reading; he said being on a lighthouse was his time to learn, so he took all sorts of subjects off with him, novels and biographies and books about space. He became interested in geology—stones and rocks, you know. He'd collect and sort them. He said he could learn all about the different eras that way.

Whatever you're doing out there, the set-off's the only bit of fresh air available on a tower. You can't just poke your head out of the windows on account of the walls being so thick: they were built with double windows, you see, an inner and an outer, three or four feet apart, so you'd have to sit in the little space between and I shouldn't think that would be very comfortable. You could go out on the gallery, that's the walkway up top that goes around the lantern, but there's not much room and, besides, you'd need a jolly long fishing rod, wouldn't you.

One of them, and I wouldn't like to guess who, but it could have been Arthur because he was one for having time away from people, being on his own, he liked that. He could have gone out on the set-off and been sitting there reading and the wind was quiet, a force one or two, then out of nowhere a big sea swells up and sweeps him away. The sea can do that. You'll know it can. Arthur was caught out once at the Eddystone, early on; he'd just made AK—that's Assistant Keeper—and he was out there drying his washing when a giant wave came out of the blue and knocked him off his feet. He was lucky his mate was there to grab hold of him, otherwise I'd have lost him years before I did. It rattled him, but he was fine. The same can't be said for his washing; I'm not sure he saw any of that again. He had to borrow the others' clothes until the relief was due.

But things like that didn't affect Arthur. Lightkeepers aren't romantic people; they don't get nervous or look into things too much. The point of the job is to keep a level head and get on with what needs to be done. Trident wouldn't hire them otherwise. Arthur was never afraid of the sea, even when it was dangerous. He told me how, on a tower, the spray from the waves can come right up to the kitchen window during a storm—bear in mind that's eighty or eighty-five feet above the water—and the rocks and boulders roll against the base, so it shudders and shakes. I'd have been scared, I think. But not Arthur; he felt the sea was on his side.

When he came ashore, he seemed, at times, out of sorts. Like a fish out of water, that's exactly it. He didn't know how to be here, whereas he knew how to be on the sea. I'd say goodbye to him to return to the tower and I could see he felt very pleased indeed at the thought of seeing her again.

I'm not sure how many books you've had published about the ocean, but writing a story about it isn't the same as writing how it really is. The sea will turn on you if you're not paying attention: it changes its mind in the snap of a finger and it doesn't care who you are. Arthur had ways of predicting it, such as what the clouds looked like or how the wind sounded against the window; he could tell you if it was blowing a six or seven just by how it sounded—so if a man like him, who is the most experienced person I can think of in these things, could be caught, then that proves it can change suddenly. Maybe he had time to shout and the others came running; the set-off's slippery, there's panic in the air, and it wouldn't take much, would it, for all three of them to get washed away?

The locked door's an oddity; I'll give you that. My only thought is that those entrance doors are thick lumps of gunmetal—they have to be to hold up against the battering they get—and they'll slam on you without any trouble at all. And as for it being bolted from the inside, that's one of those details that plagues me. But on a lighthouse, you've got these heavy iron bars that go across the door to keep it in place, so what I'm thinking is there's a chance those bars fell when it closed, if it closed with enough force . . . ?

I don't know. If it sounds daft to you, then ask yourself what other reason you'd come up with, then see which one you prefer when you start turning these things over in the middle of the night. The stopped clocks and the locked door and the table being laid, it sets your imagination going, doesn't it? I look at it practically, though. I'm not a superstitious person. Whoever was on cooking duty that day was probably being organized in setting the table ready for the next meal: there's a great emphasis on food on a lighthouse and keepers stick to routine like limpets. As for there only being two places, well, perhaps he hadn't got around to laying the third one yet.

And two clocks going at the same time? That's peculiar, but not impossible. One of those whispers that gets distorted the more it's said: some bright spark made it up, then one day it's fact, when it's not, it's just an unhelpful person saying hurtful things.

I'd hoped Trident would settle that they'd drowned so there wasn't this uncertainty for the families, but they never did. In my mind, it's drowning. I feel lucky I know what it is in my mind because I need that, even if it isn't made official.

Jenny Walker, Bill's wife, she wouldn't say the same. She likes there being no solution. If there were, then it would take away any last chance she thinks she has of Bill coming back. I know they're not coming back. But people deal with things how they want. You can't say how someone should grieve; it's very personal and private.

It is a pity, though. What happened to us should have made us come together. Us women. Us wives. Instead, it's been the opposite. I haven't seen Jenny since the ten-year anniversary and even on that day, we didn't speak. We didn't go near each other. I wish it wasn't like that, but there we are. It doesn't stop me trying to change it. I believe people have to share these things. When the worst happens, you can't bear it alone.

That's why I'm talking to you. Because you say you're interested in putting out the truth—and, I suppose, so am I. The truth is that women are important to each other. More important than the men, and that isn't what you'll want to hear because this book, like all your others, is about the men, isn't it? Men are interested in men.

But for me, no, that isn't the case. Those three left us three behind and I'm interested in what's left behind. In what we can make of it, if we still can.

As a novelist, I expect you'll make much of the superstitious aspect. But remember I don't believe in things like that.

Things like what? Come on now, you're the writer; you work it out. In all my years I've realized there are two kinds of people. The ones who hear a creak in a dark, lonely house, and shut the windows because it must have been the wind. And the ones who hear a creak in a dark, lonely house, light a candle, and go to take a look.

7

16 Myrtle Rise
West Hill
Bath

Jennifer Walker
Kestle Cottage
Mortehaven
Cornwall

June 2, 1992

Dear Jenny,

Some time has passed since my last letter. While I no longer
anticipate your reply, I remain optimistic that my words are read. I
would like to interpret your silence as peace between us—if not your
forgiveness.

I wanted to let you know that I am speaking to Mr. Sharp. This
isn't a decision I have taken lightly. Like you, I've never disclosed
information to outsiders about what happened. Trident House gave
us instructions and we followed them.

But I am tired of secrets, Jenny. Twenty years is a long time.

I'm growing old. There is much I need to let go of, much I have shouldered in silence, for many reasons, for many years, and I have to share it, at last. I hope you understand.

With my best wishes, as ever, to you and your family,
Helen

8

JENNY

After lunch it started to rain. Jenny hated the rain. She hated the mess it made when the children came in with it dripping wet, especially Hannah with the double pushchair, especially after she'd cleaned and then it was honestly more bother than it was worth.

Where was he, then? Five minutes late. Plain rude, she thought, turning up late to see someone who hadn't even asked to meet you in the first place. She'd only agreed to it because of Helen, because she wasn't having Helen Black saying things about her that weren't true—or that were true—and having them all put down in a book for the world to see. He was famous, apparently. That didn't impress her. Jenny didn't read books. *Fortune and Destiny* twice monthly did her fine.

No doubt this man expected her to roll out the red carpet. It didn't matter if he was late, because being posh and well-off, he could behave how he liked. Now he'd trample soggy shoes right through the house. Jenny found it awkward asking visitors to take their shoes off: they should know to do it without having to be asked.

She was in the mindset now of hating the rain. All those years of thinking Bill's relief was going to get put off and it would be even longer before she saw him again. In the days running up to him coming home she used to get fixated on the weather, worried it was going to change so the boat wouldn't be able to go out there and get him, and the more she watched the more the weather *had* seemed to change, just to spite her. They'd planned to move to Spain when Bill retired, buy a place in the south with what little they'd saved, a swimming pool and clay pots on the patio and pink flowers round the door, and the children would come out for holidays. Jenny was better in the sun; the rain made her mood go downhill, and the rain in England lasted for months and months, it was so depressing. She'd have been fine if they'd made it to Spain, warmth on their bones, brandy Alexanders as the sun went down. Whenever it rained these days, it reminded her that would never happen.

Helen's letter languished in the bin. Jenny ought to rip the envelopes up before she opened them. Every time one dropped through the letter box, she told herself, I'll set a match to it, I'll tear it into pieces, I'll stuff it down the drain.

But she never did. Her sister said it brought her closer to Bill, having Helen's letters to read, because they were a link to her missing husband whether she despised that link or not. Helen's letters were proof that it had been real. Jenny had been married to him once; they had been in love. It had been good. It hadn't been a dream.

The telly in the living room blacked out on an episode of *Murder, She Wrote*. Jenny pushed herself up off the settee and gave it a whack. The picture returned: the protagonist was hiding in a wardrobe from a gunman. She thought, I could do that; I could get in a cupboard and pretend I'm not home. But this Dan Sharp would be here any minute. If she didn't talk to him, there was no telling what lies that cow had up her sleeve. Even though Jenny had read all sorts of rubbish about the Maiden Rock over the years and knew to take it all with a great big bucket of salt, she still considered it her duty to care. Whenever she saw a story in the paper, she had to call in and speak to whoever was responsible so she could have her say and put them right. It was like a member of her family that she had to stand up for.

Outside, the sky grew dim. In the distance, beyond the rooftops, swam the strip of sea that Jenny clung to like a life belt. She needed that sea, to be sure it was there, the nearest she had of him. In heavy weather the view got lost and that made her panic, imagining the sea had gone, she was nowhere near it, or it had dried up altogether and her husband's bones knocked naked on the sand.

A keeper never abandons his light.

She had heard that plenty when Bill vanished.

Then what *had* he done? Over the years, she had grown used to not knowing, comfortable with it, even, a ragged pair of slippers with holes in the bottom that did nothing for her, but she never took them off.

Well, a wife never abandons her husband. Jenny would never move away. Not until she knew the truth, and then, maybe then, she could sleep.

She heard her visitor arrive on the doorstep, the shuffle of his feet and a smoker's cough. His knuckles on the door, surprising her. She clasped her shaking hands. That's right, she remembered, the bell was bust.

9

JENNY

I'd sooner have come to meet you, but the car's got a flat tire. I'm waiting for my brother-in-law to come and fix it for me. I'm no good with cars. Bill used to do everything like that. Now he's gone, I suppose I'm lucky that Carol and Ron live close by. I don't know what I'd do without them. I'm not sure I could cope.

You'd better come in. I'll turn a light on. I try not to have too many on around the house because it costs. Trident set us up with an income, but it doesn't take much for me to spend mine. I haven't been able to work so I can't get any extra. I never worked anyway; I was raising the family while Bill was on the lights, so what else was I to do? I wouldn't know where to start, in working. I wouldn't know what I'd be good at.

Go on then, tell me what you want to know. I haven't got long— I've got a man coming round to fix the TV. I'd be lost without the telly. I have it on all day; it keeps me company. When it's off I feel lonely. Quiz shows are my favorite, the ones on the shiny sets. I like *Family Fortunes* because of the flashing lights and prizes; it's colorful and I like that. I usually keep the TV on when I go to bed so it's there when I wake up, then there's someone there to say good morning to. It helps take my mind off things. The nights are the worst for that.

It's a gloomy subject for you to want to write about. Bad enough it happened in the first place without you needing to make a book out of it. I don't see why you'd want to read about the dark side of life anyway. There's enough of that in the world as it is. Why can't there be more stories about nice things? Ask your publishers that.

I suppose you want a drink, don't you. I've got coffee but I've run out of tea. I haven't been able to get to the shops because of the car and I don't like walking. Anyway, I don't drink it myself. Not even water? Suit yourself.

That's a photo of the family at Dungeness. My grandson's five and the twins are two. Hannah's lot, she didn't mean to have them early but that's how it happened. Hannah's my eldest. Then I've got Julia, who's twenty-two now, and Mark, who's twenty. I had my girls far apart because it took us awhile to get pregnant, what with Bill being away. Oh, I don't feel young to be a grandmother. I feel old. Older than I am. I put a brave face on because they don't want to come over and see their nana sad all the time, but it's a struggle. Like on Bill's birthday or our anniversary when I want to stay in bed, and I don't even want to get up to answer the door. I don't care if I'm moving on or not. I don't see the point of it. I'll never get over what happened, never.

Are you married? No, I wouldn't have said so. I've heard authors are like that. Caught up with what's in your head instead of what's outside of it.

I've never read your stories so I wouldn't know the kind of thing you cook up. One got made for telly, did it? *Neptune's Bow*. Actually, I did watch that. The Beeb put it on before Christmas. It was all right. That was you, was it? OK.

I don't see why you're interested in our business. You don't know the first thing about lighthouses or the people that work in them or anything. Lots of folk get excited about what went on, but they don't feel the need to go around making an entertainment out of it. You won't solve it, however much you fancy yourself.

We were childhood sweethearts, Bill and me. Together from when we were sixteen. I'd never been with another man before Bill and I never have since. As far as I'm concerned, we're still married. Even now, if I can't make up my mind about something, like how many fish fingers I should buy at Safeway when the grandkids are coming for tea, I ask myself what Bill would say. That helps me to decide.

I never understood other women who rowed with their husbands. They'd take any chance to moan and put them down in front of everyone else. Things like he left his dirty washing on the floor or he didn't do the dishes properly. All harping on and not stopping to see how lucky they were that they could be with their husbands every night and not have to miss them. As if any of that matters anyway, about the washing and the dishes and things. That's not what life's about. If you can't overlook those things, you're in the wrong business. You shouldn't be married at all.

What can I tell you about Bill? First thing is he wouldn't think much of outsiders sticking their beaks in. But that won't be much help to you, will it?

Bill was always destined to join the lighthouses. His mother died when he was a baby—that was a sad lot, because she died giving birth to him, so he just had his dad and his brothers when he was growing up. His father was a lighthouse keeper and so was his granddad and his great-granddad before. Bill was the youngest of three boys who went into it. There just wasn't any other option. He did resent it, yes.

Deep down I think he could've wanted to be something else, but he never got the chance because no one ever asked him. He had no power in that family, none at all.

He was always trying to please other people. He'd say to me, "Jen, I just want an easy life," and I'd tell him that was what I was here for, to make his life easy. Neither of us came from a happy background and that's what bonded us in the first place. I understood Bill and he understood me. We didn't need to explain ourselves to each other. Comforts normal people take for granted, like a nice home and a hot meal on the table. We wanted to do better for our children. Have a go at making it right.

To start with we were lucky, posted to land stations where we could all live together, or on the rocks where the housing was provided. I said to Bill when we met, right off the bat, I said, I don't like being on my own, I always like to be with someone, and if you're going to be my husband, then that's how it has to be. The service was accommodating, but I knew we'd get the tower at some point. I dreaded it. I'd have to spend a lot of time on my own then, raising the children like one of those poor single mothers. It's usually the men without families who want the towers—like Vince, the Supernumerary, he didn't have anyone to take care of, so he didn't mind what he got. Not us. We minded. I feel so angry that we never wanted that horrible tower, but we got it anyway—and look what happened.

The Maiden's the worst because it's so far off and it's ugly and threatening looking. Bill used to say it was dark and stuffy inside and that he got a bad feeling off it. "A bad, heavy feeling" was how he put it. Obviously, I think about that a lot now. I wish I had asked him more about it, but usually I changed the subject because I didn't want him getting upset. I also didn't like him thinking about the tower too much when he was ashore. That tower had enough of him as it was. We had to wait to see him for so long that when he was here, he had to be here in every way.

The nights before Bill went off again were difficult. I felt sick about him going as soon as he came ashore, which was a waste because I didn't enjoy him like I should have when he was at home. I was too caught up in the idea of him leaving again. We always spent those last nights the same. We'd cozy up on the settee and watch *Call My Bluff,* or some other show we didn't need to think too hard on. Bill said he got the Channels before he went off—that's what he called that feeling he got, of nerves and sadness was how he described it. He said it comes from when sailors used to go back on their boats after a spell at home and it took them a few days to feel better about being away, and until they did, they had that sensation of missing their real lives and having to adjust. Bill had it before he'd even left home. It was the expectation of it that was almost as bad. He'd stare out the window and see the Maiden waiting for him all that way away, and as it got dark, she'd light up, like she was saying, Aha! You thought I'd forgotten about you, didn't you, but I haven't. It was worse for us being able to see her. It'd have been better if we'd lived out of sight.

We'd check the weather in case the relief was getting delayed; we half hoped it would and half hoped it wouldn't, because that just made the waiting longer. I'd cook him his favorite dinner, steak pie with arctic roll for dessert, and bring it to him on a tray to eat on his lap, but he wouldn't eat much of it, due to the Channels.

I had a calendar that I crossed the days off on until he came back. The children kept me busy. When Hannah was a baby, we were together on a land station, but not with the others. Bill got the tower when Julia was a few months old and I was on my own with a five-year-old and a newborn daughter with colic. That was hard. I'd feel so angry whenever I clapped eyes on the Maiden. Standing there all pleased with herself. It wasn't fair that she had him when I didn't, and I needed him more.

Hannah liked having a lighthouse keeper for a father because it made her stand out; her friends' dads were postmen or shopkeepers. Nothing wrong with that, but those jobs are two a penny, aren't they? She says she remembers him, but I don't think she can. I think memories are very intense when they first start up and they keep a powerful grip on you your whole life. You can't always trust them, though.

When Bill was due ashore, I'd go out and buy his favorite foods and make his special chocolates. It was a little ritual I had. I didn't want anything to be different. I wanted him to know what to expect when he got home and for it to be there, ready for him. Just like I was ready for him. It's the small things that keep a marriage going: things that don't cost a lot but that tell the other person you love them and don't ask for anything in return.

I've got no idea what happened to my husband. If they'd left the door open, or if they'd taken the boat, or if the oilskins and gum boots were gone, then I could maybe believe that Bill was lost at sea. But the dinghy was there and so were the sou'westers and the door was locked from the inside. Think about that. A block of gunmetal can't lock itself. Then you put in the clocks and the laid table; it's wrong, that's what it is.

Bill was on the radio transmitter the day before, the twenty-ninth. He said then that the storm was on its way out. Said they'd be ready for the relief on Saturday.

Trident House have a good recording of that R/T, although I'd put money on them not letting you near it. Trident keep themselves to themselves and they don't like to talk about what happened because it's obviously embarrassing for them. But Bill said, Let's do it tomorrow; get Jory's boat sent out in the morning. And they said, All right, Bill, that's what we'll do. Now, I'm aware what Helen thinks—she thinks a big wave came up on them in the meantime. It doesn't surprise me she thinks that because she never had much of an imagination. But I know that's not right.

I'll never forget Bill's voice on the radio. Everything he said and the way he said it. That voice sounded like my husband. The only odd thing was that there was a longer wait at the end before he signed off. You know when you're watching TV and the reception cuts out for a second and the picture jumps ahead of itself? Like that.

I'm a "what if" person. I say, what if it wasn't a freak sea the day they disappeared? What if Bill was taken? I don't know by what; I don't want to say by what. All the things it could've been—what happened, how it felt, who was there, if it was one of them that did it—not a day's gone by when I haven't thought about those things, but I always come back to the same. It sounds crazy when you say it out loud. It's just what I believe. A tower light, out there on its own, it's like a sheep away from the flock. Easy pickings.

You don't look like someone who gives a fig for that. I don't care. All I'll say is you try losing that one person who means the world to you, then see how easy it is to draw a line and say, That's it, it's over, they're gone. I still hear my husband's voice, you know. Still hear it now, plain as day. Like when I'm pegging out the darks, I'll hear Bill inside the house calling my name, just saying it like he would if he'd been busy in the back fixing the chain on his bike and he came in to ask if I wanted a cup of coffee.

I know that's not possible. We're not where we were before. I've moved to a new house; he wouldn't know where I was. We couldn't have stayed at the cottage anyway—they're for keepers' families, not missing keepers' families. All the same, it felt like I was admitting he was never coming back. It makes me sad if I imagine him turning up on our doorstep, only I'm not there. But one of the caretakers at the Maiden cottages now would tell me. These sorts of fantasies go through your head.

Helen's not one for fantasies. She's too cold and matter-of-fact. That's why, when you speak to her, I bet she doesn't tell you the truth. I don't think she knows the meaning of the word. In all the time I've known her, the only thing she's been good at is lying. Helen writes me letters and sends me Christmas cards, but she might as well not bother. I never read them. I'd be happy never to hear from her again.

You'd think she'd have wanted a friend or two, given the state of her life before. But Helen never talked about that. Living next door to each other, we could have been close—that's what PKs' wives across the country were doing, looking after the families and leading the charge when the men were away. If we were getting along in the cottages, then they'd be getting along on the tower. That's the rule we lived by in the lighthouse service.

But not Helen. She thought she was special. Too grand for it, in my view, with her expensive scarves and fancy jewelry. I think even if I had all the money in the world to spend on what I looked like, I'd still be plain, because it comes out of you, doesn't it, prettiness? I've never felt pretty.

In ordinary life, we'd never brush shoulders. I'm sorry our paths crossed at all.

It is bad luck for Helen, not believing in anything. Without my faith I'd have ended it a long time ago. I still think about ending it sometimes, but then I think of the children and I can't. If I knew I'd find Bill there, then maybe. Maybe. But not yet. I need to keep our light shining.

Trident House tried telling me once that Bill did it on purpose. That he jumped on a French ship and floated off to start his life new. Now, I'm not a violent person, but it was all I could do not to cause a scene when they said that. Bill would never do it to me. He'd never have left me on my own.

Oh, right, there's the door. That's my man come to fix the TV.

Is that everything? You'll have to come back if it isn't. I can't have you staying because it makes me nervous having two things going on at once, and I need to give my attention to the TV man now. I hope he can fix it because *Come Dancing*'s on tonight. I really hate not being able to see things properly.

10

HELEN

Every summer she made the pilgrimage, on his birthday or there-abouts. She left the dog with a friend and went by train to the nearest station, half an hour or so from the coast, and by taxi the rest of the way. Nothing much changed; nothing was different. Though the business of life went on across its surface, the earth beneath moved slowly. Waves rolled to shore, forever and ever, patiently; the leaves of the beech trees wafted like a Chinese fan.

Helen turned off the high street and walked up the lane. Midges hovered in trembling clouds and the scent of cow parsley rose ripe and heat soaked from the busy hedgerow. Warm shadows leaned across her path, an orange sun divided by the dark stems of trees. She passed the sign for Mortehaven Cemetery. Crumbling headstones sloped from their rows, staggering down toward the lip of the prom-ontory, beyond which the sea shot far and wide in a dazzling celebra-tion of blue.

There had never been a grave. A bench on the headland bore the inscription:

ARTHUR BLACK, WILLIAM WALKER, VINCENT BOURNE
HUSBANDS, FATHERS, BROTHERS, SONS—BELOVED, ALL
"BRIGHTLY BEAMS OUR FATHER'S MERCY
FROM HIS LIGHTHOUSE EVERMORE"

Many times, she had heard Arthur sing that sea shanty. Sitting on the rim of the bath, the tune fluting out of the steam; humming it at the basin while soaping his face or in the kitchen grilling rashers of bacon, hacking a loaf of bread into slabs that could stop a door slamming. *Let the lower lights be burning / Send a gleam across the wave.* He'd come home smelling of seaweed and sit in his chair eating chips soaked in Sarson's from a nest of greasy paper, his hands large and cracked like terra-cotta pots, with halos round the nails. Arthur caught whole fish with his fingers—or did he? There'd been magic in him: sea magic, half man, half born in the brine. She hadn't known at first that she would marry him. It wasn't until he had taken her out on a boat on the water that she had looked at him and known. She'd just known. He was different out there. It was hard to explain. Everything about him made sense.

A fingerpost pointed TO THE LIGHTHOUSE COMPOUND, beyond which the winding lane narrowed, overtaken by greenery, bursting from the verges in jumbles of primrose and nettle. Farther on, after a climb, the Maiden Rock appeared for the first time.

The tower shimmered on a cobalt sea, a line as clean as a pen mark. A handful of lighthouse enthusiasts might come this way during summer, Helen thought; they'd get to this point, their legs grazed by blackthorn and dog violet, and admire the lighthouse from afar, a silver streak on a silver mirror—before turning back, tired and thirsting for cool drinks, and they'd have no need to think of her ever again.

Into the dappled glade of the ongoing track, the sign on a metal gate read: MAIDEN ROCK LIGHTHOUSE: NO PUBLIC ACCESS.

They were holiday lets now, only tenants allowed. The track was too tight and twisting even for rubbish collection; instead, plastic bins were clustered by the gate with numbers streaked on in white paint.

It was here that Helen expected to see him, every year, walking toward her. Perhaps there would be another with him, two shapes, their hands raised, and she would raise hers in return. She had to hope that was what happened: that people who belonged with each other found their way back in the end.

III

✦

1972

11

ARTHUR

Ships and Stars

The time I think of you the most is when the sun comes up. The moment before, the minute or two, when night yawns for morning and the sea starts to separate from the sky. Day after day the sun comes back. I don't know why. I've had my light safe here, shining through the dark, and I'll keep it shining: the sun needn't bother today. But still he comes and still come my thoughts of you. Where you are and what you are doing. Even though I'm not a man who thinks about things like this, it's now, in this moment, that I do. A man alone through the lonely hours, I nearly believe that because the sun keeps rising, and because I extinguish my light dawn after dawn as soon as it's no longer needed, you might be there when I go downstairs. You'll be sitting at the table with one of the others, older, perhaps, than when I last saw you, or maybe the same.

EIGHTEEN DAYS ON THE TOWER

Hours turn into nights turn into dawns turn into weeks, and on and on the wide sea rolls and the sting rain beats and the sun shines into evening, morning, conversations in the half-light, the never light, conversations that never happened or are happening now.

"*Mastermind* was on again," says Bill in the kitchen, fag in his mouth, hunched over his seashells. Every keeper needs a hobby, I told him when he started, and more's the better if it calls for useful workmanship, a pursuit you can go at day after day until it's perfect. An old PK I worked under taught me how to make a schooner and put it in a bottle. Personally I found it nitpicky, having to glue the sails just so. It took weeks of prep before I could slide it in and pull the rigging, and if I'd glued a whisker out of place, the whole lot was wrecked. Loneliness pushes a man to his standards. I know this because I've been on the Maiden twenty-odd years and Bill's done it for two.

"Anything good?"

"Crusades," he says. "*Thunderbirds*."

"You should have a go."

"With what?"

"Whatever it is you know about."

Bill blows his shell carving and sets it aside, then leans back in his chair with his arms behind his head. My Assistant has a studious, timid look, his hair lopped close round his ears, his features small and precise: if you saw him ashore, you'd think him an accountant. Smoke travels up his nostrils and escapes in twin jets from the corners of his mouth, where it joins the ghostly haze of whoever was puffing away in here last.

"I know about a lot of things," he says, "but not enough about any one of them."

"You know about the sea."

"It needs to be specific, doesn't it. You can't just say to that old bastard Magnusson, ask me about the sea. It's too big a topic, they'd never allow it."

"All right, then, the lights."

"Don't be a prick; you can't have a specialist subject on your own job. Name: Bill Walker. Occupation: lighthouse keeper. Subject: lighthouse keeping."

He stubs out his Embassy, lights another. Given how cold it is this time of year, we have to keep the windows fastened, and seeing as this is where we do all our cooking and smoking, and all our smoking cooking, it's heading for a proper fug-up.

"Looking forward to having Vince back?" I ask.

Bill expels air through his nose. "Can't say I'm fussed either way."

I take his mug and switch on the kettle. Out here our days and nights are organized by cups of tea—especially this time of year, December, heart of winter, when it gets light so late and dark so early and always so numbingly cold. Waking at four for my morning watch, back to bed after lunch, waking again later on, the curtains drawn, the afternoon gone. Is it today, tomorrow, next week, how long have I been sleeping?

The mug's one of Frank's, red and black with *Branderburger Tor* written across it. Frank's so finicky he'll certainly take it with him when he goes ashore tomorrow, in case one of us nicks it. We all have our tea different, so whoever's making it has to remember. Even with Vince coming back, and he's been away weeks, we'll make sure we get it right. It shows we pay attention. At home Helen never gives me sugar, but I don't complain, just go along with it instead of having the argument. Here we'll get to teasing. *You fucking half-wit, that fishing net holds on to things longer than you do.*

Bill says, "D'you know Frank puts the milk in first? Bag, milk, water on top."

"Fuck off. Milk goes second."

"That's what I said."

"The tea can't infuse in the milk otherwise."

"If you're using words like 'infuse' you can get fucked."

"If I were that PK at Longships you'd be wise to watch your language." But the swearing's like the tea, all the effing and blinding helps the conversation along. If you're swearing at someone, you're saying you're friends and you understand each other. It doesn't matter who it is, or that I'm the one in charge. We'll slip back into it as soon as we're here and put it aside as soon as we're ashore. If the wives could listen in on five minutes of it, they'd be appalled. At home, we've got to bite our tongues off before we ask how the fuck she's been getting on and how fucking nice it is to see her and by the way what the fuck are we having for our fucking tea?

"There was this woman last night," says Bill, "she did the solar system."

"There you go, then, that's bigger than the sea."

"Yeah, but it's bloody obvious what they'd ask, the planets and whatnot. They'd ask about Neptune and Saturn and they'd definitely ask about Uranus."

"Never gets tired, Bill, you fucking idiot."

"But with the sea it's less obvious. Everything about the sea's less obvious."

"I like that."

"Not me. Don't like what I can't see."

When Bill first came to the Maiden, I thought, How's this going to go? Some men open up to you and others don't. Bill was quiet, contained. He reminded me of a silverback I saw once, in London Zoo, staring out of a plastic box where the visitors came in. I've tried since to work out what exactly I saw in that animal's expression. Anger and boredom, long burned out. Resignation for itself. Pity toward me.

There's a lot of time for talk, especially on middle watch, midnight to four, when you find your conversations sloping down all sorts of dark alleys that you never mention again come the morning. Whoever's coming off watch before you will get you up, fetch you tea and a plate of cheese and digestive biscuits and bring it all up to the lantern, where he'll sit with you for an hour before going off to his bed. He'll do this to wake you up, get your brain engaged so you don't fall back asleep when you're there on your own. When it's Bill and me, he'll tell me things he'll wish he hadn't in the light of day. How he should have been a different man and had a different life and said no at the points he said yes. How Jenny asks for the seashells he's done, but he doesn't want to give them to her. He'd sooner keep them to himself, like so many other things.

Upstairs for a sleep. The banana bunks took some getting used to when I started. Land men marvel at the idea—"There was me thinking it's a joke, you've really got to sleep on those bloody bent beds?"— but over the years my spine must have curved to accommodate them, because I used to get back pain after two months on the tower and when I went ashore I'd have the aches and soreness of a man twice my age. These days I barely feel it. Lying in a normal bed feels rigid and unwelcoming. I have to make an effort to fall asleep straight on my back, but when I wake up my chest is on my knees.

I should be gone as soon as my head hits the pillow. Whether the chance comes about at a backward hour of the night or early morning, or a brief, shadowy submersion before the middle watchman exhibits his light, we take what we can get.

Or I did, once, on lights gone by. These days sleep skitters away from me on dry, clawed feet. My mind turns to visions of the deep sea, and of Helen; visions of the tower as I see it when I'm ashore, just visible in the distance, and the vertiginous, disbelieving sensation of being there and here at once, or in neither place. I turn from the curtain that separates my bunk from the room; I watch the wall in the dark, listening to the sea, to my slow heartbeat, my mind turning; I think, and I remember.

NINETEEN DAYS

Brilliant sunshine means ideal conditions for Frank's relief, which turns up late, just before lunch, seeing as the boat wouldn't start. All in all, it's a good getaway for him and a good landing for Vince, who even on a rough sea seems to step off the launch and onto the set-off with barely any trouble at all. Vince is young with black hair and a Supertramp mustache. It doesn't take long for him to settle in. Everything's got its place and we're practiced in unpacking our belongings swiftly so we can slot back into our responsibilities as efficiently as possible. Letters from home arrive in a sealed waterproof bag. There's an official one for me, marked for the Principal Keeper.

"That's the end of it, then," says Vince. "No moon for Brezhnev."

We're waiting for our grub while Vince talks about the Soviet rocket launch that exploded in the sky last month. It's disorienting to hear about things in the real world, the other world. That world could cease to be and for a time we'd be none the wiser. I'm not sure I need that world. Any city, any town, any room wider than the length of two men lying down, seems frivolous with light and noise and unnecessarily complicated.

"Bloody communists," says Bill. "Talk about a bunch of wet fucking blankets. What's worse—the threat of war or just getting on with it?"

"No way, man," says Vince. "I'm a pacifist."

" 'Course you bloody are."

"What's wrong with that?"

"Pacifism's an excuse for doing fuck all. Except maybe growing facial hair and shagging your way across London."

Vince sits back in his chair and smokes. He's only been with us nine months but he's as familiar as the kitchen dresser. I've seen dozens of keepers come and go, but some you grow to like more than others. I'm not sure Bill likes him.

"You're jealous," he says to Bill.

"Fuck off."

"How long since you were twenty-two?"

"Not as long as you think, you rude prick."

This is how it is between them, Vince ribbing Bill for being an old man even though he's still in his thirties and Bill coming back like he's put out. It's meant to be good for a laugh, but it gets to Bill, I can tell. He never lived like that. He was married by twenty, Jenny already talking about having his babies. The lighthouses calling him in.

Vince has brought gammon from the mainland, which smells unbe-

lievable frying on the stove with a cracked egg, spluttering and popping. It's two weeks now since Bill or I have had meat that hasn't come
out of a can, and canned meat's better than nothing, but it's not a patch
on the real thing. Soon enough everything that comes out of a can
starts to taste the same, of the can, whether it's fruit cocktail or a slab
of Spam. Actually, the Spam's OK if it's cooked, but if it's just cold
dumped out on the plate like Vince or Frank would do, it's enough
to turn you vegetarian.

Bill's cook today: he makes the best meals out of any of us. Vince is
useless and I'm all right, although less enthusiastic about it because I
do a lot of it ashore whereas Bill doesn't do any. His wife does everything for him. Bill says that's what it must be like being in prison,
having everything done for you "save wiping your arse," then Vince
says it's not like being in prison, since there wouldn't be orange me-
ringues or rum baba or women offering to rub your feet, would there?
Bill says, S'pose you'd know, you crook. Then it's up to me to smooth
the waters, before it stops being a joke.

Vince says, "What do you think, Mr. PK?"

"About what?"

"Keeping a lid on it, or letting it blow?"

I want to say that all this about the Cold War, about Nixon and the
USSR and Japanese planes crashing out of Moscow, strikes me as pointless. If we all had a tower to be on and a couple of people to be with,
just to be, without expectation or interference, to put in the light at
night and extinguish it at dawn, to sleep and be awake, talk and be
silent, live and die, all on our islands, couldn't we avoid the rest?

Instead I tell him, "You've got to keep the peace if you can." And
hope I can do that on this particular spell.

But Vince's talk of spaceships reminds me of a time years ago. It was dawn at Beachy Head and I was alone in the lantern, about to let the sun step in, when I saw an object fall into the sea. It was a soft, foggy morning, early enough for lingering stars left behind, a morning so beautiful you wonder that heaven isn't already here if only we took the time to look up and see, and then there it was, shimmering metal, shot out of nowhere, digested by the water and leaving no trace of itself. I couldn't know its size or how far away it was because the sea looks eternal from way up there.

I did see it and I couldn't explain it. A piece of aircraft, a flap or spoiler, that's the explanation, I know, I do know that; but there was something in the way it moved, some dynamic in its falling, that had more grace and purpose than I can describe. I told no one, not the men I was with and not Helen. But I thought it was you.

Such a precious gift that you gave me and I thank you for that.

The bedroom's kept dark because there's usually someone asleep in there, or trying to sleep, at any time of the day or night. In winter the constant dark is disorienting, our single window indicating dawn as easily as dusk. When I close the door my hand rests there, soft edged, inanimate, and it looks as if this hand belongs not to me but to a younger man, who might in another universe be opening a door, not closing it.

The book I'm reading is called *Obelisk and Hourglass*, about the history of time. I found it in the Oxfam charity shop on Mortehaven high street. I have this idea that later on I'll see the things in person that I've read about, the Egyptian pyramids, the temples of South America, the Hanging Gardens of Babylon. When I'd do it doesn't matter; it's holding the possibility in my mind that's the important thing.

After we were married, Helen and I traveled to Venice. We spent a week eating oily bread and ham as pink and thin as tissue paper. We wandered through dank passages and under bridges that smelled of eggs and salt. It seems unreal to me now, a sunken world of shadows and water, ringing bells and roofs of gold.

The *Obelisk* paperback is soft, with a sundial on the front. On the tower, we measure our time in days: how far each of us is into his eight-week spell. Helen says it's like prisoners chalking the walls, and maybe it is a little like that. In ancient China they had a way of telling the hours with a candle. They marked the wax with lines and saw how much of it had melted, and in that way the hours never got lost. You could collect the wax and remold it and relight it if you wanted. Have that time all over again.

Helen doesn't know and I would never tell her. I would never speak about you. Some things are off-limits and you are such a thing. But I wonder about the candle and about time burned through; and if hours, when they pass, are gone permanently, or if there is a way of bringing them back. What if I can get you back?

I've been out here too long. Lonely nights and reels of dark, spooling and unraveling to the black sea, the sky blacker still. Put a man, the most cynical of men, on morning watch when the sun comes up and the bloodshot sky bursts orange and have him tell me this is all there is. This isn't all there is.

In the screen behind my closed eyes, a throbbing flashlight occults from the shore. It calls from the darkness, shining, shining, insisting that I turn and see.

12

BILL

Crossing

THIRTY-FIVE DAYS ON THE TOWER

How many times have I put in this light? Eight months of the year, every year, give or take an overdue, so that's two hundred and forty days; multiply that by the number of years I've been in the service and that's getting on for fifteen, which makes it three thousand and six hundred times that I've lit this light or some version of it. As for the number of hours I've spent on a lighthouse in all that time, I'd rather not know.

Brew the meths, warm the vapor, turn the tap, and set a match to the mantle. I could do this blindfolded, though I doubt Trident would allow it. The flames flap in their glass cage. On the Maiden the illumination itself doesn't move; instead the lenses around it rotate, magnifying the beam across the sea.

It's eight o'clock. I'm off at midnight. In having the "all night in," I'm able to sleep the hours that ashore would make up a normal night.

Between now and then I'll watch for the burner getting bunged or the pressure dropping; I'll log the weather, temperature, visibility, barometric pressure, and wind force. Aside from that, and those aren't things I need to pay attention to anymore, I'll sit and think about how a man could shake up his life if he was unhappy with his lot. There are plenty of hours to do that. When I'm putting in my lights and extinguishing my lights, the whole world relies on me. Dawn and dusk are mine alone, to do with as I please. It's a powerful feeling.

Vince brought back a parcel from Jenny. If I don't read her letter now, it'll hang over me, watching me in the same way as if she were here. Sometimes up top with the light you can feel another person, if you try. You can feel they're here with you whether you like that idea or not. They could be sitting right next to you: you start to feel it in the hairs on your arms. Or they're behind you, looking at the back of your head, thinking all sorts of thoughts about you that you'd rather they didn't have. You turn to check and there's no one there, the lantern's empty, just you. But you checked.

She's put in the usual box of homemade chocolates. I see her spooning each one into its paper case, *The Archers* on in the background. Jenny Heaton. The first time I saw her coming out of school with her hair in plaits and her skirt hanging over her knees. Jenny's never liked her knees; she says they're lumpy. Her sister told her they looked like Cornish pasties and she never got over it. A bit like when I went out with the girl who lived next door, Susan Price, and months down the line she broke up with me, saying, "You're too short, Bill Walker, I need someone taller."

It wasn't bad with Jenny at first. We'd lie in bed at her mum's house, her mum pie-eyed on the sofa downstairs, Jenny's cold fingers gripping mine. I could feel her knees under the quilt, told her I liked them, there was nothing the matter with them, why didn't she let me kiss her again? We didn't talk much. I've never been a talker and she didn't mind that; I thought that was a good thing about her, different to other girls. Then one time she whispered, in the dark, "You're just like me, Bill," and I lay there till morning, worried. The main thing had been to go to bed with a girl, so I could tell my brothers I had. Now I felt this neediness creeping up on me. The key in the lock.

Jenny's written the letter on the paper she nicked from the fancy hotel in Brighton where we stayed on our honeymoon.

Bill, love, I miss you. It's been more than a month. The house feels so empty without you in it. I wish you could come home and be with us. The children ask me every day when you're coming back (which has made me even more upset!). I'm crying all the time. So is the baby, all through the night. I try to be strong, but it's hard. I feel hopeless that I won't see you for such a long time and we are only halfway through our time apart. I'm not doing anything until you get back. I don't want to go anywhere or see anyone. If I do, I'll only cry, and it takes me such an effort not to cry.

I feel her fingers in mine, in that bed.

Other people don't understand it, do they, Bill? How much I need you and miss you. It's a pain to be on my own, an actual pain in my heart. I was sick after you left this time. Hannah heard. I lied and said it was the meatballs we had for tea, but it wasn't. I have to lie to everyone when you are away. I'm not myself, Bill. Are you?

Down in the kitchen I make toast with the processed white bread Vince delivered. *Mother's Pride's a family, a family of bread.* You can't make toast with the loaves we bake, which half the time come out like crumpets and the other like scones. The grill burns the edges, but I prefer that, and someone once said charcoal was good for you, didn't they, just a bit because of the carbon. I cover it in Marmite so you can't tell. When I bite the toast the sound it makes reminds me of sticks on a bonfire, cracking.

There're only so many excuses a man can make for himself. I'm a coward. Must be. When I was ten, my dad found me reading by torch-light in my bedroom. He boxed me on the ears and said, "You'll go blind squinting like that; the service won't look twice at you in glasses." I trusted him about the glasses and that being on a lighthouse was the only thing I'd be good at, so I had better bloody manage it, otherwise what else would I do? The old man got ill years after and took to his bed, where he grew thinner and thinner until one day he disappeared, apart from the sour hole where his mouth used to be, rasping, *"It was your fault."* And it was. I'd come out upside down and twisted round, like a kitten in a drowning sack.

The sea infected us all. We couldn't get away from it, even in death. The old man had a cousin in Dorset who lived in a flat overlooking West Bay. Inside she had paintings of the sea, Old Testament ones of violent skies and frothing waves; ships flung to and fro on slinging seas. I hated going there, the whirling pools and battle scenes, can-nons firing, red flags on masts slapped by the bitter wind. The place smelled of dry sherry and the flaky shortbread biscuits she baked and stored in plastic. When she died, we took a boat out from Lyme and scattered her ashes on the water. A lot of it blew back in my face and I thought, then, I'll never get away from this bloody sea.

It didn't matter that I never learned to swim. Dad said, You don't need to swim to sit on a light. In lessons the teacher threw in a brick;

I struggled at the surface with my eyes closed and my nose held, the children's taunts echoing in my blocked ears.

Up top, the hours creep round. Time passes, invisibly. Hours get lost, and even though I'm paid to be awake and to all intents and purposes I *am* awake, there's no doubting I go into a semi-sleep state, because when I'm up in the lantern on my own all sorts of weird ideas go through my head and I can only say they're part of my dreams. Jenny ashore with the baby crying and the girls fighting; toys on the carpet, a Sindy undressed, her head turned on its shoulders so the breasts are at the back because Jenny won't buy them the male version on account of they'll soon be getting up to all sorts. Screaming at teatime, over fish cakes. How would it be to never go back?

My wife counting the days to the relief and when it comes the boat sets out and the weather's good so she's getting excited, getting the bits in that she always gets, food and drink I liked ages ago but don't anymore. Only I don't go back. I don't know where I go or how this happens, but that's the good part, not knowing. Just happens.

Before midnight I fetch Vince from the bedroom. I jog him awake with the heel of my hand and the usual greeting—"Come on, you lazy shit, time to get up"—before going down to the kitchen to make our tray. Vince needs that first nudge and then another after I've made the drinks, and then finally he'll get his arse up to the light.

I'd never bother putting biscuits on crockery at home and God knows why I do here. Two fat wedges of the old Davidstow, which is growing waxy at the edges, speckled white, meaning we'd better eat it quick.

Vince is up there already, surprising me; he's got a leather jacket thrown over his pajamas. He and Arthur are poles apart, Arthur dressing for duty like he's anticipating the Trident inspectors any minute, bristles shaved, hair combed, shoes shined, while Vince loafs about in BHS bedwear and a pair of slippers approximating dog fur.

With keepers you've worked with, you soon get accustomed to their pattern of doing things. Vince hasn't been out here a year yet, and what with the chopping and changing of who's on with who, I've only spent a short time in his company. But a month on the tower is a decade ashore for how well you get to know someone. Vince'll drink his tea straight down before he says much, and when he does it won't be a pleasantry about the weather or the state of the light or anything else that's happened that day. In this crossover hour, the rules go out the window. Rules about what you can and can't do. What you can and can't say. This is when Vince told me what he got locked up for. Not the old, petty stuff. I mean the bad time.

"You never said what your problem is," he says.

"With what?"

"This." He picks his teeth. "The sea."

"Just don't like it, do I."

"Why?"

"Who cares why? You'd never say to a pilot, If you like flying planes, then you'll love the sky and ask him to jump out the cockpit straight into it."

"There's always a reason, though, ain't there."

"I don't know."

"It's dogs, for me," says Vince. "One of the fosters had this feral bastard rottweiler—one day it came at me, just like that, nothing I did. Got hold of my arm and started shaking it like a piece of meat—

and it was a piece of meat, my arm, to that dog. Guess what its name was? Petal. Fucking Petal, for a dog like that. Since then I can't be doing with dogs. Just expect it to go at me if I see one."

"I've got my thing about the sea and it's got its thing about me."

"I don't think the sea feels much about anyone."

But that's just it. The indifference. The old man used to look at me in the flat in Dorset, when we visited that cousin of his. He never blinked. He'd come into my room when everyone else was asleep and take off his belt and sit there, on the end of my bed, his wrists pale in the moonlight, unsure what to do with it next, or with me. The sea glared at me from the walls. It didn't help me then and it won't help me now.

"I'm sick of it," I tell him. "Sick to my stomach."

"You mean seasick."

"No."

Although I get that too. Coming out here, I fucking hate that crossing. Even if it's fair it doesn't agree with me, bouncing around like a jack-in-the-box. If I never had to do it again, I'd be glad. I dread the way back as soon as I'm ashore and when I'm ashore I dread coming off. That means life should be best for me when I'm home or on the tower, only it's not. Life's no good for me anywhere. Except with her.

"Why ain't you doing another job?" Vince asks. I can hear his teeth on the sweating cheese. A slurp of tea.

"Jesus. What's this, the fucking Gestapo?"

"No need to go at me. Just like that fucking dog, ain't you."

"We've got the house. It's not a bad setup. Don't know what else I'd do."

"You could train again."

"Easy for you," I say. "You haven't got children, a wife, having to get food on the table. All that shit, over and over, twenty-three quid a week and then what?"

"PK, for you."

"I'm not Arthur."

"You could be."

The biscuit's turned to carpet in my mouth. "I'm not like him."

Often, I'm tempted to say it. What I've done to Arthur. What I'm still doing. Just to hear how it sounds. I could tell Vince. But the moment's gone.

"Man, I love being back," he says. "These lighthouses. More beauty in them than I've seen. That's what I'm in it for. Getting that promotion. Soon I'll get to Assistant, like you, then a cottage to call my own. PK one day. Having my life on the lights."

"Doesn't take much, then."

"Lightkeeping's a skill, in my opinion."

"What skill? All we do is light a fire and watch it go, then put it out again. There's all the cleaning but a monkey could do that if it was trained long enough. Check in on the R/T. Cook a bit. What else is there?"

"Aw, it's more than that," says Vince. "I've said to you before I'm used to life in a cage, and there're people who can hack it and people who can't. And it's seen as bad to be OK with the cage. You know? As if the whole point of everything is to be on the outside. But if you're content when you're banged up, whether it's in Wandsworth or out on a lighthouse, where you're not behind bars but you're still trapped in every other fucking sense of it, that's enough to see you through. We had boys in the nick who were like lions in there. They'd be fighting and smashing stuff or killing themselves all cos of this thought they had about being free. Tell you what, Bill: I felt free the entire time I was in there. Never once did I feel like I wasn't. It's more than that, ain't it? That's all I'm saying. If you don't like being on a tower, it's not cos it's the tower that's wrong."

My first landing on the Maiden was the worst. I'd heard stories about the Maiden Rock, she'll rough you up, keep your eye on the ball or you're fish food, mate. The Occasional I was set to replace was already overdue by a fortnight and his wife was sick: under other circumstances they wouldn't have sent a relief with the weather as it was, waves toppling and rain bucketing, but Trident made the decision, so we did it.

I spent most of the crossing hunched over the side, the smell of the boatman's cigar mingling with salt spray and the sting of bile. I thought of the brick at the bottom of the swimming pool and how I'd be thrashing, deaf and blind, while I drowned.

We had a heavy, slugging sea, yanking us up and thumping us down, whumping and wheezing, the prow scarcely making headway against the wind. The sight of the tower on the open water fascinated me in a morbid, avid way, like how other large man-made structures do, giant pylons or cooling chimneys or the massive beached hull of a steel container ship.

There wasn't a lot of prep. You just arrived and let the men in the boat and on the set-off do the rest. I grasped the mechanics of it, had been told to consider myself the same as the supply cartons being lifted off, just to hang there and trust I'd be carried. You've got to trust the people on either end of the rope. But the problem that day wasn't the men or the winch; it was the sea, because the sea couldn't make up its mind what it was doing. I made a mess of the harness, a flimsy loop that went under my armpits, and the bit I held on to chafed between my palms.

I was hauled up in the air, sick as a dog, inched higher until the tower came close at last. I tried not to look too long at the spitting sea beneath my feet and what a distance seemed to have opened up there.

Suddenly there was a drop, the sea plunging thirty feet and sweeping the boat too far from the tower. The air filled with hollers and a blind sense of urgency. I squeezed my eyes shut. I didn't care at that point what became of me. For a time, I swung on the harness at the mercy of the elements, the waves skimming my shoes, then pitching back down. There were bellows from the boat:

"Bring him in, bring him in!" Then:

"Bring him back, are you trying to kill him?"

Rain bit my face, the wind battering and ripping through my clothes. I opened my eyes and saw a man leaning over the set-off, Arthur Black, my Principal Keeper, his hand within reach. I lunged, but the sea beat me to it, slamming me into the concrete with such force it would be minutes before I could breathe properly again. "Well done, lad," said my PK, "you're all right there." I grabbed the dog steps, freezing slippery cold, and began my ascent to the hot, dim mouth of the entrance.

Arthur made me tea and fed me fags till I'd warmed up.

Poor Bill. Pathetic Bill. I could see him thinking it. Bill, who never came in easy, without vomit down his front and terror in his soul. Bill, whose hand was never the one that stretched for a lesser man's but only the one that received: never the stone from which PKs were carved. Drowning at the surface and he never reached the brick.

Sometimes, after I've done one of my seashells, even if I'm happy with it, I'll drop it into the ocean from the bedroom window. The wind carries it off and I like the idea of that shell being returned to the sea. All that traveling over millions of years, all that effort, rolling in the grind of the prehistoric wash, only to be spat up on a distant shore and have a man like me scratch his imaginings into its body, defile its shape for his own satisfaction, then when he's done he puts it right back where it started.

13

VINCE

Lonely Type

TWO DAYS ON THE TOWER

Tuesday morning. Three weeks till Christmas. A light won't take days off or give you holidays; it wants you all the time. The others'll soon start thinking what their families are doing and feeling pissed off they're stuck here while at home the fir trees are going up and the mince pies getting eaten. That's the done thing, so I've heard. I don't think I've ever celebrated Christmas right. In the clink we had a sloppy dinner and paper hats, but as for the so-called magic of it, I don't know what that means.

This time of year, you can't extinguish your light till gone eight. But when the sun makes it through, I set to dismantling the burners, replacing them with clean ones in readiness for the night. Then I hang the curtains round the lenses. Unlikely once you get into December that the sun ramps up proper enough to start a fire, but it's second nature, and anyway it keeps them clean. It feels like you're getting the light dressed for the day and then at night you take its clothes off again. I'd never tell the others that.

As the morning watchman, I'm on breakfast. We've got a nice pack of bacon from when I came off, so I fry that up, then keep it warm in the Rayburn till the others get up. Normally the smell gets them up, and no matter what anyone says there isn't a better smell on the planet than frying bacon. It's not bad being chef on the Maiden cos the PK's nearly as crap as I am, so I don't feel self-conscious about the meals I put up. On my first island post the keepers there were really stuck-up about the food and sarcastic whenever I set a plate in front of them, which was rude since they never taught me any sodding thing about cookery even when I asked. It's only a knack you pick up, for me anyway. I don't even know what half the ingredients are before I get started.

"Anyone hear the birds?" I ask once we're sitting round tucking in.

"What birds?" says Arthur.

"Last night. Whole load of 'em came flying in at me."

The PK's up then, going to check upstairs cos it's his lantern; even if we're the ones keeping watch, it's still his light to look after. He checks on it like it's his child.

Bill's got his head low to the plate, which he always does when he eats, right down close to whatever he's eating, and a fag smoking in the ashtray next to him so he can puff and chew and puff and chew. He looks at Arthur's empty chair.

"Why'd you let him talk to you like that?" he says.

"Huh?"

"Like you're a fucking dimwit."

I wipe my mouth. "You're the one who calls me that."

"Did you see what he did?"

"What?"

"Rushing off to see what's been fucked. What *you've* fucked. Thinks you can't be trusted with your watch. Thinks the same of me."

It's fair game for a couple of keepers to have a moan about whoever's not in the room—like unscrewing a bottle, a way of letting it out, just to say, "Did you notice how annoying it was when he did this; he can be such a stingy prick from time to time, can't he?" Not meant unkindly, but it just keeps things bubbling away instead of bubbling over.

Bill's edgier than normal. Tired. I watch him smoke the last of the Embassy, grind it out, then push his plate away. The PK comes back.

"Didn't think about cleaning them up?" he says to me, a bit sharp.

"You wouldn't've had any grub till lunch if I had. Bill'll do it, won't you, Bill?"

"Fuck off."

Arthur clears the table with a "Thanks, that was good."

After breakfast, I get the bucket and shovel and go on up there to the gallery. In fairness I hadn't realized how many birds there were cos they came in like moths in the early hours, sometime around five, and who's to say what you're seeing then or if you're seeing it straight. What with all the feathers and flapping it could've been ten or a hundred. I smoke a cigarette in the harsh cold: dead gray sea and dead gray sky and my hands look dead gray too while I scrape them up. Shearwaters—they're pests anyhow, says Bill, no great loss, but I don't agree with that while I'm looking at them all flattened and twisted round on their necks. On the Bishop Rock once, I heard the keepers there found the gallery stuffed full of birds, living, squawking ones. There'd been nowhere to set foot, not a spare inch, it was like Noah's bloody Ark. It wasn't till darkness fell and the birds got the full glare of the lantern that they flew off, dozens of them. The lighthouse beam drew them in and dazzled them, or else it frightened them away.

THREE DAYS

I thought I'd find it hard coming back to the tower this time, what with things going strong between Michelle and me. But actually, once I've done a couple of nights it's a good thing. I've got all the time in the world to think about her, here. What I said to Bill on middle watch was right—I want to make Assistant, it's all I want, and to get that security cos Trident look after you for life. Then I'll be able to say to her, All right, how about it? I'll be a man with prospects for once.

It's me on lunch, then the PK does the washing-up, then his usual thing of sitting in his chair with a cup of tea and opening a crossword puzzle. He spares me a fag. Arthur's a good one for sharing. When I got my station at Alderney, the PK there never shared a single thing he had, didn't see the point in it. He'd sticker his jars and packets with KEEP OUT and HANDS OFF: it meant he was fine for butter and tobacco and HP Sauce, but nobody wanted his company. Arthur doesn't give a lot of thought to possessions, comestible or otherwise. It all passes, he says; it's stuff, it doesn't last. The feeling you get when you're all sitting round having a fine old time, that lasts.

"Miserably failing to meet expectations," he says.

"Piss off, the spuds weren't that rough."

"Two words. Six letters, five letters."

"One of those fuckers; I'm no good at those."

"You've got to think of it two ways," says the PK. "There's the literal clue, the one on the surface, then there's the clue inside. That one takes some special thinking."

"Don't think I've got much special thinking in my brain."

"It's a question of how you look at it."

"Give me another."

"Brew some magic up, pal."

"Just made you a cup," I say.

"That's the clue, you prat. Five letters."

"Bollocks."

"That's eight." He smiles. "You nearly said it a minute ago. Here, look here."

Arthur shows me. It goes over my head, truth be told.

"I can't see it."

"Near the end. Look."

"Oh," I say as he writes it in.

Bill was wrong about the PK. Arthur's one of those that wants to help you be better than you are, instead of getting shirty or uptight about your being younger than him or taking over or any of the things I reckon Bill thinks about me. The PK's patient. He'll show me how things are done. I admire him, how he feels about the sea; it's how it should be for a lighthouse keeper. It's a shame it isn't like that for everyone.

I don't know if Bill knows that I know. That Arthur told me once on graveyard watch what happened to him years ago, when he started on the Maiden, before Bill had joined the service, before I was even walking. I lost my tongue when he said it. Didn't know how to react. I hadn't been expecting it. Why would I? You don't expect it.

I just looked at Arthur and thought, That's the kind of man I want to be. So's you'd never guess what he'd lived through. You spend your time looking up to the PK, thinking he'll have the answers, then he isn't at all what you thought.

✳

Neil Young on the Sony and my bunk curtain drawn. Bill's downstairs with his drill whistling; it's somewhere between night and day and I'm glad of the music that takes me to another place. Back in Michelle's crammed studio on Stratford Road, Neil or John Denver or King Crimson. Wine bottles with candles stuffed into them and wax down the sides; cushions with diamond mirrors sewn on. A cat in the doorway, licking its paws. *Blue Ridge Mountains, Shenandoah River* . . . Shenandoah. Now that's got no business being a word. Ought to be a magic spell or a distant moon. Everything washed in the orange of canned peaches. Lots of my thoughts of Michelle come with their own light. Purple smoke in the bedroom. Bright green when she goes out barefoot to the garden and yells the puss in for tea. What's the cat's name? Sykes? No. Staines? Poor bugger. Steptoe? Can't be.

Michelle's too good for me. 'Least I've got the brains to know it.

I never would have had the balls to go after her if it weren't for Trident House signing me up, and that only happened by accident. There aren't a lot of keepers my age at the moment—there're better wages to be had on the North Sea oil rigs, but it depends what kind of work you like doing and what shape your history's in. April '70 I'd been out in the world a couple of weeks when I bumped into this bloke in the pub;

he bought me a pint and told me he'd kept lights up on Pladda and Skerryvore back in the day. Like the other times, I was waiting to get nicked again. That was what I was used to, so I knew I'd fuck up on purpose once I was done with the outside. But the more this bloke went on about the lights, the more I thought they'd suit me. All he said was, You can't be the lonely type—you've got to think that being on your own is a good thing.

I didn't bank on Trident letting me in once they found out my record, but a few weeks later I got my letter in the post. They must've thought, He'll do, thick as a brick but he's keen. Fact is, there's not a lot to be getting on with on a lighthouse. The simplicity of it's what does it. Small tasks that absorb your mind. The illumination at night, then cleaning, cooking, checking in with the other lights in the group. Making sure there's no bad feeling between you and the men you're with, cos that's the thing you can't predict. You have to keep the atmosphere friendly, and that to me seems the most important part. Making the best of it with the others, cos if you let that get one over on you, it becomes a virus, spreading and multiplying, then by the time you realize, you're all infected, the rot's set in, and there's nowhere to go.

I look back on meeting that old keeper in the pub and it feels like I was getting sent a message. I wasn't a lost cause. The world hadn't given up on me yet.

Soon, I'll have to tell Michelle. It's been long enough now. Have to be honest about myself, cos what's the point in carrying on and making this life for us and asking her to marry me, if we can't do any of that cos I've got this big bloody lie sitting between us? Not the stuff I did before—she knows about that. I'm talking about the last time.

Trouble is, it's not the sort of thing you drop in on a first date, or even a third, then after a while it gets too hard to bring up. With me being away so much, it means when I come back it's like we start all over again. Back to the beginning, the holding hands, the wondering, the wanting. I'm not going to ruin that.

The more I like her the harder it is, and I don't want to like her too much, but you can't help these things.

Lies are easy to make. You just say nothing. Do nothing. Let the other person decide what's real. I wouldn't want to know if I were her. Every day I try to forget.

When I close my eyes, I can still see it, as clear as if it happened last night. Blood and fur, a child's high scream: and my friend in my arms, grown cold.

My whole life I've looked over my shoulder to see who's coming. I still look behind me, even out here on the sea where there's nobody but us.

I live with the knowledge I've got enemies. Bad people who do bad things and they want to do bad things to me. I get afraid of going to sleep sometimes because of the nightmares I have. That they'll find me here, on this rock. *You thought you had it in you to get out from under, but you're wrong, son. You'll never be more than you are.*

I'm never going back. Not to prison. Not to my old life.

That's why I brought it off with me. Hid it in the wall cranny under the sink where the others won't find it. It's safe there. You'd have to know where to look.

At some point I fall asleep, cos next thing I know Bill's shoving me awake in the thick, groggy dark and telling me to get upstairs cos the light's not going to watch itself and if he doesn't get some bloody kip soon he might do something he'll regret.

IV

·

1992

14

HELEN

A mile farther on, past two padlocked gates, she saw them at last: four single-story keepers' cottages nestled on the peninsula, painted green and white, with factory-black chimneys and slate roofs. The Maiden Rock cottages were as close to the lighthouse as it was possible to be, but still so far away, and this had always struck Helen as sad, unrequited, a hopeful heart reaching out to indifference.

It could be yesterday; Admiral could still be theirs. The biggest of them, purpose-built and utilitarian, a cross between a school boardinghouse and a P&O ferry. Inside it had corridors like a hospital and small box rooms, whose hard, antiseptic edges no quantity of personal belongings could soften. In winter a chill crept through the cracks in the windows, which were fastened with iron latches that made her palms smell of coins. Above the oven and shower, Trident House issued laminated reminders that the property was not theirs: USE EXTRACTOR FAN and CAUTION: HOT WATER. A notice in the hall read IN CASE OF EMERGENCY DIAL 999. At the front, beyond the barren, windswept veranda with its concrete picnic table, garage doors advised

DANGER—DO NOT USE IN HIGH WINDS. And always, always, the monotony of it—that was what had done her in. Day in, day out, the weeks, the months, the years, with only the sea for company.

Jenny and Bill had lived in Masters. Today there was a red hatchback parked on the tarmac with a BABY ON BOARD sticker in the rear. Helen supposed it was a unique getaway for people, a glimpse into a lost world, and the Maiden Rock's infamy ensured a one-off attraction. That was why the cottages had been converted so quickly after automation, a money-spinner for Trident House. She could see the advert now:

Experience what life was like for the Maiden Rock Missing!

The third cottage, Pursers, had been Betty and Frank's. Frank had been First Assistant on the tower, having been in the job longer—when Arthur was ashore, he'd be made Keeper-in-Charge. Frank had been off duty at the time of the vanishing. Helen always thought it must have felt to him as if he'd turned up five minutes late for a flight that wound up crashing into a mountain.

Gunners, the last, would have gone to Vince. He had wanted that promotion so badly. The reason why he'd never got it was a secret only the lighthouse knew.

As the Maiden glimmered coolly on the horizon, Helen could not shake her suspicion that the tower knew yet more. It knew about her.

Now it returned her gaze in quiet accusation, as if to say: You can't deny the truth, Helen. You are not the innocent.

※

She gave him the address and he put out his fag and jerked his head to the boot.

"Any bags, love?"

"No. I'm just here for the day. I need you to take me to the station after."

"Right you are."

The sun was dropping, molten peach as it dipped into the horizon. Helen was glad he could not see her properly, in the back of the taxi, drowsy in summer shadow. Mortehaven drivers were Mortehaven born and bred: the story was forever at the forefront of their minds, as they were called upon by tourists to recap the disappearance or identify their part in it, where they had been when they'd heard, the Trident House official they'd carried once from A to B, the friend of their daughter who knew one of the Walker children. She shouldn't think he would recognize her anyway, not all these years on, but equally expected strangers to greet her as they had in the past, when she was Mrs. PK, asking how Arthur was, when he was due ashore, how she was getting on in his absence. In return they would tell her their personal business, their problems, her position as the Principal Keeper's wife issuing a public service akin to that of a reverend or pub landlord, interested by default in the lives of people she didn't know.

"Are you picking up a friend?" he asked from the front.

"We're not stopping," she said. "Well, we are, but only for a moment. I'm not getting out."

He turned the radio on. They passed the church with its slender evening spire, and the smugglers' inn where she and Arthur and Jenny and Bill had gone for supper on a rare occasion both men were ashore. After a bottle of wine, Jenny had cried and told her she was lucky she didn't have children because it was no good looking after them when you were stranded back here on your own; Bill had got it in the neck, then Jenny had been sick in the ladies and they'd left. Winding up past the hotel and park and through the climbing terraces.

The same address Helen had visited for the last nineteen years, whenever she came back, a rite of passage even if she never went inside. One of these days she would pluck up the courage to get out and walk up to the door.

"Here," she said. "Anywhere's fine."

A gift at this late hour to be able to glimpse into windows: squares lit gold, life glowing within. "What do you want to do?" he asked. "Shall I turn the engine off?"

"It's OK. Keep it running."

The house was the only one in darkness. Perhaps Jenny had gone away or didn't live here anymore. The thought panicked Helen—of being unable to contact her; of never again putting to paper those things she could only ever say to this woman, about their loved ones, their lost ones, the breach between them that twenty years later had calcified to stone.

Jenny had thought she could put her trust in the PK's wife. Why shouldn't she? Trust had been the foundation of Helen's job. It had been her role to give support, to pour drinks and hold hands, to wipe tears when life became too much, because she understood, she did, and she cared. She knew when to stroke an arm, saying, "There, my love, it's not forever, he'll be back before you know it," and think of ways she could make it better, because lonesomeness was a friend of hers and she knew its tricks and wiles.

Instead, Helen had deceived her.

"All right," she told the driver. "We can go now."

"That's it?"

"Yes. I'm ready to go home."

The train was late; the soporific chug of its wheels closed her eyes before Truro. She dreamed, again, that she was following him in a crowd—the back of his head, only when the head turned it wasn't the right person after all. His eyes came to her in drifts of sleep, looking up from underwater or otherwise in broad daylight, sitting opposite her at the kitchen table, or at the end of her bed, keeping watch over all that she did.

15

HELEN

You'd like to know why I don't speak to Jenny Walker. Rather, why she doesn't speak to me. Are you interested in the truth? You say you are, but you're also very good at making things up. I'll admit your novels aren't my sort of thing. I haven't read any, in fact— although I know the one about the brothers on the barrack ship, *Ghost Fleet*, that's right: a friend of mine got quite into that one when it came out.

That's what I'm saying, without wishing to be rude. Alpha men, fighting, all that testosterone flying about. If you're looking to tell one of your adventure stories, I doubt you'll see what happened between Jenny and me as relevant, if I'm honest.

Who knows if it was relevant? Over the years I've gone half mad asking myself if it was. If Arthur and the others disappeared because of how things were with us.

First, I'll tell you that I never expected to marry a lighthouse keeper. I was aware there must be people doing it, but it always sounded marginal to me, a job someone might take if he didn't fit in with any other part of society, and it turns out I was right. It takes a special temperament. All the keepers I've known have had that shared thing in common, and that's to be all right with their own company. Arthur was content with himself. I thought that was very attractive in someone and I still do. You can only get so close to that person because he has something inside him that only he knows about. My grandmother had a saying about that. It was to never show your full hand—you know, to whomever you're with. Never show your cards, always keep something back. I don't think Arthur showed his full hand to anyone, not even me. That was just who he was.

I'm not sure I'd describe him as lonely. As I said, he had a contained way about him, but that isn't the same as loneliness. Being on your own doesn't mean you're lonely and the other way around: you can be with lots of people, all chattering and nattering and demanding of your presence, and you can be the loneliest person there is. Certainly, on the lighthouses, Arthur was never lonely. I'm confident about that. That was one of the questions people asked, they'd say, Doesn't he find it lonely out there? But he never did. If anything, I'd say it was here, on land, that he felt lonely.

When you think of it like that, it isn't any wonder I made a mistake. I'm not justifying it, and Jenny wouldn't either. But nothing's ever black and white.

I'm not sure Arthur ever wanted to come home to me. When he came ashore on his relief, I could see as soon as he stepped off the boat that he was already missing the light. Not missing being there—missing *her*. Land life wasn't for him.

What we went through, Arthur and me, of course that was part of it. I had a lot of feelings about that, a lot of complicated feelings to come to terms with. I blamed Arthur. He blamed me. We blamed each other, but there just isn't any point in blame when something like that happens, is there? There just isn't any point.

I felt so angry after he disappeared. That he'd found this way out for himself. He had no right to do that, just upping and leaving one day without a word. He always said I was strong, and I am strong, but sometimes I think I should never have let him know it.

When Arthur first got his post to the Maiden, I thought we'd be happy. The tower made him happy, so I thought we'd be happy too. Arthur was pleased because for him she was the best of the lights. He'd done spells on the Wolf, the Bishop, the Eddystone, the Longships, all the major sea stations, but the Maiden was the one he coveted: big, old-fashioned, the sort of lighthouse he'd dreamed about when he was a boy. Arthur said a sea tower was "a proper lighthouse"—the proper experience of one. Boys don't dream about the ones stuck on land, do they? They want boats chucked about on the waves, brigands and buccaneering, camaraderie and starlight.

For a while after Arthur died, I consoled myself by thinking that at least it was the way he'd have wanted to go. He wouldn't have wanted to die in any other way than on the sea. In a sense it's fitting, and that actually makes me feel a bit better about it.

The Maiden always had her eye on him. Does that sound silly? Don't put that in your book, will you. Lighthouses don't have personalities; they don't have thoughts and feelings and dangerous ideas, and they don't bear ill will toward people. Anything like that's fantasy—and that's your department, not mine. I'm just giving you the facts.

But I never liked the look of her. Some lights look friendly enough, but she never put me at ease. I never set foot on her and I didn't like that either, that Arthur stayed somewhere I'd never been. But you can't land on a tower any day you feel like it; you can't drop in to say hello. Seeing as Arthur was a private man, this suited him. I think he liked having something away from me. Perhaps all husbands do. They need something that their wives know nothing about.

Oh, be quiet! The dog needs letting out. Will you excuse me for a moment?

Right, here we are. Sorry about that. I spend my life waiting for her to get on with things. I got my first dog right after I lost Arthur because I needed another heartbeat about the place, and I suppose I was used to having a quiet companion, or at least one who wasn't here for much of the time. Unfortunately, this one's been on a digging spree, but that's the way of it, and she's as entitled to the garden as I am. I never used to bother with planting, but that's helped me too. It's about watching what you've put in the ground grow and flourish. If you've been through an ordeal like ours, you need to see the way life has of coming back again and again, against the odds, against the frost and the dog paws. There's a certain stubbornness in it that I admire.

Arthur was always fascinated by nature. Right from childhood, he was sensitive, with a full imagination. Like you, in that way—the imagination part. I'm not saying you're insensitive. I haven't spent enough time with you to tell one way or the other, and anyway, what business is it of mine? I'd assume you have to be sensitive to be an author, getting inside your characters' minds and coming up with what makes them tick.

His father kept birds, that's what started it. The poor man wasn't well, it was shell shock after the war, an extremely bad case, and the birds soothed him.

Arthur didn't like to talk about his father. Wouldn't or couldn't. Whenever I asked, he'd change the subject, or tell me he didn't wish to discuss it. There was much my husband didn't wish to discuss, and I came to learn that's all well and good until the person you're with wants to talk. When your wife wants to, she deserves to have a conversation, doesn't she? Because how else does anything ever get solved?

I do think, sometimes, how we might have avoided everything that happened: those twists and turns of life that evolve from a single decision. If Arthur hadn't seen the Trident advertisement in the paper, if we hadn't bought that particular paper on that particular day . . . If I'd never met him, because that was a chance encounter as well, in the queue at Paddington Station when I was short of change to buy my ticket. A single to Bath Spa, to visit my parents. Even then, when it was the done thing, I didn't assume a man would pay for me. I thought about Arthur the whole way there.

We met a week later so I could pay him back. The attraction was a slow burn. It wasn't one of those lovestruck, thunderbolt situations. Part of me was pleased at imagining my father would disapprove. He was headmaster at an all-boys boarding school and he wanted me to marry a doctor or a lawyer, someone with a "reputable" job. He never told me so, but I'd put money on him thinking lighthouse keeping was for men with a feminine way about them. I don't think my father ever read a single line of poetry. Does that explain it better?

Trident offered us a good salary and starting package, housing was thrown in, and bills were paid—it all sounded highly agreeable. Arthur thought he'd fit in well and I thought it was the kind of lifestyle that would be a good conversation starter at parties—that my husband worked on a lighthouse. I didn't realize then that parties didn't come too far out of London and they certainly didn't swim down the

Severn Estuary and emerge in the Bristol Channel, around which we spent the best part of those first years.

The routine wasn't easy on either of us to begin with. As an SAK they send you all over the country and you never know where you'll be sent to next. Every few weeks you're at a new light. It's because Trident wants to give you as much experience as they can, so you learn the job fast. But they're also testing you. They want to know if you're able to get along with the different personalities, if you're flexible, if you're willing and reliable. We used to joke that Arthur was parceled from here to kingdom come—only kingdom never came, until the Maiden, that was. But yes, it was tiring. I never stayed anywhere long enough to settle, and Arthur was off for long stretches at a time. It was harder than I'd been prepared for. I felt him slipping away from me even then.

Not everyone found the training as hard as we did. Vince, for instance, he was used to being moved around and never staying put; he grew up in foster care and I don't think he ever had a permanent home. Vince appreciated the spontaneity of it, getting a posting through, then you pack your bags and go where you're needed. You could be called up north or down south or out on an island somewhere. The Maiden was Vince's first tower. It's an extreme post for a novice anyway, but then when you think how it ended . . . Just terrible. A young man with his whole life ahead of him.

I'm not surprised Michelle Davies won't talk to you. As his girlfriend she had a bad time of it after the disappearance, with everyone saying Vince had been responsible for it, he'd killed Arthur and Bill, some plan he'd been formulating weeks in advance, then he made a clever escape for himself. Trident implied it too. They weren't allowed to say so, but they definitely encouraged people to believe that.

Michelle's married now. Two daughters. I shouldn't think she wants to revisit that period in her life. She and Vince were very in love. He used to come down from London before his duty was about to start. I'd see him in the harbor with his cassette player, all arms and legs and one of those big mustaches you see in American TV shows. He would've got keepers' accommodation once he'd made Assistant.

Arthur spoke highly of Vince, said what a nice boy he was, decent and down-to-earth. It's a shame for a person, when they've had a difficult start in life, and they can never get out from under because people always think the worst of them.

Trident got blamed for hiring a man with a criminal record, but they were always taking people who needed a way back into society and it was never frowned upon or worried about. Lighthouse keeping is the best job for someone who's used to being closed off and living in confined spaces. They're normally a very disciplined sort too, in being accustomed to a strict way of life. It wasn't unusual to be on a light with a borstal boy, or someone who'd been in jail. The trouble was when something went wrong, which it did, it was easy to point the finger. Michelle couldn't argue back. She couldn't speak up for Vince, because that wasn't what the Institution wanted to hear. It went against their party line. That'll be why she doesn't want to see you. She doesn't want all that scraped up and all those horrible things being said about Vince again. People went ballistic at the time, when they found out he'd been in jail. There was every rumor circling you could think of—that he'd been a murderer, he'd murdered ten people; he was a serial killer, a rapist, or a pedophile. I can tell you he wasn't any of those.

You don't have to go to prison to know you've done wrong. Aren't we all accountable, to a certain extent? What I did. What Arthur did.

What Bill did. Just because someone didn't put bars around us, it doesn't mean those bars weren't deserved. Or that they didn't exist.

Michelle told me once that Vince did many things in his life that he wanted to forget. Now you know about Arthur and me, I can admit to you that I did too.

16

TWO PAPERS

Daily Telegraph, April 1973

PRISON EVIDENCE IN MAIDEN
ROCK INVESTIGATION

As hopes fade for three men who disappeared from the
Maiden Rock Lighthouse last December, new facts come to
light that sources suggest implicate the youngest of them,
Vincent Bourne, as a possible agent in the event. Mr. Bourne,
the Supernumerary Assistant Keeper, was twenty-two when
he vanished from the remote Southwest station between
Christmas and New Year, along with his colleagues Arthur
Black and William Walker. It emerged yesterday that before enrolling with Trident House Mr. Bourne was detained
on charges of Arson, Common Assault, Assault Occasion-
ing Actual Bodily Harm, Trespass, Theft, Incitement, and
Attempted Escape from Lawful Custody.

Sunday Mirror, April 1973

SCANDALOUS SECRET LIFE OF CRIMINAL LIGHTHOUSE KEEPER

Loner lightman Vincent Bourne has been EXPOSED as a repeat offender in a series of leaks made by a former jail mate. "You name it, he's done it," says our source; "he's capable of anything." Unmarried Vince went missing from the Maiden Rock four months ago with two others. All three men remain unaccounted for. "He shouldn't have gone anywhere near that tower," says our source. "Whatever happened, he did it."

17

MICHELLE

She hadn't been his girlfriend for a long time, she thought as she bent to tie the fifty-sixth shoelace of the day. "Stay still," she told her daughter, whose hand grabbed a clump of hair in response. A lot of the time Michelle couldn't tell whose hair it was, just that hair got grabbed in angry fistfuls and when it hurt it was probably hers.

"Now keep them on," she said. "Please."

The sisters went off to play Snakes and Ladders, or empty the game across the carpet and feed the dice to the dog. Michelle stayed in the hall, watching the phone.

He had called once already this morning, and again yesterday, and again last week. "I'm not Vinny's girlfriend anymore," she'd told him, which was stating the bleeding obvious, since Vinny would never again have a girlfriend as long as he lived—and he wasn't living, was he? Or was he? To cope with uncertainty long-term, to let it get inside her and make its nest there, was the worst kind of limbo.

Dan Sharp might think he could get to the bottom of it, but Michelle couldn't say if there was one. It just went down and down, like the sea. Why Vinny disappeared and how—these were things she would never discover. And if he wanted her to say that Vinny had been all the things he hadn't, all the things the public hated him for, well, she couldn't. She had her own family now. Her husband wouldn't be glad to come home to find her talking to a stranger, breathing life back into the man she'd loved when she was nineteen, the only man, truly, she'd ever loved.

The author should go sniffing round somebody else's door. He had no idea what he was getting himself into, dredging up memories from people who'd rather stay out of it. He should stick with his thrillers. Michelle had borrowed one last year from the library while they were in there looking for *Esio Trot*. Roger had called it rubbish, but he didn't like her reading. Said it put fancy ideas in her head.

"Mummy!"

Two minutes, the average time it took before one of the girls shouted a complaint. What would it be this time? Accusations of snatching, cheating, Fiona taking her knickers off and sitting bare bottomed on the board game. She went in, comforted the crying, and tried to take her mind off Vincent Bourne. That was another world, one she no longer lived in. Even if she wanted to, she couldn't find a way back.

People hardly talked to her about it now. Marriage had helped, since she didn't have the same name so they couldn't recognize her; they couldn't say, "Oh, *that's* who you are, you'll know all about that, then," to which her reply was always the same. No, she knew nothing, no more than they did. But still they'd get that look in their eye, nudge-nudge, wink-wink, as if she did indeed know why those men had vanished, but of course she couldn't tell. It had been her man, after all. His secret.

"Mummy, want a biscuit."

"What do you say?"

"Please."

The children put up a wall, but that was as good as it got. Walls stopped her feeling. Hurting. Except when she managed to scale them, usually first thing in the morning when she opened her eyes and the day was a blank white page, and she had an image of Vinny in her mind that was so real it could have been a photograph. She couldn't believe it had been twenty years since they'd touched. How had her mind held on to these details? She never talked to Roger about it. He was the jealous type anyway, wasn't interested in past relationships, especially not that one.

On the way back from the kitchen, the telephone rang. Michelle stopped, malted milks in hand, paint stains down her top. It would be him again.

There were things she could tell him. Sometimes she almost wanted to, just to be free of them. But that was in the dead of night, and by the time the alarm clock shrilled, and the girls needed getting up, and there was breakfast to be made and Roger's sandwiches to go in a bag and the school runs to be done, she saw sense.

Michelle picked up the phone.

The writer started talking, but she cut him off.

"I told you to leave me alone," she said, gripping the receiver. "I've got nothing to tell you about Vinny. If you contact me again, I'll call the police."

18

JENNY

The sand got everywhere. Jenny disliked how it felt between her toes, how it made the skin there squeak, how it got into the picnic basket and the cheese-and-pickle rolls she'd prepared that morning, careful to cut them into quarters as her grandson preferred. Later she'd go home with grit in her teeth and it would be there in her food for a week.

The beach reminded her of that scene in *Jaws*. Little ones in sun hats patting out buckets, squealing in the shallows, and shivering in towels. Jenny had seen *Jaws* at the Orpheus three summers after Bill went and God only knew why she'd put herself through it. Bad things coming up out of the sea, things with teeth that smelled of blood.

Jenny didn't like to be scared. It was like being a child again, afraid of the dark and the creak on the stairs; the shadows in her mum's garden on Conferry Road that came closer day by day. When they were little, Carol used to tell her stories about vampires and werewolves, and others she made up too, about the shriveled thing that lived under the bed. Jenny thought there'd been enough to be afraid of in that house.

No wonder Carol had left as soon as she could. She had cut her ties. Jenny, the younger, had stuck around longer.

Hannah came back with the ice creams. "Sorry," she said. "They melted."

The cones were soggy and green. The grandchildren got the best of them, then dropped them in the sand. Jenny felt her shoulders burning.

"Not still thinking about it, are you?" said Hannah.

"No."

"You're paranoid."

"So what if I am?"

Jenny looked out at the lighthouse, cloaked in mist, the sort there is on the sea after the weather's blown over. The more she peered into the steam, the more the tower materialized. It would always concern her how these two scenes could be part of the same world. Children on a beach, carefree and licking ice creams. And that place.

"You think that man's spying on you."

"No, I don't."

Jenny moved under the parasol. A couple strolled past, his hand on the small of her back. Bill had used to walk next to her with his hand on the small of her back. At the beginning, anyway, when he'd still wanted to be near her.

"You've got to stop curtain twitching, Mum. It's unhealthy. And turn some bloody lights on at home; I'm sick of coming round and finding it like a mausoleum."

"Then don't come round."

Hannah sulked for a minute, then said, "What are you worried about anyway? He's only going to write up what you tell him."

"What's that supposed to mean?"

"I don't know. I'm asking you."

Jenny pushed a hole in the sand with her finger. It felt cooler under the surface.

"Stop talking to him," said Hannah.

"I can't."

"Why?"

"If she is," said Jenny, "I am." She would avoid saying Helen's name at any cost. She hated that she even had to think it, that the woman existed at all.

"For God's sake—" Hannah jumped up and ran down the beach, where Nicholas had fallen in another child's sandpit. Sometimes Jenny wished she had never told Hannah about Bill's affair, back when Hannah was barely a teen. The right thing would have been to keep it to herself—for her daughter to have had nice, unspoiled memories of her dad as loving and caring. After a while, though, Jenny hadn't been able to stop herself. She couldn't share it with anyone else because she was embarrassed.

On the outside, she and Bill had been the perfect couple, the envy of their friends. After he went, it seemed a shame to ruin it. Tragedy on top of tragedy.

Hannah came back with a bawling child. A sour taste filled Jenny's mouth. She thought about what Bill must have tasted when he'd eaten those chocolates.

"Who cares what that cow's doing?" said Hannah, sitting down next to her. She shielded her eyes from the sun. "You were the one who knew him, Mum."

Hannah put a hand on hers and Jenny worried she might cry. She'd have no one left, if Hannah found out. She had only meant to teach Bill a lesson. Remind him where his loyalties lay. Just the tiniest amount of household bleach—"limited vomiting when swallowed in small quantities"—disguised by the soapy flavor of violet.

It was her own fault. She hadn't made an effort with anyone in years, just hidden herself away, eating microwave dinners in front of reruns of *Blockbusters*. Julia and Mark were good enough to her, but Hannah was the special one: the older she'd grown, the more like friends they'd become. Hannah believed her mother was the innocent victim. Jenny couldn't risk her discovering that both her parents had failed.

Now this Sharp person would push and prod until she gave in. Or maybe he already knew. Maybe Helen knew; maybe Arthur had written it in a note sent back from the tower. The worst part would be explaining it to Hannah. She couldn't.

"You were married fourteen years," said Hannah. "Three children, Mum. Helen knew him for what? Five bloody minutes. She can say what she likes. If raking up what happened is making you miserable, don't do it. I mean, shadowy figures waiting outside your house in cars? Come on."

Hannah was right. Only Jenny had felt it the night before last, really *felt* it, someone loitering on the road. And sure enough, when she'd peered through the nets, she'd seen a car there with its engine purring. It had sat for a long time, watching her. No one had come to meet it; no one climbed out. Moments later it drove away.

Jenny stood and shook the sand off her towel. It blew back on her, stinging. She wanted to go home, but the children were coming back too, and she'd have to put the oven on for chops and get to peeling potatoes, and she'd miss *Neighbours* now at the least. She helped to pack the bags, call the children, dust off their feet—and all the while the Maiden stood obscenely at her back, her ghastly companion.

The intruder was opening doors she needed to stay closed. Doors she'd spent years blocking, because the place beyond was one she could never set foot in again.

She had already lost her husband. She wasn't losing her daughter too.

19

JENNY

I don't see it as a downside, not knowing. It's good not to know. Mum used to say, "Jennifer, you don't know anything." She meant it meanly because she was a mean woman, but actually, it's helped me a lot in the course of my life. They've never found Bill's body and until that happens, there's a chance he's alive. As long as there's a chance, there's hope. It gets less as the years go by, but it's never completely gone.

Until Trident House can show me what's left of my husband, I won't accept he's dead. Why should I? His vanishing was a magic trick. He could come back the same way. Surprise! Like that Paul Daniels off the telly. It'd be no harder accounting for Bill popping back up than it is accounting for how he got lost.

Authors are meant to be open-minded, aren't they? Well. Let's see.

You'll remember I told you about Bill's bad feeling. He had these extra senses; he was that sort of soul. Tuned in, like me. It's no surprise, in my opinion, what with his mother dying like that. It meant Bill got to believing—at least, he wanted to believe—that there was more to life than the skin and bone we're given in this one.

When we first started going together, he used to leave notes for me. He'd put them in my desk at school, saying what time to meet. We had to do it in secret because of Mum. Carol had gone by then, so it was just Mum and me at home. She'd lock the door as soon as I got in and wouldn't let me out again. There was a tree in the park, with a hole in the trunk he put presents in. A bag of sherbet lemons or a plastic ring he'd got off the market. I still think I could find one of those notes one day, from Bill. Under my pillow or propped up by the kettle. The cottage where we used to live, Monday, four thirty, he'll meet me there.

I'm not saying Bill's off sunning himself on a beach somewhere. Just that if it *was* something supernatural that took him—better to say, *borrowed* him—then something supernatural might just as easily return him to me. It's possible, and that's enough for me.

I don't trust people who say they've never experienced something they can't explain. They must be very closed off as people and it's a waste to live a life where you only think about what's in front of you and you never consider what else there is.

You have to look beyond all that. Stretch your mind out a little, if that's what it takes.

Did you ever hear about the Silver Man? He's a bit of a Mortehaven local legend. I never clapped eyes on him myself, but plenty I know did. Trustworthy people who you'd swear were telling you the truth. They said they saw him just wandering about as plain as day, easy as you like, just as if he belonged.

God, your publishers really picked a bright one with you, didn't they? Because he was silver, obviously, his hair and clothes. Even his skin, sort of silvery, like a fish. And the weird thing about him, as well as what he looked like, was that he showed up in places he couldn't have got to. Like he'd got there more quickly than he could; like there must have been more than one copy of him drifting about. There were folk who said he seemed like he was on his way to work because he was carrying a briefcase and that was silver in color too. Some would see him at the bottom of the high street, then they got in their cars and minutes later he came out in front of them at the top of the climb or up on the cliff, three or more miles away. Pat in the Seven Sisters said she saw him one time waving at her from down on the beach, and if you ever meet Pat, you'll know she doesn't know how to tell a lie. He was far off and carrying his little silver bag, and she said it was just like he was inviting her over because as she got closer, he walked into the sea and carried on walking till he went under and that was the end of that.

You're right that I'm Christian, but I think the more you understand religion, the more you see it's part and parcel of the same thing. Heaven and hell—that's supernatural, isn't it? Angels and devils. Bushes on fire. Seas split in two. If you trust God, you should be broad-minded about the possibilities in His universe.

There's more than what the textbooks tell you. It's not like science for all its cleverness gets the answers. Take that about Creation. Science goes back with its theories about the Big Bang, but then it can't get any further because there's no reason why any of the stuff that was needed for the Big Bang to happen was there in the first place. All these particles and atoms or whatever was meant to go bang, they don't come out of nowhere, do they? Bill said that's why a lot of scientists believe. They know better than anyone that you can't get something out of nothing.

My mum believed in both. Growing up, we had crosses and psalms all over the house; everywhere you looked there was the baby Jesus, you couldn't get away from Him. Mum lit candles and kept the cur-

tains closed so it was like a chapel inside, but we also had wind chimes
and dream catchers, and she saw shamans sometimes. One of them
was called Kestrel. He came round and put his hand on Mum's head
and spoke gobbledygook, then they went upstairs. I remember he had
a big ink of two crossed feathers at the top of his back. I saw it one
morning when I came into the kitchen in my nightie and there he was,
making toast like he lived with us.

When I was nine, the Virgin Mary turned up in our garden. She
arrived one day lying facedown by the shed, in between the fridge
and the pile of bin bags. Mum said she'd fallen out the back of a van
at church, so she'd brought her home to watch over us—because we
needed watching over, Carol and me. The fact she'd fallen out the
back of it that's just a turn of phrase, now I think of it that's just a turn of phrase, not actually
what happened, but in those days I had an image in my head of the
van doors coming open and a life-sized Madonna smacking her face
on the pavement. You could see where she'd smacked it; her cheek
was chipped on one side. Mum had this plan to bring her in and clean
her up, but she never did, so I went out there and put her upright.
From then on, every night I made myself open my bedroom curtains
and see her standing there like a real person. I'd scare myself into
thinking she moved, from one side of the garden to the other, then
toward me, nearer each day.

Even though Mum said she was religious, she must have sworn by
a different God to mine. Let's just say the plaster Mary wasn't the only
one who got a smacking.

Living with her made me understand the difference between good
and bad. How you can't always see the difference with your eyes—
you have to feel it, you know, here. The way I look at it, there's light

and dark in the world and that's what the whole world revolves around. There has to be light in order for there to be dark and the same the other way. It's like a set of weighing scales, up at one end, down at the other. It depends which there's more of—the more light you have, the harder it is for the dark to get in. The thing about God's light is it's easy; it's not hard to find. There might be moments in your life where you get a little bit of light, say if you have good news or a nice thing happens to you, and I think that's like flicking a torch on. It's bright while it lasts but it doesn't last forever. God's light lasts.

Bill was the only person I confided in, about that and lots of things. When we got engaged, Mum told him she was glad he was taking me off her hands because she'd had about as much as she could stand. Apart from that I don't think she ever spoke a word to him. At my wedding reception, she locked herself upstairs at the pub with a bottle of Jameson, crying about how I was leaving her.

I did leave her, in the end. She fell asleep in the WC and I left her there, with her head on the toilet roll dispenser. I haven't spoken to her since. I don't know if she's dead or alive. I don't waste time thinking about it. After Bill went, she didn't try to contact me, even though it was all over the papers so it wouldn't have been hard. I didn't want her to find me anyway. I'm better off without her. It takes a lot to say you're better off without your mother, but that's the fact of it for me.

I'll never have my girls hate me like I hate my mother. I'll never be a mother like that. Not really a mother—that's a holy word and she wasn't a holy woman, just a person who put me in this world, then washed her hands of me.

It was fate I found Bill. I'd be in a shelter, or homeless, if it weren't for Bill and the lighthouse service. Now do you see why he would never have left that tower of his own accord? We'd come so far for what we had. That's how I know it was something else that went on.

I could tell when his bad feeling got one over on him. He'd stop eating or sleeping. He'd wake at five o'clock in the morning; I could hear him swallowing in the dark. He'd lie there so still. If I said anything, if I said, "Bill, love, are you awake?" he wouldn't answer, and that's when I knew he was under one of his clouds.

When he did talk to me, which wasn't often, I always listened. He'd never had that. His dad and brothers were always making fun of him, and if there's anything Bill hates, it's being made fun of. He'd be another man, if he'd had his mum. Then again, I wouldn't have wanted another man, so that's a problem it's best if I don't think too long on.

Do you believe in coincidences? You must. You've got a big fat one at the end of *Neptune's Bow* with those two characters of yours walking into the same hotel. What are the chances of that? You could've found another way round it, but you didn't. Maybe you and me aren't so different after all.

Well, here's another one for you. You'll know the light was burning the night before Bill disappeared—the night of the twenty-ninth. The papers made a lot of that at the time, because it means that whatever happened must have happened the next morning, before Jory Martin's boat went out. It means there was someone there, at least one of them, at least *someone*, putting the light in and tending it through the night—and it just so happens they vanish right before the relief gets there?

I don't think coincidences like that happen without there being more to it. It makes us think if only that relief had got out there sooner, if only the boatman had gone against the weather, and it just seems extra cruel that way. But that's what it boils down to: whether you think coincidences exist. Is it just the way the world has of working, or is it something else? For me, it's clear which one it is.

Anyone who knows the first thing about tower reliefs knows that when relief day comes, everyone's on the radio transmission, anxious the landing should happen and talking about whether or not it's going ahead. But that day, they couldn't get through. Ashore they were ringing in, but no one was picking up. The engineer wrote up storm damage, but I don't accept it for a second. A transmitter going just as three men vanish off the face of the earth? You'd have to be a fool.

At the end of the day, people wouldn't keep talking about the Maiden Rock if there was nothing strange about it. Nothing supernatural. They wouldn't if it was the sea, like Helen says, or the Supernumerary losing the plot.

There've been people who said they saw lights in the sky the night before Bill disappeared. Red ones that hovered over the tower, then darted away. Or the captains on ships who say they've seen a keeper waving at them from the balcony rail, when there hasn't been anyone living there for years. Or the birds—you'll have heard about them. Fishermen who swear they've seen three white birds, perched on the rocks at low tide or flying round the lamp when it's rough. The maintenance mechanics who go out there now say so too. They've put a helipad on top of the lantern, to stop them having to try and land the traditional way. The birds are right there waiting for them; they're not fussed by the rotors or the noise, they're just staring straight at them.

That's why the thing about the mechanic bothered me. Everyone says it didn't happen—that there was no one out there but them. Trident threw it out with the rest of the hearsay. They said it was as unbelievable as those captains saying they'd seen a ghost. But it depends what you believe. I said to you before, I believe in what if.

It was Bill's bad feeling. It was the lights in the sky, the birds, the transmitter, the coincidence. Maybe it was something I haven't thought about yet because like my mum said, I don't know anything. All I know is I don't know anything at all.

20

8 Church Road
Towcester
Northants

Helen Black
16 Myrtle Rise
West Hill
Bath

July 18, 1992

Dear Helen,

Can we meet? It's important. My new telephone number is below.
I need to talk to you in person. It's about Vince and what happened.
Call me if you can. Please.

Michelle

V

.

1972

21

ARTHUR

Sad Song

TWENTY-THREE DAYS ON THE TOWER

When I'm ashore, Helen and I take turns with the washing-up, and when it's my turn it's a chore to be done as quickly as possible. Afterward, there might be an episode of *Paul Temple* to watch on the telly, or if it's a clear night I'll walk the short distance from the cottages to the cliff edge, and look out at the lighthouse and miss her.

Here it's a ritual, a task to take my time over because my time doesn't need to be anywhere else. I might do it with a post-supper fag in my mouth, and every so often one of the others hovers an ashtray under to let the ash drop off. Otherwise it drops into the sink and I'll have to fish it out and start again.

In spite of the fags, we take cleanliness seriously. Ask any one of us and we'll say we don't mind so much at home, partly because a lot of the time the wives look after that side of things (Helen doesn't, but that's what I like about her) and partly because at home it's not important. If you're living on a tower there isn't much space, so that space has to be spick-and-span. You could eat your lunch off any floor here, any surface. So, if I drop my ash into the washing-up, I'll drain it out and do it again. It's a nice spot to spend half an hour in, at the window looking out at the sea, as sheer and silver as Bacofoil. Before now I've done the plates twice because it's been so agreeable.

"D'you read any poems?" Vince asks, smoking at the table with a game of Clock Patience. He's got "Supersonic Rocket Ship" going on the player.

"Sometimes."

"They say there's a poem for anything that happens in your life."

"I think that's true."

"Still, when there's nothing much else to do."

"No, nothing much else."

He's waiting for me to take the mick. Even if you have a dream round here that you want to talk about, you'll get called a soppy prick. But Vince isn't what you'd guess him to be. Rock bands, pens, fags, that's his lot. The Kinks, Deep Purple, Led Zepp, T. Rex. Bill and I don't bother with music; we're content with the wireless on the dresser that on a good day picks up *I'm Sorry I Haven't a Clue* on Radio 4. The reception's patchy, but just hearing Barry Cryer's voice reminds us there are other people out there and other lives happening. For that reason, I don't always feel like listening to it, but if I don't, I won't tell Bill to turn it off; I'll just go somewhere else.

"Who do you like, then?"

"Got to be Thomas," I say. "'Do not go gentle into that good night.'"

"Don't know it."

"You ought to."

"A lot of these guys are poets," he says. "Davies and Bowie and that; the stuff they write, the tune's only part of it, the words stand out on their own."

"Bob Dylan."

"Right on."

"Have you read Walt Whitman? *'Out of the cradle endlessly rocking, . . . Out of the Ninth-month midnight.'*"

"What does that mean?"

"Not a lot without the rest of it. Even then it's what it means to you."

"My girl at home," says Vince. "I wrote her a few lines."

"What did she think?"

"Chicks dig poetry." He smiles. "So that ended up meaning something pretty decent for me, if you catch my drift. I was making it up in my mind to start with. Nights banged up go slow. I just had these thoughts and they fit together here and there, quite nice some of the time. I think it helps to get whatever it is inside your head and put it down on paper so you can look at it and then it seems smaller than before."

"What were they about?"

"You'd need a drink in me for that."

"You wouldn't show me one?"

"Maybe," he says. "Since it's you."

"Good."

"It's likely shit. It's trippy but I think you'll get it; that's why you'll get it. I don't want stuff bottled up. It ain't good to bottle stuff up."

"No."

"Got to let it out."

"Anytime, Vince; you know that."

"Thanks, Mr. PK. And don't tell Bill, will you?"

"About the poems?"

"Yeah."

"I won't."

"It's not his thing."

"How do you know?"

"Just do. He'd pull it apart. He wouldn't mean to, but he couldn't help himself."

TWENTY-FOUR, TWENTY-FIVE, TWENTY-SIX DAYS

Suns rise and moons rise. Lamps lit and lights put out. Stars swing on the night frame, ancient patterns reordered, saucepan on the tilt, crab upside down, Scorpio and Mazzaroth and equinox. Wind waves and horses ride, froth and spume, then calm and calm; endless sea, rapidly changing mood, whispering and whistling its sad song, soul song, lost song, gone but never for long, up again until it's rolling, and at the heart of it our Maiden, rooted down like a centuries-old oak, hunkered right into the rock.

Big swell, bright day, grease the fog jib and oil the lenses. Tinned steak tastes better than it smells, and I take a photograph of sky and sea on the Nikon because there isn't anything to separate the two. An RAF fighter goes past about a quarter of a mile off, at lantern level; I wave, but he won't see.

Sleep, or try to. In the stuffy dark there go the planes again, but they don't come past, Bill tells me, it was just that one. I need to sleep. Not sleeping, so hours become days without my noticing, days into nights, strike them off on the calendar so we don't get lost, it's today, it's tomorrow, it's Whitman's Ninth-month midnight.

Friday. A boat comes past. Day-trippers loop the tower, calling, "Hello, anyone up there?" They're out of their minds this time of year, bundled in hats and scarves, but if there's a fisherman willing to do it, then good luck to him. To the tourists, we're a novelty: "Home for Christmas?" they shout. I can't tell if they're asking it or saying it because of the noise of the foam on the rocks, and anyway only one of us is. Bill's ready; he'll be ready by then.

You start to see it in a man, after a while. Forty days for Bill and counting. He'll need to stretch his legs and hold his wife and children. You see it in a friend, when he's getting to the point of forgetting all that, when he's forgetting there's life outside and this one wall isn't the end of the earth. Bill gets flinty and loses his sense of humor—that's how you know it's forty days. It's always forty days.

TWENTY-EIGHT DAYS

There's a strip of white paint on the floor of the oil store that needs recoating, so I spend a careful hour doing that, making the line perfect and better than it was before. When that's done, I clean the brushes on the set-off until they look brand-new. I often think how there's painting to be got on with in the cottage ashore, but it doesn't interest me much, and Trident sends a man out every once in a while for that. Here, I'll seek out things that need doing, even if they could probably last awhile longer without looking shabby. I'll get to fixing or improving whatever it is right away.

Before we joined the service, Helen and I lived in a bedsit in

Tufnell Park. On Sunday mornings I'd go and buy the paper and take her back a roll from the bakery on the corner. She'd eat it in bed, sheets tangled round her legs, and afterward we'd shake the crumbs off and drink grainy black coffee, then go for a walk on Hampstead Heath. I question what our lives would be like if we'd stayed there. Helen would be happier. She wouldn't think she had given up her life for mine, because that's how she feels, and once or twice she's said she might as well have married into the army.

Longings and regrets I get on middle watch. I once heard a tale about a keeper who got infatuated with this girl from his hometown. They'd blown hot and cold all summer and he didn't know what the situation was until a boat came out one day and there she was, standing in the fore, knee-deep in ropes and life jackets, and she cried out that she loved him. The mates I was with, we all pissed ourselves laughing, as that's how it goes when there's anything to do with feelings or romance or anything like that. But privately I thought different.

It isn't easy for some people to say what's inside them. It isn't easy for me.

I thought about doing that for Helen, but it wouldn't work as well coming into land, and besides there isn't a boatman I'd trust. I overthought it and by then it seemed daft. The kind of thing you do when you're twenty-five, not fifty. There comes a point where too much has happened. Water under the bridge: too much of that.

Back inside for a bath. Vince is in the living room listening to his records and I call in to him, the wind's blowing up, but he doesn't hear, and it isn't important enough to repeat. The bath's in the kitchen, a tin bucket and flannel: I stand there in my underpants and soap as quickly as possible. It isn't pleasant, just functional. Dry and get dressed and immediately make a cup of tea because I'm cold and my hair's wet.

The first memory I have is to do with wet hair. My mother toweling my head dry with no-nonsense strokes, the rough practicality with which mothers spit on their fingers to wipe dirty mouths, impatient and concerned. Later on, she did it for my dad. He was a child by then, so I stopped being one. I grew up, grew past him.

It's a heft to lift the bucket through the wall cavity and empty it out the window, so I go up to the gallery and do it off there, only once I'm tipping it over the rails a northwesterly comes out of nowhere and gusts me aside. I almost lose my grip, which would have had me groveling to the others all over Christmas—sorry, lads, no bathroom facilities, I'm afraid—but I manage to hold on and get drenched for my efforts. My trousers are soaked and the belly part of my pullover.

The wind's freezing, my knuckles pink and cracked on the rim of the pail. Quickly I go back inside and down to the bedroom, dropping the bucket back first, to get changed.

Bill's asleep in there. His curtain's open; he's on his side so I can make out the line of his ear and the thick muscle of his shoulder. I've always thought of Bill as slight—small and flighty, like a thief on the Underground. Recently he's bulked up. Or has he always been like this? Sometimes, when you look at a man, you see him afresh: proximity cheated you into thinking he's someone he's not.

He's snoring, gently. Occasionally it strikes me how much time I spend with men I'd otherwise have nothing to do with. At home, I don't make friends easily. I don't have the knack. People come and go; there's no time; I can't find a way in. Here, it isn't a choice. We learn to live together in a narrow column with no way out. Men become friends and friends become brothers. For only children, this is as good as it gets. When I was a boy, I heard it as "lonely children": I thought it was that through to when I was fourteen and saw the right thing written on a medical pamphlet.

Moving quietly, I take a jumper from my locker, but that pair of trousers was my last so I reckon Bill won't mind if I steal a pair of his. We're about the same size if I don't wear a belt. Mine will be ages drying and the Rayburn's all we've got for that.

Once I've got the trousers on, it's force of habit to feel in the pockets. When I do, my hand meets a familiar object. I'm not sure at first in what way it's familiar—what it is, exactly, I'm feeling, just that it's known to me.

When I asked Helen to marry me, I couldn't afford a ring. At least not the one she deserved, a sapphire from Hatton Garden, set between two diamonds. It was another five years and a sizable bank loan before I could give her that. But weeks before, we'd taken a trip out of town and she'd seen a necklace she liked on a bric-a-brac stall. It was nothing special. A plain silver chain with a pendant in the shape of an anchor. It had cost me ten pounds. Even though the ring she wears now is worth more than that, it's this chain that always meant the most.

Helen thinks I haven't noticed that she's stopped wearing it. But I notice everything about her, all that's changed when I go ashore.

I should have sent a boat for her, I think, the anchor chain running through my fingers in the final moments of a life that's mine, a wife I recognize: I should have sent a boat for her with a message shouted from the front. So she knew.

On the stairs, in the dank daylight, I take the necklace out of Bill's trouser pocket and look at it, then in at him, trying to fathom what to any other man would be obvious but to me is an impossible hiding, a lie too devastating, the series of events that must have unfolded to which I've been ignorant.

Constellations changed. The sky fell. The man I thought was my friend.

22

BILL

Silver Man

Sharks are blank. That's why they frighten. They're cool torpedoes of blubber, sliced at the gills, equipped with teeth. Fat and teeth, that's the thing. Needles in a bowl of curd.

I saw one once. Sitting there fishing when all of a sudden there he was, a big gray lozenge coming at me through the water, like one of the pills Jenny gives me when I can't sleep. I got my line up quick, but all he did was circle the tower a couple of times, then swim away. I'd thought him a basker, but Arthur said a great white. Arthur knows better. There'd been sightings on our neighbor lights too.

When I came ashore and told Jenny, she grabbed me, her breath sharp with wine, and said, "Bill, promise me you'll never go fishing off that set-off again." Then at night she tried for me with her eyes full of sorry and why not.

I didn't tell her it wasn't fear I'd felt for that shark but admiration. If he had a family, he'd left them behind. If he had a wife, he'd eaten her by now.

FORTY-FIVE DAYS ON THE TOWER

The gale hits us midweek. Sometimes I can see the heavy weather coming in from far away, hulking clouds marching on the tower and the sea getting ready to do its thing, but other times the rain and wind attack us out of nowhere. Before I know it, I'm eating breakfast in the kitchen with the spray smacking the window.

"Fuck," says Vince, who normally acts unconcerned, but I've noticed he's smoking his next fag off his last. Even with the shutters closed, the noise is off the scale. Rain rinses the glass and the sea's gone sickly like someone put too much milk in it. The tower shakes, vibrating from bottom to top, a queer feeling as if we're caught in an electrical current, rippling from the base through the soles of our feet, out the tops of our heads, and up. Boulders slam in at fifty miles an hour. I can't believe we'll stay standing.

Arthur's reading an old copy of *National Geographic*. He isn't worried. What happened to him makes it unlikely he'd be afraid of much, in the long run. That's why I don't feel guilty. Helen shouldn't either. He's already been through the worst.

Usually in the weather Arthur will have his reassuring words to say, such as everything those engineers learned from Smeaton's stump, and all the lighthouses over hundreds of years that were built and fell and built and fell until they learned how to do it properly, with dovetails and metal joints and granite dug into the bedrock.

All it does is talk down to me. Makes me feel like the novice he hauled onto the set-off that day. Arthur knows best. What do I know?

Today, though, he doesn't speak. He carries on reading *National*

Geographic, looking up once at Vince to say yes, please, to a cup of tea. The magazine must be from back in '65, at least. The clock keeps ticking. Four minutes past eleven. The fags get smoked and on it goes.

·

Midday. Up to the PK, the afternoon watchman. The fog gun's deafening. It's a rum job operating the jib; you'd think it would be a break in the monotony, but all it is is sitting inside the doorway pressing a plunger, and what could be more monotonous than that. In low visibility, whoever's watch it is has to sit pressing that bloody plunger every five minutes for hours at a time. The rest of us have to listen to it, have our meals or try to sleep, all with these ruddy blasts ringing out twelve times an hour. Trident give us earplugs for it, same as they do for families on rock or shore lights, but that's a bastard in itself. You can't do anything with it going off. You can't think straight.

The action comes when I've got to get back out on the gallery, wind down the jib, and reload the charges. I don't like being out there with the sea chucking itself about and the wind shrilling so sharp it gives me earache. When I'm ashore I can still hear that wind tunneling through my head, sighing and creaking on a fair day or whining in a squall. Arthur likes it. He likes being out on the gallery, seeing it in motion. He's in the lantern now on one of the kitchen chairs, his thumb on the trigger.

"All right, Bill?"

The horn blasts. BURRRRRRRRR.

"Brought you tea," I say, putting the cup by his feet. He isn't wearing shoes and his socks don't match. He doesn't say thank you. Just goes on staring at the sea.

"What's for supper?" he says after a minute.

I stop at the stairs. Put my hands in my pockets.

"Steak and kidney."

"Good day for it."

"Ashore'd be better."

Arthur lights a cigarette. "Not long now for you, matey."

"Thirteen days."

Thirteen days until I see her again. The smell of her hair, like cloves. The first time her lips met mine, a snowflake passing through the light beam.

"What'll you do when you get back?" he asks.

"Have a beer. Sleep in a proper bed."

BURRRRRRRRR.

"Say hello to Helen for me, won't you?"

"Always do."

The PK runs his thumb around the plunger. "What was in the parcel?"

"What?"

"Jenny's, what Vince brought off."

"Usual. Letter. Chocs."

I could smoke, but I haven't got my fags and Arthur isn't in a sharing mood. He gets this way, in the weather. Dazed. Half here. Like the old man he is.

"Makes me guilty," I say. "That's why she does it."

"Jenny's a good wife. Helen would never do that."

BURRRRRRRRR.

"Do what?"

I know all the things Helen does. Or that I'd like her to do, and that she will do for me, sometime soon, when she realizes she doesn't owe him a thing.

"The good wife," says Arthur. "Not for me."

He might see now if he looks at me, but he doesn't look.

Helen says he never looks at her. If she were mine, I would never take my eyes off her. I already do that. Quietly. When Jenny can't see. I watch for the front door to Admiral to open and for Helen to step out and pat her handbag for the house keys. Her eyes cross the glass; she's saying hello and she hasn't forgotten, she's thinking about me just as much as I'm thinking about her; she wants us to be together, as quickly as we can. Then Jenny yells at me from the kitchen for not checking on the baby, who's gone and dropped his scrambled egg on the floor.

In the time Arthur's been my Principal Keeper, it's been right here in front of him. Helen said they don't touch. Don't talk. Still, he's never suspected a thing.

Some feelings you can't help. I said that to Helen the first time, when she stood at the washing machine before we said goodbye, I said, I just can't help it. It isn't to do with Arthur and if he weren't married to her there'd never be a problem. But he is. They were married while I was still in short trousers, having my dad sit on the end of my bed and run his belt across his palm.

"Jenny could be more independent minded," I say. "Like Helen."

It's a dare to say her name out loud, in front of him. I want to keep saying it.

"You like independent women, Bill?"

"Better than the alternative."

"Is it?"

"That time we went out in Mortehaven," I say—pushing it, just to see, "it was Helen's birthday. She wore that blue dress she'd bought up in London. We got a sitter and went to the Seven Sisters and shared that fish platter."

"I bought that dress for her."

"It suited her."

"Still does."

"Helen complained about the wine. Didn't put Jenny off drinking it. When we came home, Jenny was crying over me. Said she felt ugly and stupid next to Helen. I said if she hadn't drunk so much, she mightn't be feeling so bad about it."

"She's protective."

"She's drunk."

"Why does she drink?"

"Fucked if I know. Whatever it is, she's an incoming missile. When I get ashore, I don't know what I'm going to get."

"Neither does she," says Arthur.

"What?"

"Helen told me once it was like a stranger coming back."

"With me?"

Arthur meets my eye, at last. He's smoking down into the filter, the gritty bit, the sour bit. "No," he says. "With me."

BURRRRRRRRR.

"Tea's getting cold," I say, backing away.

"Get some sleep, Bill." He puts out the fag and goes to reload the charges.

FORTY-SIX DAYS

Two hours to go till my watch. Got that feeling in my stomach, or is it just a deeper version of what's already there, the queasiness that puts me in the in-between place? Not on land or sea, not at home and not away, in between but I don't know where, just floating. Helen tells me not to think about the bad places. Sometimes I can't help it.

I tell her things I've never told my wife.

How I was twelve when I saw him. In the passenger seat of my neighbor's car, Mrs. E; her boy was in my class, a little shit if ever I knew one. My hair was still wet from swimming. I was thinking about the brass tin where my brother hid the smokes, in the old man's gun chest. I'd nick one, smoke it under the porch before they got back.

At the bottom of the hill, there was a sharp bend going down into Mortehaven. Mrs. E slowed the car almost to a stop, and as she did a man crossed the road right in front of us. He was so strange looking, I soaked up every detail about him. He had silver hair and carried a briefcase. He wore sunglasses, even though it was February and freezing. It struck me that none of his outfit fitted the time. This was the start of the fifties, and the styling of the suit, as silver as the hair, was, even to what the old man called my "dumb boy's brain," from another decade, the twenties maybe. He looked relaxed but purposeful, like he was expected somewhere but was comfortably on time.

The man went down a side street. We moved on. Mrs. E drove the Sunbeam like a ninety-year-old, blinking and twitching, her nose pressed up to the windscreen. Five minutes passed, which is a fair distance when you're traveling by car, so I couldn't believe it when we came down past the post office and the same man crossed the road ahead of us. Again, from left to right. Again, the weird hair and suit, the sunglasses and the briefcase. He stepped right out of the hedge, right out of nowhere, so Mrs. E had to swerve onto the verge and the horn blared, pointlessly. He didn't see us. Didn't see the car, or the fact he'd nearly been hit. Didn't seem to notice us at all.

It wasn't possible he'd arrived there before we did. Even if he'd
come by car or bus or bike, he couldn't have overtaken us—nothing
had overtaken us—and there was no other road into Mortehaven. He
couldn't have walked; he'd barely have got past the mount. Unless he
had a twin, dressed the same way, who moved identically, there was
that—but I knew in my gut that wasn't the point. The point was we
had seen not just the same man but *the same moment*: his crossing from
left to right, the angle of his head, the swing of the briefcase, the winter sun glancing off his eyewear, even the number of steps he took, as
if it weren't a road he was on but another, invisible surface, transposed
over the top of the high street like a badly developed photograph.

Mrs. E turned to me and said, "What in God's name was that?"

That. Not he.

To this day, I don't have an answer to her question.

I never told the old man about it. Never told my brothers. Through
the weeks that came after, the stranger with the briefcase faded slowly
from my mind. I didn't even speak about it when Mrs. E died, unexpectedly, when she was out one morning buying her husband's *Valley
Echo*. The newsagent said she'd come over curious, seen someone she
recognized through the window. The paper fell to the floor.

Only now, twenty-three years later, as I'm sitting on a tower lighthouse with *Coronation Street* on the telly and Vince boiling some
god-awful-smelling cauliflower stew two floors down, I'm thinking
about him again. Too much time out here for thinking—that's what
the old man didn't reckon on. It depends who you are, if you let your
mind get one over on you. Hauntings that won't let you go.

Weak boy, wet boy; the sooner you get on the lighthouses the better.

The moon pale eyed through the window. Weird moon. Weird

thoughts. Moons out here so bright it hurts. Against everything else they're brighter than they should be. Imagining the moon is the sun and the whole world turned inside out.

This time I'm the one in the silver suit. I'm the one stepping into the road; I can feel the curves of the case, the weight of mysterious things inside, and I look over at the car, the boy in the passenger seat of a Sunbeam-Talbot, and I say to him,

Run.

"Bill?"

Arthur's at the door. There's a knife from the kitchen in his hand.

"Sorry. I fell asleep. Fuck. What time is it?"

"Seven." He points the blade at me. It glints. "You can help me if you like."

23

VINCE

Black Magic Marks

FIFTEEN DAYS ON THE TOWER

Coastguard Hart Point calling the group, how do you read me, please, over?

Hart Point, Tango, going down. Hart Point, Foxtrot, going down. Hart Point, Lima, going down. Hart Point, Whiskey, going down. Hart Point, Yankee, going down.

Tango, Tango, hello from Hart Point, how do you receive me, please, over?

Hart Point, Tango replying, receiving you loud and clear and a fine afternoon it is too, are you receiving me, over?

Hearing you well, Tango, thank you and it is indeed a fine day. Hart Point to Foxtrot, Hart Point to Foxtrot; good afternoon, are you receiving me, over?

Foxtrot, Foxtrot to Hart Point, afternoon from us all, receiving you clearly, over.

Roger that, Foxtrot. This is Hart Point to Lima, how do you hear me, over?

Lima to Hart Point, hearing you loud and clear, hello to the group, this is Lima to Hart Point, nothing else to report, thank you, over.

Thank you, Lima. Whiskey, this is Hart Point to Whiskey, are you reading me?

Whiskey, Whiskey to Hart Point, reading you fine, Steve, over.

Thanks, Ron. Hart Point to Yankee, Hart Point to Yankee; are you receiving me, please, over?

Yankee, Yankee to Hart Point, Vince here, happy to hear your voices, reception good on both wavelengths, hearing you well, thanks, over.

Thank you, Vince. Best wishes to the group, Hart Point over and out.

SIXTEEN DAYS

I pinched a couple of the chocolates Bill's wife sent him. Had a chance to last night while Bill was watching telly. I'll admit I take a peek in their stores from time to time to see if there's anything I fancy, and if there's enough, it's finders keepers. Even if Bill noticed, I don't think he'd mind. He doesn't talk about his wife with much affection.

"Wait till you're married half your life," he says whenever I mention Michelle. "It's not the same once you get that ring on her finger."

Out on the set-off with my fishing line; unlikely I'll hook much, but you never know, pollack or mackerel, that'd be nice, bit of garlic rubbed in like Bill showed me and some dried parsley. Might have a lemon still knocking about. My fingers sticking out of my gloves are stiff with cold, so it's a pain to fish the chocs out but worth it.

Dark coating, lilac cream inside, salty on the tongue after I've swallowed. I wonder if I'll ever have a woman who makes me things like this, just cos she can, just cos she wants to. Before I went off, Michelle and me talked about how we'd stay together and not have anyone else on the scene. I think about it more than she does, cos what exactly am I getting up to on this sorry rock with two other blokes? It's her who's back in town with the nightclubs and those eyelashes. When I play "Waterloo Sunset" I see us walking over Waterloo Bridge and her turning to me and saying, "I never knew a man so well that I didn't know at all." She shouldn't mind about that. No one knows. Not even the PK and Bill and I'm with them every day. That's all right. What I show people and what I am—those are two separate things. Isn't it the same for everyone?

Fishing's as much about sitting there as it is about getting a tug on the line, even in the bitter cold with my coat pulled up to my eyebrows and my balls frozen solid. I feel like the most minuscule person when I'm surrounded by so much sea. I used to fantasize about water while I was locked up, not baths or drizzly rain but Olympic-sized pools of it, and oceans that stretched for miles. When you can't have it, you want it.

Better not let the PK see me without the safety line attached, but honestly, it's a faff, and then you have to sit with this knot under your arse and it hurts like buggery. Every PK's got his way of operating depending on what he thinks is going to be a risk to his station: Arthur says we've got to have the line reeved cos there was that time he nearly got swept off the Eddystone, and if he hadn't had Lady Luck smiling down on him, he'd never be here to tell the story.

Whatever happens on a lighthouse falls back on the PK. Arthur told me about a young keeper who got lost that way off the Scottish coast, one of those that gets passed down as a warning, but if the same thing happened on the Eddystone, then there's no reason why it couldn't here. The PK in charge on that tower never got over it. It went that this young keeper fancied doing some fishing one day and the weather was fine, not a cloud in the sky and the sea was as calm as you like. He told the Assistant he was off to do just that, and the Assistant says, "Right you are, bring me back a catch for my tea." Meanwhile the PK's fast asleep in his bunk, none the wiser, so this keeper goes down to where I am now, sitting here like I am with his legs dangling down off the set-off, and that's the last we know of him. When the Assistant goes to fetch him awhile later there's nobody there. 'Course they're all bamboozled. The Assistant didn't hear anything, nobody shouting for help, and it seemed that even if this bloke had fallen in, he'd still be there in the water, calling for them. But he isn't. He's just gone, fishing line and all. It was only the PK's and the Assistant's word that each other hadn't been to blame.

The PK in charge took responsibility. The way he saw it, it was his to bear. Then the Landmark Board found these books in the keeper's bunk, about the devil and the occult, all sorts of spooky shit you don't want to be getting near. Black magic marks scratched across the bedroom, pentagrams and horned hands; symbols picked into the walls. Sends a shiver down my spine just thinking about it.

I bring up the line and go back inside.

As I do, I see a shape on the water, bobbing away from me. I squint; it isn't driftwood or a buoy or a bird; it's a shoal of tuna near the surface or a plastic bag, a few plastic bags, billowed out. Or is it bigger than that, more solid, the size and shape of a man—is he facedown, faceup, arms out? Not sure. The water vibrates. I can't be certain whether I've seen it at all, and even though I'm trying I can't catch it any longer.

✳

"What's for lunch, then?" Bill's doing the brass between the kitchen and the bedroom. This is the only bit that ever needs doing: we must've got grubby hands from smoking or checkers, then being too tired going upstairs to bed so we forget ourselves.

"A bit of seaweed and a crisp packet, if you want it."

"Bloody hell."

He's scrubbing viciously, even though the rails are clean as new pennies. When I said to Arthur yesterday that Bill looked ready to get gone, he gave me one of his sideways looks and said, down in his throat, "You're right about that."

"I think I saw a body," I tell him.

Bill stops polishing. "What?"

"Just now."

"Where?"

"Where d'you bloody think? In the sea."

Bill wipes his hands, slowly. "Who was it?"

"I don't know. Some swimmer."

"You sure?"

"No."

'Course when we get outside, there's nothing to be found—it was gone anyway before I said anything to Bill, and I don't know for certain what I saw, only that it's put me on edge. I want to ask the PK what to do but Bill says don't bother, the PK's up in his bunk, he's not had any rest and it's starting to turn against him. Arthur's showing the strain—haven't I noticed? He doesn't need this.

"He had goggles on," I say.

"Who?"

"The swimmer. Red ones."

"Get on the R/T," says Bill. "They can deal with it if they want. Bugger'll be long dead anyway. He was dead, wasn't he?"

"I don't know. Don't want to make a song out of it. It could've been a seal."

"In goggles?"

"I don't know if it had goggles on."

"You don't know much, do you?"

I think about the gun hidden under the kitchen sink. Thankful it's there. Just in case we're not alone.

Up to the kitchen and Bill makes tea, strong, two sugars, which get dumped in with a tablespoon so it's actually more like six. All this sea makes you see things that aren't there. The PK told me that. If you look at the same picture for long enough, the mind comes up with an object to disrupt it, to test if you're concentrating. Desert mirages, you get the same on the sea. Colors like you wouldn't believe; splashes and whirlpools; shapes on the surface that flitter and vanish. Even on a flat sea the water gets chopped about and broken, black and shivering up close like a bag of rubbish left out overnight. You could peel a hole in the sky and stick your finger through, to touch whatever's behind. It would feel soft and needing. It wouldn't want to let you go.

When you're with the sea every day, it takes whatever's inside you and shines it back. *Blood and fur, a child's high scream: and my friend in my arms, grown cold.*

"Drink up," says Bill.

The hot, sweet tea makes me sick. Or it's the body.

"Arthur ever tell you about the sailor up north?" Bill clicks his lighter, singeing the end of his fag. I say no, go on. "Bugger's boat got wrecked on the rocks round the light. Everyone on it drowned; the shipment was lost. This sailor blamed Arthur. Said it was the fault of the lighthouse. His crew'd been out at sea for so long, looking at a bloody great horizon with nothing on it, when they finally saw the beam, they couldn't tell how far away it was. Distances change." He taps his temple with the butt of the smoke. "You think an object's farther away than it is, then all of a sudden you're on it."

"You think I made it up?"

"No. Just you can't always trust what's real."

"The PK's seen it all."

Bill sucks long on the stick. "Arthur isn't who he used to be."

"What do you mean?"

"He's not the same person."

"I didn't think you knew him before."

"I didn't. Helen told me."

I say, "He can't be chipper all the time. Would you be, after . . . ?"

"It's not that," says Bill. "It's when people go wrong and you don't recognize them anymore. That's what Helen says. It comes up on you like the bloody lighthouse on that shipwreck, all of a sudden you haven't a fucking idea who you married."

◼

In the afternoon, it starts to snow. Snow on a tower's weird because there isn't anything to give you bearings. You don't see it piling up on the roof of a car or covering a farmer's field, so you can't guess how much of it's fallen, just that it keeps coming from the sky and the sky's the color of bone. The sea accepts it quietly. Water, way below, metal dull and motionless. Before I worked on a lighthouse, I thought the sea was always the same color, didn't think much beyond it being blue or green, but actually it's hardly ever blue or green. It's a whole load of colors and they're mostly black or brown, yellow, gold, sometimes pink if it's churning.

Up in the lantern I put my entry in the weather log, sign my initials, then leave it on the desk for the next watchman. The PK's taught me all sorts about how the sea works and what the weather does to make it a certain way on some days and not others. S for snow, O for over-cast, P for passing showers. The pages before are a whole alphabet of letters. It'll never not strike me as magic how the weather changes in no time at all. It's like a person who shouts and then sleeps, and the snow is its dreaming.

Letters to Denote the State of the Weather. Drizzling. Gloomy. Light-ning. Squall. Thunder. Wet dew. Haze. I like the feel and look of them, how some of them feel how they sound. Thunder sounds like a boulder rolling toward you. Haze is slow and lazy. Squall's like you're thrown in a tizz. Same as the names of the things that live in the sea, which sound like pebbles clinking on the beach. Periwinkle, mussel, sea squirt, whelk. Every few months we get a pile of books brought out that we share with the other lighthouses in the group, a traveling library. I read the lot.

I had a foster mum who was big on books. About the only one who was. She'd make a point of reading to us and it was down to those words sounding different from the words I knew in my life. The words that made up my life were short, hard words like *oi* and *fuck* and *you cunt*, bricks for bashing you over the head.

Every time I heard a word I liked, that I felt something for, I memorized it. It felt like the more I read, the more free I was in my mind, and if you're free in your mind, then it doesn't matter what else is going on. In prison I got a dictionary and found odd little words that I thought were terrific. Birds, there are lots of those. Kittiwakes and cormorants. Curlews. Pipits. Sound like they've got the wind running right through them. I copied words down and learned that when you put them together and messed around with them a bit you could get something new out of it again.

But I'm still stumped when I'm writing my letter to Michelle, propped up in my bunk when my watch is done, notepad on my blanket, pen in my hand, figuring out how to put it all down and I don't know where to begin. A is for apology. D is for deceit.

It's time to tell her the truth.

I see her in her London flat, toes grazing her calf as she opens the envelope.

VI

·

1992

24

HELEN

The cathedral was the place to meet, being large and anonymous. In pews, in cloisters, in the red velvet seats up by where the boys' chapel sang, whispers had steeped the rank stone for centuries. Now theirs, hers and Michelle's, could join them without remark.

"Roger and the girls are in a café round the corner," said Michelle. "I can't be long. I didn't mean to bring them. They wanted to come. I mean, he did."

"Where does he think you are?"

"Buying a birthday present. For him. I'll have to go to Debenhams after, pick out a tie or something."

Helen suspected this was how things were for people who had shared calamity: they got to the heart of it immediately, doing away with niceties and preludes about the traffic. She and Michelle hadn't known each other before. They had met after the event, at the funeral Trident House put on—a "farewell service," they'd called it, and it had been more for the newspapers than for any of them. In the years since, they made contact when they could, if one or other woman happened to be passing that part of the country. They would send letters whenever the sadness of that winter got the better of them and the urge hit to express it to someone who understood: letters that were sometimes answered, sometimes not, but the comfort was in writing them.

"Thank you for coming," said Michelle. "Thank you for calling."

"It's all right."

"I wasn't sure if you would."

"Why?"

"I don't know," said Michelle. "Jenny never gets back to me."

"She doesn't get back to me either."

Michelle unzipped her handbag and took out a tube of Polos. Inside the foil, the sweets were cracked into pieces, all down the length of the tube. Helen could picture her dropping them at the village store while her daughters selected packets of fruit gums and cola bottles. How old would the girls be now? Eight and four, about that. Helen didn't know how it would be to watch a child of hers thrive, healthy and sturdy, little limbs fattening, hair growing, suddenly as tall as you.

Michelle offered them, despite the bits.

"Thanks," said Helen.

"Please stop talking to Dan Sharp."

She was taken aback. "That's what you came here to say?"

An elderly couple came to sit on the pew in front of them. The man lowered his head. Michelle moved close enough that Helen could smell her shampoo.

"Sort of," she said. "Do you even know who he is?"

"Not really. He writes about boats and bombs."

"Under a fake name."

Helen crunched the Polo. "I'm not surprised about that."

The woman in front turned round and shot them a glare. Helen thought she had a bob like a motorcycle helmet.

Michelle whispered: "Why does a novelist want to write about us?"

"I don't know. Why does anyone write about anything?"

"There must be a reason."

"He likes the sea, he said."

"Then he should go on holiday."

Helen felt unsure why she was having to defend a man she hardly knew; why she wanted to. "He's looking for the truth. He cares about it."

Michelle put the sweets back in her bag and zipped it shut.

"*Shh!*" The woman threw them daggers.

Michelle signaled they move across the aisle. When they were sitting again, she looked up at the altar. Helen noticed she'd had her ears pierced once.

"Do you believe in Him?" Michelle asked.

Christ's feet were crossed at their bridges: an eruption of coagulated blood. It was a particularly gruesome one, Helen thought. Whoever had modeled it had driven the thorns in with unnecessary force.

"I've tried."

"Me too." Michelle rotated her wedding band. "I feel jealous when I see people coming in here and they just know, don't they? They know it's going to be all right."

"They believe. Which isn't the same."

"Isn't it?"

"I don't think so."

"I know Vinny didn't hurt the others," said Michelle.

"I know Arthur didn't."

"But we don't know, do we?"

"If it matters, I never thought of Vince as the villain."

Michelle took her hand briefly, then let it go.

"Yes," she said. "You were the only one."

Helen saw she'd been picking her fingernails, which were painted red but bitten short. She was taken back twenty years, to the anxious teenager Michelle had been, trembling at the farewell service, during questioning, or when pinioned by journalists in the street. People didn't change that much. Jenny would assume the same of her.

"Aren't you afraid of what Trident will say when they find out?"

"I don't care what they say," said Helen.

"They'll stop your money."

"So?"

"It's different for me," said Michelle. "I've got people to look after. A family." She stopped herself. "I didn't mean—"

"That's OK."

"Just that they're young still—"

"I understand."

"Don't tell me you've never felt scared of them? All that about not talking to anyone or giving away their private business. There was always a threat in there, never said outright but it was obvious what they meant."

"If that's true," said Helen, "then I think talking to Sharp is our best chance at honesty. It's always suited Trident to blame it on Vince, you know that. It's never been fair. He went to prison; he was thought of as a bad lot, so it was easy. People could get their heads around it. All they had to do was admit they got it wrong in giving him a job; they never should have done it; let that be a lesson learned. But it matters, doesn't it? To say what he was really like. I'd have thought it matters to you."

Michelle closed her eyes.

"Why are we really here?" asked Helen.

After a moment, she said, "Vinny wrote me a letter. Right before they disappeared. One of the tripper boats picked it up. He told me what he'd been in prison for. The final time. I never told anyone about it."

"All right."

"It only made him sound worse than he was—and there was already so much against him that it didn't seem kind to rub salt in the wound. That's all it would have been, for it to come out straightaway afterward. Do you see?"

"Yes."

Her eyes met Helen's, and the look communicated in them was urgent and pained. "But there was another thing in that letter that I should have shared, Helen. It did matter. It could have helped. Only I was too scared to say anything."

Helen waited.

"Vinny told me there was a man out to get him. He thought he'd be able to get away from his past with this job on the lighthouses, but actually it was the opposite. Now this person knew just where to find him. Vinny was a sitting target, out on the sea."

"Who are you talking about?"

"The one he'd done it to. The last thing."

"I don't understand."

Michelle checked behind her, as if her husband might be standing there, or an official from Trident House. Out in the vestibule, a baby started crying.

"This man worked for Trident," she said. "Vinny found out right after he got offered the job. His mate back home told him; said he'd never believe it, but guess who else had found a way in? Not as a keeper—he was office administration, but under the same roof, if

you can call it that. He had this funny name for himself. Called himself the White Rook. That's what the gangs back in London called
him. It was 'cause of him having all this white hair, since he was a kid.
What's that again?"

"Albino."

"His real name was Eddie."

"Eddie took the job as a way to get at Vince?"

"He must've discovered Vinny got work at Trident, then decided
that'd be as good a way to do it as any, so he wormed his way in."

Helen felt light-headed. This was how it worked with the vanishing. Whenever a new idea surfaced, or the event tilted to a fresh angle
in her mind, or a possibility occurred to her at three in the morning so
fully formed that she had to sit up, clammy and disoriented, and turn
the bedside lamp on to get her bearings, the lighthouse shook in its
snow globe. The pieces fell in a new pattern each time.

"Are you talking about revenge?"

"I think so."

"What happened to Eddie?"

"He left the Institution," said Michelle. "No one saw him again.
But I don't think it was Eddie that did it anyway. I think he paid someone. He had people all over. Dangerous people who could get things
done and do it under the radar."

"Did Trident know the connection? They must have."

"If they did, they never said anything to me about it. But it's like
Vinny *knew* it was going to happen. He said he was seeing things out
there. Imagining stuff that wasn't true, and he said that happened
sometimes, with the loneliness of it, but this was new. Then when
they disappeared, the more I think about it, the more it seems clear as
glass to me that that's what happened. It wasn't the sea or spies or any

of that. It was this man, this White Rook. Eddie. He's still out there, and if he gets wind that I've been talking about Vinny, whatever I say, he'll come after me and my family."

Helen thought about the birds Arthur's father had kept, long ago. Her husband had used to recall going up the hill in the early mornings, before school.

They get better, then they fly away.

In a sliver of an instant, she saw the dimple in Arthur's smile as he looked up at her from the book he was reading.

How did the mind hold on to such things? She could never remember which number bus to take to the city center from home, but she could remember that.

"It's easy to feel responsible," she said carefully. "I feel it too. I expect Jenny does. Our own stories are always going to feel the most significant. But listen—for your White Rook there are a dozen more. Things that make us worry we had more to do with it than we realize; that we're all to blame in some way—"

"This writer following me," said Michelle, "it brings it all back. How it was in '73. I can't live through it again, Helen. I was nineteen, bloody hell, I was a baby. Didn't know what hit me. I'd lost the man I was mad for." Her throat closed; her voice broke. "I miss Vinny. Every single day. And you miss Arthur too, and Jenny misses Bill. With Roger, with marrying him, it isn't the same. If I'd been your age, I'd never have got with anyone else, like you haven't, 'cause there wouldn't be any point. But I had to get on; I couldn't give up on life. I wouldn't change the girls for the world, but maybe it's true that you never love again like you love the first time."

"It is true," said Helen.

"I'm safer if I keep my mouth shut."

"That's what Trident wants you to think."

"What difference is a stupid book going to make?"

"None, maybe. Except to me."

A couple of schoolboys in the next aisle were looking at them. Michelle said: "Tell it to Jenny instead, then. She is who you're doing it for, isn't she?"

"Of course," said Helen. "And believe me, I've tried."

"Where's she living?"

Helen told her. "Trident gave me the address."

"Mrs. PK still gets the perks." But she said it with a smile. "Twenty years is long enough, isn't it? We've all moved on. She can't hold it against you. It wasn't as though—"

"Yes, she can."

Michelle took her hand. "I'll help you, if you want."

"I don't know how you're going to do that."

"If you help me. Be careful, Helen. That's all. Be careful what you tell him. Will you?"

"I will."

Michelle looked at her watch. "Oh God, it's half past. I've got to get to Debenhams and back before Roger sends out a search party."

She collected her bag and jacket; then they stood and hugged each other. Helen wasn't used to hugging, it had never come that naturally to her, and besides, there was no one these days who needed it.

"It was good seeing you," said Michelle.

"It was good seeing you too."

Helen put on her coat and watched the other woman leave, down the aisle and out into the bright afternoon light.

25

HELEN

It would have been normal to meet one's new neighbors on the doorstep or when slamming the door to one's car. Instead she had met Bill and Jenny Walker at a charity dance in Mortehaven village hall one summer when Arthur was off on the light. She had spent much of the week crying in the bathroom, Monday to Thursday anyway, because she felt that was a safe place to cry. Normally she did not mind when Arthur was away, the empty cottage, but she felt it then. It depended on the time of year.

Frank's wife, Betty, dropped in with a shepherd's pie and asked if she would be kind enough to help in the cloakroom. One of their number had fallen away; they'd be so grateful. As usual when put on the spot, she felt she couldn't say no; the instinct was to be helpful, even if, after Betty left, she wondered why on earth she had agreed. But the village hall cloakroom was a dim-lit place, and putting tickets on hangers on coats made a plodding, harmless sense. "Have you met them next door yet?" Betty asked. She hadn't. The Walkers' car had arrived yesterday, the new Assistant Keeper and his family, chaotic with luggage and children. Helen should have been round already. It

looked unfriendly that she hadn't. She was Mrs. PK, it was her obliga-
tion; she ought to have been leading the charge, offering her services
as she had when Betty moved in.

Arthur couldn't help when his spells of duty fell, but yesterday was
a mighty and dreaded obelisk. For three hundred and sixty-four days
of the year it rolled toward her from a foul horizon. She had an instant
to meet its living eye before closing her own.

The dance was successful. Helen stayed with the coats, soft and per-
fumed. She smelled the men's cologne, which was warm and spicy, and
the women's musk like flowers and sex. In quiet moments she smoked
to stop herself crying and fingered the velvet sleeves that hung in their
rows, closely packed and frilled like gills on a mushroom. He came to
her near the end, to collect the jackets his wife had put in.

"You're Helen," he said, and introduced himself.

She was thankful for the dark. Bill Walker wasn't what she had
expected, although she hadn't expected anything in particular; he was
neater and younger, with a long nose and even features that reminded
her of one of Raphael's cardinals. He gazed at her as she hadn't been
gazed at in a very long time, and she could almost believe she was
another woman, and none of the things that had happened to her had
happened.

"Those two," he said. "The buttons, yes; no, next one along."

In the end he came and pointed them out himself. The closeness of
him, his skin fair and unlined, felt inexplicably comforting. She had to
have twenty years on him, at least.

Like spectators, the coats gathered round. It was a few seconds; it
couldn't have been more. For all the times she would relive it, it must
have been more.

"Are you all right?" asked Bill, for he could tell.

"Yes," she said, because she would never. She didn't know where to start, nor should she start, with someone she had only just met.

His wife was still at the bar; she wouldn't come back of her own accord, he'd have to go out there and fetch her. They danced to "A Whiter Shade of Pale," there in the cloakroom, the only two people in the world. In the sooty darkness he drew her to him, or she went without persuasion, it was hard to say, and they held each other, her cheek on his, and the room was humming harder as the ceiling flew away.

26

HELEN

I don't know what drew me to him. If it hadn't been Bill, it might have been someone else. At that time in my life, it could have been anyone.

That sounds selfish, but I hope you'll stick with me. If you're putting this in your book, you need to get it down right. I don't want any mistakes.

Will Jenny believe me? I shouldn't think so. But this is one story I can give you and know it's true. I'd rather leave it written down than not at all.

That was how Bill and I met. The temptation was more about how it made me feel than any such thing toward him. It felt good to be wanted. That isn't an excuse; I did what I did; it was my decision. But when we had that initial connection . . . I wonder if that isn't too grand a word—*connection*; what is that, anyway, a fussy way of saying "attraction"? I wouldn't say I was even attracted to him; it was just that he had seen me crying; he had seen a secret part of me, and once that happened it seemed logical that he might as well see the rest. I was lonely and sad. It had been a long time since a man had held me—

since he'd touched any part of me—and then there was Bill. He made
me feel all the things affairs are supposed to: young, desired, cleansed
of past misdemeanors, even if the misdemeanor in the present is the
worst of the lot.

Did I·feel for him in return? No. Not for Bill. I felt for someone
who wanted to be kind to me. Who'd listen, after my husband had
stopped.

Living in the cottages, we couldn't avoid getting close. We lived
all over each other; even when the men were away the women were
stitched together constantly. You couldn't decide one day that you
didn't feel sociable because there'd always be someone doing their
weeding in the front or calling out the window asking if you wanted
to come over for a cup of coffee; so if you didn't crop up at least once,
you'd have them banging down the door asking if you were all right.
Some people might like that, but it wasn't for me. I like my front door
and it's closed for a reason.

When Arthur was off it sometimes meant Bill was home, and the
other way around. That was how it worked with the roster. For each
man it was eight weeks on the tower, then four at home, rotated among
four of them, if you count in Frank. So, in a way, it would have been
the ideal ground for it. When I didn't have my husband, there was a
chance I'd have Bill. It could have worked beautifully . . . if that was
what happened.

Of course, when Jenny discovered it, she thought the worst. I don't
know what gave it away. She never said and I never asked. She'd had
her suspicions for a while, I suppose. Bill made no attempt to conceal
his feelings about me, and to be honest I'm not even sure it *was* about
me. Not deep down. I believe Bill wanted a way out of a life he didn't
get on with. Our "affair" was a choice he could make on his own.

She told me she knew on the day of the memorial. She said the oddest thing to me then; she said: "He got what was coming to him." I did too, in a way.

Trident House held the service once they'd decided my husband was dead. They didn't consult me or ask for my blessing or understanding or anything like that.

Have you made any progress with them, by the way? No, that makes sense. I'd imagine you could ring them six more times and you still wouldn't hear back. Trident will want to distance themselves from what you're doing, so I doubt they'll comment on it much. I don't mean to be offensive, but they'll be dismissive about the stories you've had published. They'll say, What's a man like him going to know about a matter like this? They'd be right. But in twenty years, you're the first person who's asked me for my part in it. All the journalists who've thrown their hat in, not one of them ever knocked on my door and asked for my own words.

Trident would sooner blot the event from their history. They've never engaged with any aspect of the aftermath, as far as I know: no interviews, no release of records, no transparency whatsoever. These days, it wouldn't be like that—there's more demand for that sort of thing now. But back then it was all about covering it up. Unluckily for the Institution, people don't work that way. Feelings and memories don't either. It isn't something you can hide away in a filing cabinet. You can't keep people quiet however hard you go at it.

The day of the memorial stays with me for all the wrong reasons. It was cold, on the fringes of spring, and windless; Mortehaven Beach was smooth and brown, pitted with pebbles, and I can still see very clearly the lip of the sea as it dragged into shore; it had that rotten-froth quality, fermented like beer. There were men in uniform standing by boards covered in flowers. They had photographs of Arthur and the others, staring back to us, to land. A simulation of a burial when there was nothing to bury.

It rained and rained. I wore heels because it seemed disrespectful—stupidly—not to, and my shoes kept disappearing into the sand. Arthur's face on the placard didn't belong to him. You know when you see a picture in the paper of a murdered girl and you search her eyes for a clue as to what happened to her, some inkling that she'd *known*? Well, that day I looked at Arthur and I understood this was his secret and it always would be. Families and friends urged us to "fight"—for answers and resolution—but the definition of fighting is that you're up against something, aren't you, and it was just too exhausting for me. It wasn't Trident House I was fighting. It was him; it was Arthur. He didn't want me in on it. There's the assumption you have to seek answers for your loved ones when they die. Suppose they'd prefer silence?

Afterward, Jenny went for me. I couldn't blame her. I was trying to help her with the baby because her daughters were off running riot on the beach, and I could see she'd been crying and not sleeping, just like me, and then out of nowhere she smacked me across the cheek. The worst was seeing Arthur's and Bill's faces on the billboards, and the look in Arthur's eye was one of, Thank God I'm out of that.

Right then I'd have swapped with him in a heartbeat, just about wherever he was. Chained up on a ship or pecked to death in a cove, anything was preferable. I envied him his privacy. It isn't easy to disappear. For the life of me I don't know how he managed it. The problem is that Jenny never listened to my side of the story. You might say the problem is with me and your readers will, I'm sure. There's nothing so hateful as a woman who gets involved with another woman's husband. Never mind the husband's part: he was tricked or seduced, most likely, and it's funny how men insist on power in all aspects of their lives except when it does not suit them, and then they're content to be feeble and let the women take responsibility. Jenny carried on loving Bill and that's her business, that's her prerogative. Bill was a husband and a father, and the meaning in those roles is greater than I have privilege to know.

The truth is, I did dance with Bill at the charity ball when Arthur was away on the light, and I did get close to him in the weeks after that. On one occasion, after I became upset at their house, he kissed me.

The kiss was quick and meaningless. It felt completely wrong. That was the turning point. I asked myself what I had been doing—this wasn't me; it wasn't at all—and what exactly I'd been hoping to get out of it. Flattery was part of it, I admit. I couldn't think what a young man saw in me. I'd been a fool and I regretted my mistake. I wished that Bill would regret it too.

I told him it couldn't go any further. I thought he'd agree, but his reaction was astonishing. He became hostile at the same time as swearing his devotion. He said he was in love with me. He very nearly spat those words, as though he hated his position but could do nothing to change it.

After that, I did all I could to avoid him. I made excuses to Jenny and felt thankful when Bill went back to the Maiden, so I didn't have to see him. When he was ashore without Arthur, he behaved frighteningly. That's the only word I can use. I'd find him in my cottage, saying he'd come to fix a light that Jenny told him about, and afterward I'd notice possessions of mine were missing. Underwear and soaps, shoes and jewelry: to this day I'm convinced he stole a dear necklace of mine, a chain Arthur gave me when he proposed. I can't think where else it went, and naturally I couldn't tell Arthur, so he must have thought I'd lost it or didn't want to wear it.

It seemed Bill wanted us to be a couple so much that in his mind, at least, it came true. He talked about holidays we might take. Local beauty spots he'd show me when he was next ashore. Suppers he'd treat me to at his favorite restaurants.

It was as if I had told him that day not that I wished to end it with him—whatever "it" was, a single intimacy, our getting to know one another, the confusion of our meeting, things that, all right, might amount to infidelity in the mildest sense of the word but not, in my view, the obliterating sort—but instead that I had resolved to end my union with Arthur and begin again with him. Bill would be flagrant about it, taking my hand with Jenny in the room, or slipping his arm round my waist while I was in the kitchen slicing the fruit cake she'd brought round. No matter how many times I told him no, he refused to leave me alone. And the shells! Those bloody seashells he brought back for me, the ones he chiseled on the tower; they filled up my house, my drawers, anywhere I could think of to hide the damn things because I was terrified someone would see them. I couldn't throw them away in case Jenny found them in the bins. She often added her glass to the collection at the last minute. I couldn't risk it.

I was trapped. There was no escape. Not unless I confessed to the short-lived attachment we'd had—which would anyway be Bill's word against mine.

You can argue that one kiss was enough. But I wish Jenny knew it was nothing more. Bill and I were not in love. Love is pure and clean and kind; it comes from a noble, gentle place. It doesn't come from frustration or blackmail or hatred or dissatisfaction. Bill didn't love me. I want to tell Jenny that and I've tried, over the years; I've written her letters, I've gone to see her, I've called her up, but it's no use.

Now you're here. And you think I want to find out what happened to Arthur, that I'm hoping you'll hit on what's never occurred to us before. Well, I don't. Twenty years is more than long enough to dwell on what you can't change. I'd rather focus on what I can.

My husband is dead, but I'm not. Nor is Jenny. And this thing I share with her, it isn't a dead thing, it's living, and if that's the case, then it can change, it can grow, it can find a way out. I'm tired of death and loss; I've had enough of those.

I told you before about the garden. The way life has of coming back again and again, out of the cold. That's what I'm hoping for. That's what I want.

27

JENNY

Ron must have left the Metro in gear because when she turned the ignition it jumped backward like a startled rabbit. She hadn't driven in a while and felt shaky behind the wheel, her brain confused by messages. Indicate, mirrors, check her blind spot. She used to do it without thinking. At points the whole thing felt too overwhelming.

She wasn't looking forward to today, her grandson's sixth birthday party. Jenny had never enjoyed social occasions, but with Bill by her side it had been bearable.

Now she was on her own, fending for herself at family events, mixing with people she didn't know, whose silent judgments followed her round the room. Did they remember her from years ago? Their parents would. She had been the hysterical one, scrapping at the cameras and swearing in the news. But Hannah said she needed to get out of the house; she'd been cooped up too long; she was starting to "go strange."

She turned the fans on and thought the air emanating from them smelled of fish. She should use the car more. But where would she go? Apart from her children's houses or the supermarket. Join the WI, suggested Hannah. But the thought of crocheting blankets with a gaggle of old dears left her cold. She could imagine how it would be, once they realized who she was. Gossiping over their knitting needles.

She was steeling herself to pull out of the space when she spotted a woman in her wing mirror, walking up the street.

Jenny ducked down in the driver's seat. She was prone to this. Whenever she saw a person she knew in the park or the shops, she wouldn't approach them with glad surprise and a word of greeting, as other people might: she'd hide behind a lamppost or the nearest display of toilet roll and wait until they'd gone by.

Only this wasn't a person she knew. She didn't think so, anyway. Blue jeans, big jacket, yellow hair scraped back in a bun. Jenny couldn't get a clear view of her face.

Maybe she recognized the height and build of this woman; yes, maybe she did. The fish air grew stronger. She turned the fans off.

The woman passed the car and stopped outside Jenny's gate. She took a piece of paper out of her pocket and checked an address. Then she knocked on the front door and waited some time, a good two minutes, before stepping to one side and nosing into the living room window. Jenny felt pleased she had closed the curtains.

Another knock, another wait: whatever it was she'd come for was important.

Still sagged in the seat, Jenny shoved the car into first and drove away, leaving her blind spot unchecked.

◼

When she was a girl there'd been Marmite wheels and a game of musical chairs; now it was bouncy castles and balloon artists at the village hall, the whole class of thirty invited, then back to Hannah's semidetached for a cake the size of a wall tapestry.

Jenny drifted on the periphery of the gathering. While Hannah rushed about after the children, filling paper plates with slices of soggy Margherita pizza and some depressed-looking carrot sticks that had been sitting out for too long, she avoided conversation. The parents looked tired and annoyed, positioning themselves close to the bowls of cheese puffs and ogling the Teenage Mutant Ninja Turtles cake when it was finally unsheathed and lit ablaze with enough candles to fire a rocket into space.

"Mum, can you help clear away?"

She was relieved to be given a task: in the kitchen emptying ketchup-stained disks into a black bin liner. Back in the next room, a child's argument flared. She heard crying, soothing, then a gently closed door. She put the kettle on for coffee.

First, the car outside with its engine running. Now Michelle Davies.

Two decades on, older and knackered looking, but still, undoubtedly, her.

"Why did you do it?"

A question for herself or for Bill—it didn't matter, really. Better watch out for that, though: Hannah had caught her talking to herself last weekend and told her off. "Don't get batty on me, Mum; I haven't got the space, so it'd be Cedars Retirement and there's only one way out of there." But if Jenny didn't say these things out loud, then Bill would never hear them, and she believed, somehow, wherever he was, that he did.

If she concentrated, she could see her husband clearly, standing there at the kitchen cupboards, getting the coffee cups out, a thin pleat of cigarette smoke trailing from his hidden face, like a chimney smoldering in a wood.

She always saw Bill as he'd been when she had lost him. She could not update him, nor imagine him aged. The human face changed in mysterious, spontaneous ways, not just by genetics but by the living of life. Unless it was known what had happened to a person, it couldn't be done. So Jenny preserved him as the man she had married, before the disappearance, before they met Helen Black, before they had ever set eyes on the terrible Maiden Rock.

She took out a mug and filled it, although Hannah was low on Nescafé, so it was a weak brew and had to be improved by three teaspoons of sugar.

It was Bill's fault she had done what she did.

Hannah poked her head in. "We're cutting the cake in a sec."

"I'm not feeling well, love."

"What's the matter?"

"Just a headache. I'll be fine."

Hannah looked concerned. "I've got paracetamol in the bathroom."

"It's all right. You go ahead. I'll have a sit-down."

Jenny leaned on the counter and willed the tears away. There were the quietest triggers to despair: the shortage of coffee, for one. In these moments of trivial difficulty, it felt as if the world were against her, unwilling to compensate.

Bill's affair had been worse than his disappearance. At least in the second he'd been the victim. Although, as Jenny told herself time and again, he'd been the victim with Helen too.

It had started with those cups of tea. As Jenny stirred her mug, repeated refrains of "Happy Birthday" seeping through the walls and the bin bag slumped against her legs like a homeless person in a shop door, she recalled returning to Masters one afternoon when Bill was ashore. Helen sitting there, glossy and groomed, in their good room; Bill had his arm round her on the settee and their cups of tea had gone cold in front of them. Jenny thought a lot about the tea, afterward: that they must have been talking for a long time and forgotten about the tea. The fact those teas were cold bothered her.

Later, when she asked Bill why Helen had come to the cottage, he'd poured scorn on it. When she'd asked again, he'd shouted at her that if she spent less time at the bottom of a bottle, she might be able to work it out. His insult pierced her as sharply as if he'd said it moments ago. For days Jenny hadn't been able to look at him, hadn't been able to speak to him, and the separation after that was a hard one: when he went back off to the tower, she didn't know what to think. Each time she saw Helen she turned away, afraid of confrontation but at the same time desperate to understand.

Instead she drank and tried not to worry, but the more she drank the more she fretted and the same the other way. Jenny had promised herself she would never turn into her mum. But it had started quietly, as these things do. To start with drinking only when Bill was off because it helped to keep her company, or if the girls were fraying her nerves, or after Mark was born and then she never got any sleep. Soon, a glass turned into a bottle.

Jenny went into the hall. The party had moved to the garden. Through the patio glazing, she saw a group of children gathered round a tasseled creature suspended in a tree, which they were whacking with sticks. After a while, some sweets fell out.

Bill had accused her of being unsympathetic. After what Helen had gone through, shouldn't she be able to rely on her friends?

Jenny didn't understand why *she* couldn't be the friend. Why did it have to be him? They did everything together. He didn't have friendships she didn't know about.

It was never easy, from then, when Bill came ashore. Every time Jenny left the house, she assumed he was sneaking over to Helen's or Helen was sneaking over to theirs. When she got home, she'd check the water glasses to see if they were dry, and the tap in the bathroom that she always left askew, and smell the air in case she could detect perfume. Helen always wore the same, Eau Passionnée, only bit of French Jenny knew, and that was only because she'd been to Admiral one time and seen it on the dressing table and given herself a spritz; she never wore perfume, so she'd felt like a new lady in it. The most shameful thing was how she had driven up to Exeter one day a few weeks later and bought a bottle of her own. She had wanted to feel like Helen. To see what that was like. But when Bill came ashore and she met him off the boat, the first thing he said to her was, "What's that smell? It doesn't suit you," so she never wore it again.

A car pulled up outside Hannah's house. Jenny heard a door slam. A marble of panic rolled up her throat. She gripped the banister and fled upstairs.

Moments later, peering down from Hannah's bedroom window, she saw it was only a parent come early to collect their child, the one who'd been crying.

Hannah's right, she thought miserably. I have gone strange.

Her daughter's room was a tip, the bed unmade, her son-in-law's toiletries splashed across the bedside. Bill had never been messy. Lightkeeping had taught him standards, such as how to ball his socks and put them in a drawer, instead of discarding their wilted bodies on the carpet like a pair of rats squashed on the motorway.

If only she could describe the pain that had made her do that wicked thing.

The realization that he no longer loved her.

She had wanted to shake him. She had given him beautiful children and a loving home and still he was looking over that damn fence thinking a couple like that, who'd gone through that, were better than them?

Carol had stoked the flames. She reminded Jenny how she had raised that family all by herself, being on her own with the girls since Bill started on the tower and then when Mark came along she was on her own with him too, washing nappies, warming bottles, bent over the baby's cot at three a.m., with the Maiden Rock blinking at her through the night.

During those nights Jenny would weep with anger: she hadn't known which was worse, that Bill was tending the flame and as wide-awake as she was—awake but not helping, having no idea how ready she was to hurl the baby out the window, send him soaring across the sky like a comet in his blanket—or that he was sleeping. She could have murdered him if she thought about him sleeping. And she could have murdered him if she thought about Helen, and the less she slept the more she thought and the worse her thoughts became. She didn't sleep for months with Mark. Not sleeping drove her potty.

Helen hadn't raised his family, had she? She hadn't given him children and ironed his clothes. She hadn't cooked him arctic roll from scratch and stroked his brow as he complained about the Channels and how they made his stomach fill with coal.

But still Helen felt it appropriate to write her damn letters that were only about making herself feel better, not Jenny. As soon as Jenny

started reading them—as soon as she saw Bill's name written down—
she crumpled them up and threw them away.

I bet lots of men have loved you, Jenny had thought of Helen at the
time. *It's not fair for you to decide you want him now, when he's mine and
he's all I've got.*

Her daughter's nightdress lay in a heap at the foot of the bed. Jenny
sat and ran a hand over it. She remembered folding Hannah's nightie
when she was little, under the pillow, kissing her clammy forehead
good night.

Will you check on me? Check on me in two bits.

Yes, I'll check on you.

In two bits, Mummy, check on me. Promise?

Promise. How could Bill have turned his light out on them?

Soon, Hannah would see her innocent mother for the fraud she
was—pretending all these years to be the victim when she was
anything but. She would cut Jenny off, as coldly and permanently as
Jenny had cut off her own mother.

"Mum?" Hannah appeared at the door.

Jenny jumped. "You frightened me."

"I didn't know where you were. How's the head?"

"What?"

"Your headache."

"Oh. Better."

"People are leaving," said Hannah, "thank God." She had a tea towel
over her shoulder with a smear across it. "Greg's doing the party bags.
Are you coming down?"

Jenny looked away. She tried to stop the tears coming, but it was
useless.

She had only intended to give her husband a scare. She hadn't meant for him to go forever.

"What's wrong?" Hannah came in. "Mum—what's happened?"

Jenny pulled the nightdress into her lap.

"There's something I have to tell you," she said.

28

Trident House
88 North Fields
London

Mrs. Michelle Davies
8 Church Road
Towcester
Northants

August 12, 1992

Dear Mrs. Davies,

Re: Annual Allowance

Please find enclosed a check for this period's Bereavement Allowance. I trust this meets with your needs.

A note of caution: the Institution has been made aware of third parties interested in researching the history of the Maiden Rock. I have no need to remind you that our position remains clear: neither we, nor anyone connected with the disappearance, are able to provide further detail on the matter. The case has been settled and does not require revision.

Yours faithfully,
[Signature]
The Trident House Fellowship

29

MICHELLE

She had noticed the bird for the first time a week ago, after she'd traveled to see Jenny. That had been a wasted trip. She'd spent the whole drive back deciding what further lies she would have to tell Roger, who'd been annoyed at needing to take the day off work to look after the girls. Already she'd made up the sick friend who hadn't long left.

It was sitting on the lawn one afternoon while she was folding away the garden chairs, and since then it kept appearing all over the place, on the windowsill while she was cooking breakfast, under the oak tree, or perched on the guinea pig hutch, its beady eye staring in at her. It was always on its own.

"Who are you?" she said to it one day. "Go away."

She grew afraid of seeing it, even if several days could pass between sightings—but this made it worse because she would think it had gone, only for it to reappear suddenly, when she least expected it, like a poke in the ribs while falling asleep.

On Sunday afternoon, Roger took the girls out. Michelle was sitting on the sofa reading *Woman's Weekender* and was growing interested in a story about a couple done over by the mortgage lenders, when a flash of white flickered in the corner of her eye. The bird was on the grass again, its feathers settling. It orbited on the spot, getting its bearings, but when it caught sight of her it stopped and looked at her probingly.

"Shoo," she said, parting the conservatory glass, but the bird didn't move until she stepped outside and went right at it, as close as a meter away. Then it flew off and settled on a branch above her head. "Leave me alone," she told it. Back inside, she drew the curtains and tried to return to *Woman's Weekender*, but she knew the bird was there, she *knew* it even if she couldn't see it, sitting there in the tree, watching.

When Roger came home, she had the curtains closed. He said, "What the bloody hell's going on?" She said it was nothing, she'd just had a migraine.

The next morning the bird was outside her bedroom. Roger had left for the office. She was glad he was not here to see her open the window and hurl a cup of water at it with a strangled noise, which prompted a flurry of wings and her elder daughter to rush in, mouth full of toothpaste, and demand, "Mummy, what're you doing? You look like a clown." Michelle met her reflection in the mirror and was surprised by what she saw: her hair unbrushed, yesterday's makeup black grit.

"Come on," she said. "Time to get ready."

On the drive to Monday Club, the radio played James Taylor's "Fire and Rain." Michelle thought about the night she had met Vinny, of his lips when he smoked.

With both girls dropped off, she drove to Sainsbury's even though she didn't need anything. She put her head on the steering wheel.

The song made her ache.

February '72. She had only gone to the party because Erica made her. There'd been nothing to wear, so she'd gone through the laundry basket and found a pair of flares, which she'd doused in her mum's Rive Gauche. She'd been dumped a week ago and wasn't in the mood. "Come on; it'll be fun," said Erica. When they arrived, she thought, I've seen too many scenes like this. A girl was being sick into a flowerpot outside and the end of her plait kept getting caught in her mouth.

"This is Vinny."

Michelle had heard about Erica's jailbird cousin. She wondered then why she hadn't listened harder. Vinny had a head on everyone else, with dark hair and slightly uneven teeth. She could look at him only when he wasn't looking at her. Meeting his eye gave her a humiliated sort of shock.

With Erica gone, he said: "*Michelle* . . . Makes me think of that Beatles song."

"Do you dig the Beatles?"

"More of a Stones man."

"I never liked my name," admitted Michelle. "It reminds me of the sea. It's the shell part. The sea scares me a little. Too deep, maybe." She was talking too much.

Vinny had a nice smile, warm and sincere, and it traveled up to fill his eyes.

"Do you want to celebrate with me?" he asked.

"What are you celebrating?"

He picked up a bottle of Babycham. "Come on."

It was fresher outside on the steps, once the girl and her plaits had gone in.

"I got a job today," he said. "As a lighthouse keeper."

She could see his eyelashes in the dark. "I've never met a lighthouse keeper."

"Now you have."

"And there was I talking about the sea."

"That's how I knew you'd be the one to celebrate with."

She smiled. The drink tasted sweet. "Do you have a smoke?" she asked.

Vinny fished around in his jacket. "It's grass." When he struck the match, she glimpsed the insides of his hands, which seemed an intimate part of him to see.

"It doesn't sound like a real job," she said, wanting to stay out here with him.

"What's a real job?"

"I don't know." She passed him the joint. "One where you don't get lonely."

"I won't be any lonelier than I am now."

"Do you feel lonely now?"

He smiled back at her. "Not exactly."

Michelle thought, There'll always be a bit of me that gets drawn to the wrong one. Maybe there's a bit of that in every woman.

In the car park at Sainsbury's, a VW's horn beeped behind her. The driver wound her window down. "Are you going?" she said impatiently. "I've got two kids in the back."

Michelle realized she was parked in a mother-and-baby space.

"Sorry. Yes. I am." She reversed and drove out of the car park the wrong way down a one-way route, prompting an unpleasant cyclist to shout that she was a blind bloody cow. Indicating left at the roundabout, she saw the bird again, sitting on the island in the middle, on its own, staring at her.

She was woken in the night. Her toes were cold. Two thirty-three a.m.

Roger's bulk was soothing next to her, his fleshy back rising and falling on a snore. She got up and put on her dressing gown, which felt stiff because she'd dried it on the washing line and the sun had cooked it.

Downstairs, in his study, she reached for the file hidden under the desk. Roger had encouraged her to throw it away: "What do you want to keep that crap for?" He'd called it junk that was taking up much-needed space, an objection he did not throw at the arrangement of chrome "stress relievers" scattered across the veneer.

Michelle sat in his chair and opened the folder. Letters from Trident, all variations on a theme: *Our deepest condolences . . . shocked and bewildered . . . if there's anything we can do . . .* Then the bereavement allowance that was better read as hush money: cash for keeping quiet and they'd keep her in exchange.

Finally, their verdict: *We've investigated all we reasonably can. . . . Prison changes people . . . the isolation . . . not the best place for Vincent to have been, in his state of mind.*

State of mind? To this day Vinny had the finest mind she had come across.

Interviews: 1973.

Michelle leaned over in the queasy glow of the overhead and ran her nail around the lip of the file. When the inquiries were happening, Helen Black had insisted on getting copies of everything. Trident hadn't a leg to stand on: the last thing they needed was a stricken relative going to the press.

She reread the transcripts now, words spoken twenty years ago but still alive on the page. Though she knew the text well, her head hurt and her heart hurt more.

She wished that she had been the one to talk about Vinny. Instead it had been Pearl, his aunt, the woman who had raised him. Michelle could have told them what Vinny had really been like, not these lies. Painting him as a thug and a down-and-out. To have it documented, all the lovely things about him, would have meant something.

Most of Pearl's account she could dismiss, but one part was difficult. She reached it now and lingered there, going over the words until their meaning broke apart. Mike Senner's claim troubled her. It always had. The fisherman swore he'd been out to the tower the week before it was discovered empty: he said he'd gone to fill up the water storage tanks and had spoken to Bill and Vince. They had told him about an unexpected visitor.

Why hadn't the investigators pursued that claim? It fit. And it proved what happened, surely it did.

The clock on Roger's desk said five to four. Her eyes were closing; it would be morning soon.

Upstairs, she climbed into bed, careful not to disturb her husband. A shadow moved across the wall, the fingertips of trees reaching through the curtains. She could feel the weight of the man she'd loved, loved him still, the ghost of him, sitting next to her, reassuring as a dog, and how that lightened and then left as she tripped over into sleep.

VII

·

1972

30

ARTHUR

The Boat

Helen,

I never write to you. Never have, don't know how. Lighthouse letters—did you find a book about those once? Some soft romance you picked up in a train station waiting room, back in the days before we started on the life. Keepers writing letters to their girls. Absence making the heart grow fonder. It's not like that. You said when you finished, "I doubt it's like that," and you were right, it's not, for us. Would you rather I had written? Would that have stopped you? What's in my head doesn't come out right, most of the time. I want to tell you, darling. There's so much I want to tell you.

✖

Postcards never finished; postcards never sent. I tear them up and drop them into the sea so I can watch them float away. In another life, a lucky one, I see the pieces washing onto shore. She'll find them, gather them to her, put them back together. It will all make sense.

THIRTY-SIX DAYS ON THE TOWER

"What's wrong with you?" Bill says to Vince over Wednesday's lunch of chicken soup and days-old bread, which is starting to harden and mold. The soup's canned, jellied on top, but once it's heated and thickened up it's OK. "You look sick as a dog."

"Something I ate. Feel like bloody death warmed up."

Bill smokes and grins at me, like it's all a fucking joke.

"What?" I say.

"Nothing. Christ, someone's got to keep their pecker up."

Vince stirs his soup without appetite. I can't blame him; it tastes like the inside of a pocket filled with ten bob. I'm craving fresh meat now, fresh anything. On the rocks up north, we used to keep chickens—the good ones gave us eggs our whole stay and those that didn't wound up in a stew. We'd look at the fowl when we got there and hope at least one of them was getting henpecked for the sake of our stomachs.

"My guts," complains Vince. "They're wrung out."

Bill says, "We'll get you off before the weather turns, eh, Arthur?"

I scrape my chin, running a thumbnail along the spines growing there. I see Helen, looking at me with tenderness, or what I mistook for tenderness but was more likely disdain. *What are you doing with a beard, Arthur Black? You've never had a beard in all the time I've known you, and it isn't you, it isn't you at all.*

There was a time when she didn't know me, and it might be me, after all.

"Just that it'd be you and me then, Bill."

He flicks his fag ash into the soup bowl.

"Wouldn't be for long. They'd bring someone else."

Right now, looking at my Assistant, I think I'd like to sweep the cups and plates from the table, send the whole mess flying as I launch myself against him and wipe that stupid fucking grin off his treacherous face.

"No," I say. "It wouldn't be long."

Vince glances between us.

"What do you want to do?" I ask him.

"I'll be right," he says, shoving the food away. "Rather not haul some poor bugger off right before Christmas."

Bill says, "I'm not doing your fucking watch for you if that's what you're after."

"Thanks for the sympathy, man."

"You'll get plenty of that ashore, from the doctor."

"Anyone'd think you wanted me gone, you bastard."

Bill shrugs. "Just don't want your lurgy, mate. The thunder bucket's under enough strain as it is."

Vince puts his head in his hands. "Could've been my cooking," he groans.

"If it was anyone's . . . ," says Bill.

"I thought if we all had it—"

"Which we soon bloody will—"

"I'll give it a day," says Vince. "See if it passes."

"I'll do your watch," I tell him. "Go back to bed."

When he's gone, Bill says, "Get a boat out, Arthur. He looks like shit."

"That's my decision. It'll be over tomorrow."

"If it isn't?"

"Then we call in."

"Not if there's a bloody great sea on."

"There won't be."

"Not what the forecast says," says Bill.

I light a cigarette. "The forecast isn't always right."

"And you are?"

When the time came for those hens up north, my PK showed me how. He held her upside down and told me to slit her throat. One clean slice from left to right.

"What are you getting at, Bill?"

He looks at me for a moment.

"Fuck it," he says eventually. "You're the PK, not me. Do what you want."

I gathered these dolostones at Flamborough Head. My PK back then took me aside on a quiet day and said, "Here's a penny, lad, and some vinegar, now go see what you make of it." The rocks with calcium in them fizzed with the acid; I learned how to classify their hardness on a scale of one to ten, scratching the hardest with a coin. He gave me his pad and guidebook with all his jottings inside: he'd taken up painting by then and that was him saying, This is yours now, have this for a while, then pass it on.

For Helen, the stones are morbid. For me, it's the opposite. When you're touching a rock that's been here thousands of years, you're holding hands with history.

She says I'm more comfortable on the tower than I am on land, and maybe that's right. Life ashore feels wrong to me. I'm thrown about by the unsteadiness of it all. Telephones ring unexpectedly. Local shops sell two types of milk and I can't decide which to buy. People tell me their news in detail, in shops or at the bus stop, "Morning, Arthur, back so soon? Doesn't seem like yesterday since I last saw you. Did Helen tell you Laura's Stan's finally had his bladder stones removed?" They'll talk about next week or some date in July that I know I won't be here for, but I'll nod along with it, knowing it won't make the slightest bit of difference to me. In that way it's only ever a halfway house, the land life, in that I'm there but not there, like going to a party full of people I've never met, ignorant of the dress code and having to leave before midnight.

When I'm ashore I have to pretend to be a man I'm not, part of something I'm not part of. It's difficult to explain it to normal people. They wouldn't have an interest in the endless quiet stillness of the morning watch, or in how the cooking of a good braise can occupy one's thoughts all day and the day after. Lighthouse worlds are small. Slow. That's what other people can't do: they can't do things slowly and with meaning.

My brain works differently here. Ashore it sort of goes to sleep; it isn't as sharp as it is now. Take when I'm going off on the relief, I'll know exactly how much my bag of tricks should weigh with all the bits and pieces inside—slippers, underpants, towels, comb, handker-chiefs, facecloth, working trousers, comfortable trousers, pullovers, sponge bag, fags, shaving soap. That's to do with my lighthouse life, so I'll know how heavy each item is on its own and all together, and if something's missing I'll be able to say without thinking too hard what that is. Before now I've stopped Helen on the jetty to tell her I've left my nail clippers in the cupboard in the bathroom. In ordinary life, I lose all that. There's too much to bother with and no point anyway because it's always changing. So, while it might seem like the tower demands less of me, or it's here I go into a switched-off state, that'd be wrong.

Helen will confuse me even more when I go back. She'll want to talk to me on some nights and not on others. She'll go out and I won't know where.

Though I could guess now, where. Bill mightn't be it. She could have plenty, poking fun behind my back, calling me the fool, the man who can't hold on to his wife.

I can't rest for thoughts of them together. How could she? And him, whom I took under my wing when he got here, showing him the ropes and showing him friendship, calming him after the fright and sickness of the crossing, and all along—how long?—he wasn't the person I thought.

I can't rest for thoughts of you.

Sleep is the refuge, but it won't let me close. In my bunk I get hot then cold, sweat then shiver, it's night then it's dawn and I can't remember any time in between.

*

One of our generators has packed up. I radio the mainland for assistance and they say they'll send a man out. But really I don't want him here. Don't want anybody new. Anybody at all.

By four o'clock a stiff fog advances over the sea: they've missed their chance. I go up to the gallery to load the jib. It's freezing outside, unnaturally quiet.

There's a smudge on the gallery, a single footprint.

Small. I blink. It's gone.

Fog does this. Makes everything muffled and still. I wouldn't be the first keeper to attribute a temperament to the elements, seeing as they become as close companions to us as our mates indoors, but there is a particular quality to fog. It smothers light and sound, shrinking the world until the spot you're in is the only one left.

December sun is weak at the best of times. Now it's lemonish, cream on the turn. Families ashore will be setting up their Christmas trees and decorating their homes with ribbons and candles. Helen and I used to make the effort, but we don't these days. We'll always have the teatime angel chimes because those were the ones she grew up with, and a length of tinsel wrapped around the mirror. I'm rarely there for Christmas. There's no point in her doing it alone.

I enter F and G into the weather log—G denoting "gloomy"—then read the thermometer and record the visibility, which is barely a stone's throw from the tower.

I spend a long time doing it, longer than the others. They don't inscribe much—dates, symbols, at the required three hours, nothing that belongs to them truly. I don't know why I'm writing or what I'm writing especially. Perhaps I'm writing to you. It's the fog or the hours or the endlessness of everything.

Outside, I pick up a feather from when Vince shoveled his birds. Vince says, "Stop calling them my birds, they're not my bloody birds," but they are in the way I think of them, because he was the one that found them. I steady the feather before releasing it. It hovers for a moment, held by the clotted air, then disappears. It doesn't drop, or fall, or flip away as it would on a breeze. It vanishes.

When I stand, it's to see a shape on the sea, out in the distance, emerging from the fog. So Trident did send someone. Only the boat's coming from the wrong direction, from the open water. It can't be maintenance, after all. I squint, uncertain if it's a quirk of the weather, but my binoculars confirm the boat is coming in fast. Without hesitation I wind the jib and press the plunger to fire the gun. It sounds deafeningly, splitting the smoke. The clock's on for five minutes but I fire another immediately, before winding the jib again to reload.

The boat seems not to hear. It hastens to the tower, oblivious to the explosions and to my now waving arms, hollering at it to steer clear.

Through the binoculars, my target appears faintly. The boat's mast is tall, but the vessel itself is compact. I see a head piloting it and decide that if I can see him, he must be able to see me, so I call again, "Hard to starboard, hard to starboard!"

The gun explodes. Why does he advance? Can he not detect my light?

Now I can make out his torn sail, with no more movement inside it than a sock on a line on a still day. He's coming in for help; he doesn't want to go around. I shout that I'll prepare the winch and he doesn't respond, so I use the flag semaphore. At last, he lifts an arm.

"Hello!" I call. "I see you!"

He keeps one arm up, fingers together, more like a paddle than a hand. Not only is the vessel small but he is too.

"Hello," I say again, not shouting this time.

The boat turns starboard, but the person inside is waving now. It isn't a wave of SOS but one of recognition. He passes the tower. I watch him go and in seconds the fog takes him. He's gone.

31

BILL

Bad Penny

Sid arrives on Thursday. We've barely cleared away breakfast before Arthur gives the heads-up that the dinghy's coming in and it's the mechanic to fix the generator. He looks surprised, as if he didn't expect it.

The fog's still dense. I didn't reckon on Trident shipping any man out. Why doesn't Arthur question it? This week his beard has grown dark, his eyes darker still. There are keepers who stay so long on towers they start to hear mermaids.

It takes minutes of shouting into the dead gloom before the boat's positioned and our newcomer's strapped up to the harness. His boatman is no one I recognize; he's masked in a sou'wester, his face hidden, but he does a fine job of keeping the rope taut and the boat at a steady distance, which is no mean feat because the sea round the tower's gone like bathwater down a plughole. It's the rocks that do me in: cold hunks of carbon that man's got nothing to do with. Same as the ocean, same as the sky. There isn't any feeling, no connection at all. And if that's what life comes down to, then that makes sense to me. There isn't heaven or hell or good or bad, because none of it cares.

"Pleased t' meet you," says the mechanic. "I'm Sid."

He puts his hand out. He's taller than Arthur or me, with a boxer's build. I swear if the Trident Fellows ever had to spend more than a night on a sea light, they'd stop hiring people who take up the space of two. Sid's older than the norm. He has a tattoo on his arm, of a man's skull inside the jaws of a wolf. His hair is thick and pale.

"Where're you from, then?" Arthur asks once the three of us are sitting in the kitchen, smoking, our hands round mugs of tea.

"All over." Sid shakes his empty pack, then pilfers one of Arthur's. "I never stay put. Was told I'd be good for the lighthouses, like one o' ye, because they move ye round and that. But this, nah, couldn't be doing with it. Too bloody small."

Sid looks about, as if he's never been on a tower station before and how amusing are the little table and chairs and the men living their lives inside.

Normally when people come on, they know they're not part of it. This is our world they're in, so they have to toe the line, just like it'd be ashore if you hired a plumber and he came round to do a job. But there's an unnatural feeling about Sid. I can't say what. His voice is high-pitched for a bloke and for someone that big; it's not entirely like a woman's, but not far off. It doesn't sit on him, like it doesn't belong to him, and the more because the accent is broad, northern, and reminds me of my granddad, who had fists like hams and a nose like a misshapen root vegetable.

He reminds me of someone all over. He reminds me of a dream I once had.

"Me, I need space," says Sid. "Suits me fine to pay a visit once in a while, but I couldn't be doing with living here. Got a light? Ta. Fuck, ye boys must smoke a lot; I only smoke when I'm bored. Why ain't ye got any washing-up liquid, eh? I thought ye keepers were obsessed with all tha'. But ye ain't got any."

The PK frowns. "We're waiting for Trident to approve it."

"Ye should've said. I could've brought some over; could've got some from Spar, call it an early Christmas present. Wouldn't've been a bother."

"Soap does all right."

"Don't ye lot get fed up? Sitting round doing fuck all, all day."

"It's a bit more than that," says Arthur.

"Right, but still boring."

"Not once you're used to it."

"Wouldn't want to get used to it, mate. Aye, that'd be the worry." Sid blows smoke in the direction of the weight tube. "Imagine ye still had to wind that bugger up and down all day and night. Don't half take up space, does it?"

Arthur agrees, then says about the weights on chains there used to be inside and how whoever's watch it was had to wind the weights all the way up to the lantern to turn the lenses before dropping them back down again. Every forty minutes, like a grandfather clock. Arthur would've enjoyed it, I think, before it was done electrically; it's his sort of thing: head down, get on with it, like my dad and his dad before. One of the reasons Arthur's their golden boy. Trident's trustworthy long-service veteran who's never so much as stepped an inch out of line. Arthur proves the tower life works. Men can survive it and survive it well. Every keeper I've been stationed with talks about learning from him. Like he's a holy grail they might someday get to touch.

He isn't like that, once you know. That's why whatever she says to me now about how she's made a mistake, I don't believe it.

"It's a right thing, is cancer," says Sid, stubbing out his fag. "What a riot that is. D'ye know I've had it three times? I'm the original bullet dodger, me. Must have a cat in me to have all these lives. More tea? Ta, two sugars, don't be shy about it, pal; yep, two, that's it. Dunno what I'm doing taking these tin-pot jobs—but I am, guess I need t' make a god's penny. Show me someone who's had cancer that many times, it really takes it out o' ye, it does. Dogs get it too. I never knew that, but me mate's dog had it, but the dog didn't get owt for it because he's a dog, so he died. Where's yer third?"

"Third?" says Arthur.

"Yer other man."

"Sleeping."

"At this hour? Flippin' 'eck, what's this for him, a holiday?"

"He's sick."

"If he's sick in his bed, he can't be up t' much. Ye should tell him I've had cancer three bleedin' times and see what he makes o' that. I almost want to get it again, ye know. It's turned into a bit of a game for me now. Seeing as I'm winning at it, I'll have another pot and see how I do, how many times I can beat it. It's a rough one, those hospitals. They say I'm like a bad penny in how I keep turning up."

"My mother was from Yorkshire." It's the first thing I've said to him.

"Yeah?" He turns on me. Silver eyes. "Where was your granny from?"

"What?"

"I don't need your life story, pal."

"I guessed. The accent."

"Then ye're a crap guess. Like I said, I'm from all over. Being that way, ye get to witness the whole circus o' life. Ye two ever heard of the white rook? I've a pal said he saw one once, on the Maiden Rock. It were definitely the Maiden, it was, hundred percent. Not a gull, me mate knows these things, it were a white rook. He was up on the gallery and this bloody bird comes right out of nowhere and sits down next to him, giving him the beady eye. Totally white, it was, a flippin' great big white rook."

"We don't get rooks out here," says Arthur.

"Ye did that time. It was ages ago, mind. I've got a thing about birds, can't stand the buggers. They're prehistoric in the way they look, aren't they, all beaks and feet and flapping about. Ye ever tried helping a bird when it's got itsen in difficulty? It bloody screams at ye, it does, it's terrifying."

Eventually, I get Sid down to the generator. I watch the back of his head as we go down the staircase—one turn to the oil, one to the paraffin, one to the store. His hair is the strangest color, almost white but not quite, and not the white that comes with age. There's a tremor of recognition in a dark part of my brain, but it breaks apart when I reach for it.

The mechanic's so big I can't think how we'll both fit down there with the batteries and crammed-in machinery, but we do. Arthur says I'm to stay with him. I don't want to. I don't like how he looks at me, as if he knows every thought I ever had.

"Who's your boatman?"

Sid sets to work on draining the fuel. "Ye what?"

"Your boatman. I don't know him."

"I don't know him neither, pal."

"We usually get Jory. He's our usual one."

"Sorry to disappoint." It's murky down here, thick with shadows. "Bet ye were hoping for extras, weren't you, Christmas being around the corner."

"Sometimes that happens."

"Yeah, ye lighthouse keepers like thinking of yeselves as a bleedin' charity."

"I wouldn't say that."

"I heard all the nippers at the school send ye presents." Sid's fingers work swiftly; he doesn't pay attention to what he's doing, he does it absentmindedly, like someone stirring a pot while on the phone. "And the church too. Ye're not running a platoon out in Vietnam, pal, don't feel too sorry for yeselves."

"We're always grateful for it."

"It's over the top if ye ask me. And d'ye want to hear another thing, Bill? Another thing's this tendinitis. Ye ever had it? Ye can thank your lucky stars, then—I woke up with me hand all seized up, couldn't move it a bit; and not just me hand but me wrist and all the way up to me elbow, completely dead it were, might as well've had a sack o' spuds tied to me for all the good it did. This doctor said to me—"

"The cancer doctor?"

"Nah, different one, this doctor says, Sidney, ye've got tendinitis. I say, I got what-what? An' he tells me it's where the nerve gets trapped going into yer hand, and ye have to put up with it till it gets better cos there's fuck all else to be done." He rolls his shoulders: there's a cracking sound. "'Course I couldn't work then and that were the pits, though not as bad as the cancer, that really were a thing, but turns out the quack were right, and this tendinitis did go away on its own. It caught me unawares, it did. Bit like that white rook ye've got out here."

"There isn't a white rook."

"Suit yourself. Me mate knows what he's talking about."

"Who is your mate? I might know him."

Sid takes out the carburetor. "Ye married, Bill?"

"Yes."

"Jenny, ain't it?"

"How do you know her name?"

He unscrews the float bowl. "Reminds me of a donkey."

"I'll tell her you said that."

"How's it going, then? With Jenny. I heard she's a drunk."

The smell of fuel fills my nostrils. "What?"

"Things get around." Those eyes cross mine. "Ashore, like. People talk."

"That's none of your damn business."

"Right ye are. Should mind me big nose. Only Ah'm curious as to what makes a man and woman want to stay together their whole lives, ye know. It fascinates me, like. Ah'm not married meself, never wanted it. Can't think o' much worse."

I've got to speak, or I'll punch him. Got to fill my mouth or I'll fill my fist. My dad said, *You're a boy who gets hit, Bill; you're not a boy who hits.*

"Shit, ain't it." Sid picks up a wire brush. "Being tied down all that time. Life's a long haul. Couldn't be arsed with it. Bit of a loner, me."

"You get lots of time apart in this job."

"Which you like, eh, Bill."

My head hurts.

"Ah'm sorry," he says. "Just interested. People come to me with their problems."

"I don't have problems."

Down here, Sid looks younger than he did upstairs. His hands as they wipe the gunk out of the bowl are smooth, not belonging to a man who gets his fingers covered in grease for a living. I can't stop thinking of his teeth when he smiled, bright white, the canines sharp. My chest feels like I've swallowed a bag of sand.

"Ye keep telling tha'sen that, pal," he says. "Ye'll never guess what I was before I started in this game. Go on. Have a guess. Bet ye can't."

"I can't."

"I already gave ye a clue." He sprays the jet passage. "People came to me with their problems. Once a week. On a Sunday. Bloody hell, ye're no churchgoer then!"

"You were a *priest?*"

"What's the matter—don't I look like a holy man?"

"No."

"It were a long time ago. Pass me that flathead, would ye?"

"Why?"

"I need it."

"Why a priest?"

"Reason I told ye that was so's ye'd get whatever it is off yer chest."

"I don't have anything on my chest."

He wipes his nose with the tattooed arm. "What about that bag?"

"What bag?"

"Ye said summat like ye had a bag of sand on yer chest what with everything you had corked up inside it."

I peer at him. Closer.

"Ye don't love yer wife, Jenny Donkey, but ye'd have a crack at the

PK's." Sid turns the screwdriver in his hands. "Yep, ye'd have a crack at 'er. Loved her for ages, haven't ye, ever since ye came here and yer own wife looked shabby standing next to her. Ye feel about Helen so strong ye can't look at her straight. Can't even touch her, even to help with her shopping bags; ye're worried it'll be obvious to him and then he'll know. Well, he already knows, pal. He knows what ye want, how fucked ye are over her. Surprised? 'Course he knows, ye idiot. Ye think he's old and past it, don't ye, and what's a bugger like that goin' t' do with ye? I wouldn't want t' guess at it, pal. That's a man with nothing to lose."

"I don't know who the hell you are—"

"Aye, ye do. Ye know exactly who I am."

Sid taps the pad of his index finger against the pad of his thumb. It sounds like an old telephone line connecting.

"Ye missed the boat with Helen," he says. "After what happened to 'em, she's ruined now, ain't she. She'll never get better, and ye didn't do it with her. He did."

"Don't talk about Helen again," I warn him. "You don't know her."

"Nor do ye, ye crazy fuck. But I know ye. Aye, I know all o' ye. Just enough, and enough's as good as a feast."

He wipes his hands and smiles again, showing his jaw teeth.

"Now what am I getting for me dinner? Been ages since I had me some home-cooked grub."

32

VINCE

Knock-Knock

EIGHTEEN DAYS ON THE TOWER

Someone comes to bed, but that doesn't mean it's night. It's dark, but that doesn't mean it's night. Or maybe it is night, there's always a chance. Slivers of happenings and sounds that belong in the real world: the steam off a cup of tea or the dinner-canteen stench of a tin of Heinz ravioli. Nowhere to go and nowhere to be except holed up in the same place, sick to the stomach, stomach like a net filled with crabs, worried and waiting and the days on repeat. In the nick I had a slit to see daylight; they don't want you getting spoiled on the amount of light you get, cos light's a luxury for a man with a dark heart in his chest. But when it was clear, I'd glimpse the stars, five or six of them, maybe, and they seemed the most beautiful thing to me then and they still do now. I'd be lying there with some con on the bunk above, snoring or scratching his balls, and I'd stare at those stars for as long as it took me before I went to sleep.

It's worse for the others. They've got to deal with covering my watch and cleaning up after me. Me, I'm used to shitting and puking in buckets. Bill and the PK are used to fine china and porcelain bogs, or whatever bogs are made out of. Being sick here or being sick in the clink, it doesn't make much of a difference.

❈

The PK comes in. Kneels, gets a box out his cupboard. I can hear the rocks and stones as they knock against each other, *knock-knock*, soft, cold, constant. Time passes.

❈

"Did I tell you I read palms?" Michelle said to me after she finished work. I was meeting her at Charing Cross; she came out of a busy station, umbrella hanging like something shot, and waved and smiled. I thought, How the hell did I manage this?

"Not into that crap, are you?"

"What do you mean?"

"Dead people. Thinking you've lived before."

"I don't know what I think about that." We passed over Trafalgar Square. Gray pigeons on a gray column. "My nan showed me how to do the palms."

"Yeah?"

"And Tarot."

"Those cards with the goats swinging upside down."

"You've never done it."

" 'Course I bloody haven't!"

"I'll do it for you if you like."

She didn't. We went back to her bedsit on Stratford Road and fucked instead. When I woke up next morning, she had one of my hands in hers and was looking at it.

"What is it?" I asked.

She said: "You don't have a fate line."

I said, "Should I?" She said yes. I said as long as I've got a heart line that's fine by me. You've got one of those, she said.

✕

Half awake, half asleep, drowning in a half world. Last night I heard the PK's voice on the radio. He's calling for a doctor, isn't he? Arthur will take care of me.

Knock-knock.

Who's there?

A man coming at me over the sea. White hair, white skin; feet dripping on the set-off, hands on the dog steps. Here he is at the entrance. At the door now.

I promised Michelle it was over. When I wrote to her, I swore, There'll be no more fighting now. No more danger. Trust me.

There was a bloke in the lockup, he played a lot of chess and he's the one I learned it from; he said it was like being one of the pieces, one of the big ones, let's say a horse. If you put the horse on the board, it's part of the game and there are ways the game can get it. But if you take it off it's just a horse, there's nothing else to call it, it can't be boxed in or got at or played; it isn't even part of the game anymore.

You have to take yourself off the board every once in a while. Get back to who you are—the real you, when you're alone and there's no pretending. You can do that on a lighthouse. There's no one pulling you this way or pushing you that. Just you.

When they come for me, that's when I'll know. What I'm made of. What I've got. What I'm willing to do.

My secret in the kitchen under the sink. Like the PK and his stones, that private pleasure. I imagine the weight of the gun, its curves as smooth as hers.

‡

Hours I've been floating. Dimly aware of the PK coming into the bedroom, the creak of a bunk and the swish of a curtain in the deep, deep dark, then a whisper:

Vince, can you hear me? Not long now, mate.

Drifting in that darkness, enough to lift my thoughts up to the top of the tower, part of the sky or part of the sea, or else I'm lost somewhere on land, searching for that unknowable, unreachable light, feeling I've died.

NINETEEN DAYS

A time I remember, some day in the middle of a million days when we ran out of fags. Patting a pocket like a slack-skinned cheek, realizing, Shit, we've smoked them all. Three keepers legging it between floors, raiding coats and shirts, every nook where an in-case-of-emergency fag might once have been stowed. Shaking every box and tin, thinking of that mate that gave me one once and then I went and hid it and I can't remember where. The mission for butts tossed in bins, twisting the nubs to get the innards out and rolling them into a smokable flute. One or two puffs, but worth it.

Smoking on a light's more than habit. Two and a half minutes of being in the time that you're in. Quiet heart, quiet soul. Then what? Waiting for a boat to pass by, putting in an ask for a crew to be coming, but that could be days, and the hours stretch on and on and the sea makes fun of us, tiny men with tiny desires.

Then Arthur found a pack. If it were Bill, he'd have kept it. Fags aren't like tins of sardines and they don't have to be shared. But the PK put a smoke by each of our places—one a day, no more for him, no less for us, and that fag was anticipated to the point of something divine. The three of us smoking after dinner in silence, warm crackle of paper, the soft *pup* of our lips. Nothing before or since ever tasted as good.

A nightmare jolts me, or it could be the sheets, which are wet with sweat and tangled between my legs. I was climbing, then my muscles gave out and I fell and I woke up.

Someone else, *knock-knock*—there's talk in the background, in the distance, above or below I can't tell, but someone else is here cos Bill and the PK use their smarter voices then, better and clearer instead of the grunts and swears.

I try to sit. Bump my head. My back peels off the wrinkled sheet. Blood rushes to my head. It hurts; I lie down.

Belly empty, but to think about food makes me sick. To think about the chocolates Bill's wife sent over makes me sick. Sockets hurt, sockets all over, those points in the body where round things go in round-shaped holes. There's a bucket on the floor. I don't know when I last used it or it was cleared away.

They've brought a doctor, that's it. I want a doctor. But it isn't a doctor, it isn't anyone; I'm dreaming of going on the gallery for the fresh air and to let the wind blast it out of me, but I'll never get up there, I'll never get up, and it feels like thirst, actual thirst, the need to get out, a drink I have to have or I'll die. What if I die?

※

When I wake again it's freezing cold. The wall is freezing damp. I pull the sheet and blanket and they're freezing too.

Brackish dreams I wade through up to my knees, coating my tongue in bitter liquor. Back there again, walking, the block of flats up ahead. I saw it not as it had been in real life but changed. Crooked. My mate Reg behind me, the others too: I didn't see them but I felt them, heard the shift of their jackets as they moved. . . .

Let's go back. Let's not do this.

But the dream carried on as if it never heard, and the dog was barking now. I saw its teeth. Its veined black gums and the scab that oozed when it snarled.

Blood and fur, a child's high scream. My friend grown cold in my arms.

※

The window outside the bedroom is an opaque square. I think of F for fog.

Three voices.

I need water. I expect to come to the kitchen and see myself there, with the others, the PK, Bill, and me, sitting round smoking over a game of cards, and it's my own voice I've been hearing, and the standing version, the one thinking this, isn't involved at all. He's invisible. Dead. He died somewhere back there in his dreams.

But when I make it downstairs, it isn't me I see.

It's a big, silver-haired bloke.

Arthur says, "About time."

The big, silver-haired bloke doesn't say anything, but he looks at me, and smiles.

VIII

·

INTERVIEWS:
1973

33

HELEN

—I can bear it. Whatever it is. If they're dead, I can bear it. I can bear that over not knowing. You'd tell us, wouldn't you? If you found out, you'd tell us?

—We know how upsetting this is for you, Helen.

She wished they would not say that. They could not possibly know. The idea she would never see Arthur again was bottomless and strange, a book of empty pages, a shunt off the side of a train, the stair you thought was there in the dark but wasn't.

January 2. Tuesday morning. Eleven forty-five.

Four days they had been gone. When Helen saw the Maiden Rock through her living room window, she had the uncanny sensation of watching a car drive by with no one at the wheel.

—Do you have a view as to what's happened to your husband?

The investigators sat opposite her, the bearers of bad news, of no news, of nothing. At times it struck her as inconceivable, an elaborate game played through mischief or boredom to see how it shook things up ashore, how long it would be before those clod-footed land people found them, the lizards, clinging slyly to a rock.

—I don't know. It makes no sense. People don't just disappear, do they?

—Not typically.

—You think they're dead.

—It's too early to draw conclusions.

—But you're thinking it. Aren't you? I am.

—Let's go back a little, if we can. The last communication we received from Arthur was his canceling a request for a mechanic to come to fix the generator.

—Yes.

—Why do you think Arthur canceled the request, Helen?

—The generator was mended.

—Yet Trident hadn't dispatched anyone.

—One of them must have fixed it. Arthur could have done it. Or Bill.

The man scribbled on his notepad. There were too many questions—all of them time wasting, from people who didn't know the first thing about lighthouses, what it meant to be involved in a lighthouse with someone who was on a lighthouse.

—Was Arthur behaving in any way abnormally the last time you saw him?

—No.

—Did he talk about anyone in particular, any name that was new or unusual?

—I don't think so.

—We're looking to rule out that Arthur and the others weren't picked up from the tower by a third party. Someone with a boat. Is that the kind of thing he'd do?

Helen shook her head. Arthur was pragmatic and sensible; he had a mind like an index. On their first outing as a couple, he'd told her the names of the stars. It wasn't even a romantic thing; it was just that he knew. Betelgeuse. Cassiopeia. Names like marbles in a glass bowl. He took clocks apart and put them back together again, to see how they dismantled and then how they worked, the elegance of the mechanism. He did jigsaws awash with sea and sky because being a keeper he'd learned to notice the defining detail where she saw only gray. She had always thought he had the finest set of shoulders she had seen on a man, an odd thing to be captivated by but there it was. Previously she'd been out with someone who had no shoulders to speak of and whose clothes had seemed in constant danger of dropping away, like a shirt on a hanger that was too small. By contrast, she could have steadied two baskets on Arthur's. She had been ready, then, to marry and start a family.

—Was Arthur depressed at all?

—What do you mean "at all"? Either you are or you aren't.

—Did he ever say he felt down? Did you observe a loss of appetite, or that he slept more than usual or stopped engaging with people?

—Arthur rarely engaged with people.

—So, he might have suffered with depression.

—I don't think so. We never talked about that.

Helen thought of her husband in this kitchen weeks before, standing by the oven, right there, *right there*, his back to her, and the memory was close enough to touch. He'd spread jam on bread, and she had felt irritated at how, before he ate the bread, he'd washed the knife, dried it, and put it away, and only then did he sit down to eat. She'd said nothing because a long marriage had taught her that if you didn't have nice words to say, then it was better to say nothing at all. She could have things how she preferred when he was off; when he came back, she could feel irritated and say nothing, because that was marriage, a lot of the time.

—Can I ask what you did before enrolling with Trident?

—I had a job in London. As a salesclerk.

—Quite a contrast as a way of life, then.

—I suppose so. I've been involved with the Institution over half my years, but I still think about that time and how different it is for me now and has been for so long.

—Do you like living here on your own? It's very remote.

—I don't think too much about it.

—It's, what, four miles into Mortehaven?

—Arthur said it was as if Trident didn't want us to get out.

—Isolation can be harmful, Helen. We have to consider that not just for the men but for their families too. If Arthur was depressed . . .

—I never said he was depressed.

—But it would stand to reason he might have been.

—Why?

The investigators watched her sympathetically.

—Seclusion can be very damaging to a person. Especially if they're in an existing vulnerable state.

—What are you suggesting?

—It's too early to suggest anything. We're looking at several prospects.

She had already considered the prospects. Bill had told Arthur. He'd lied about Helen's feelings and how long it had gone on: a schoolboy in knee socks prodding the nest. The thought that Arthur had believed it made something crumple inside her.

—The effects of being quarantined are serious. It isn't a normal state for a person. Were you aware that Mr. Walker had trouble with it? Or Mr. Bourne?

—I don't know either of them very well.

—But living next door to Mr. Walker, you must have been familiar with him.

—Not really.

—Are you friendly with his wife, Jenny? How long have they been here?

—A couple of years.

—And there've never been any arguments in the cottages, any fallings-out?

—No.

—I should think you and she have been a comfort to each other.

Helen focused on the oilcloth covering the table. Jenny had given it to her for her birthday last year, salmon-hued drawings of rural Devon interspersed with recipes for soup and cockle pie. Jenny was a passionate cook. She cooked fatty terrines and treacle sponges; delicacies for Bill to take off with him to the tower. Jenny prided herself on her cooking, her homeliness, her motherliness, all the things Helen was not.

When Bill was off, she sometimes invited Helen over for a home-cooked meal. Helen accepted her invitations uneasily. During the meal she talked to the little ones while Jenny ladled food into bowls, then sloshed out wine, then cleared it away, with dozens of dialogues started and not a single one finished. Helen insisted on doing the washing-up, and then there was something about the position of two women at a kitchen sink—one washing, one drying, the radio murmuring—that engendered confidence.

Forgive me, Jenny. I was alone, and lonely.

—There'll be provisions for her, as a single mother. And for you, Helen. Trident House is clear about that. Whatever it takes, you'll be looked after.

—It might not come to that. They could still come back.

But it had already come to that. On Saturday morning when Trident's people had rolled up in a pair of Vauxhall Victors, winding down the narrow track to the compound. Jenny and the children had been expecting Bill home. The officers came to the door, and Helen, watching from her window, had known straightaway. The stiff shoulders, the bowed heads, the caps dutifully removed as soon as the door was opened. In grief and shock people make smaller movements than they do normally, respectful of their proper sequence. Jenny had fallen to the step.

Helen knew how it felt to have the life go out of her, but she had never seen it in another person and found she was unable to see it then because Jenny's pain required that she turn her head at the final moment, like passing a road accident and sensing its need for privacy.

Bill must have had a heart attack, she thought, or gone over the side of the boat and drowned. She accepted it quite readily. Her first, selfish emotion was relief.

When the officers looked toward her own cottage, there was an instant in which everything around her had stilled: the ticking clock, the hum of the fridge, the rumble of the kettle in the kitchen reaching a boil. Later, after she was told, part of her questioned if she had willed it to happen, a change or revelation, and it had.

—Are you all right, Helen? Can we carry on?

—Will you excuse me; I need some fresh air.

Outside the wind was wailing, the brown sea choppy and frothing white crests. Wave clouds raced across the sky. Helen didn't have a coat, but the slicing cold felt necessary, the wind battering her dress. She could just see the Maiden, a remote vertical housing its emergency contingent. Trident thought that lodging them here where they could see the faintest smidgen of that ugly tower made them feel closer to their husbands, but it only made it worse. The men couldn't see them. As far as Arthur was concerned, his life ashore ceased to exist, but still she was able to look at him, and every day it bothered her. She would rather not see it at all.

Come back to me, she thought.

The tower faced her, unyielding. All towers were proud, but the Maiden was in particular. It was proud of taking Arthur. It was his secret place, away from her, and it liked that. She thought of the rocks he had collected from the island stations, noting their parallels and discrepancies when she'd wanted to hit him and cry, *Look at me, you stupid man, look at me; can't you see how much I need you?*

She couldn't remember starting to love him, because it seemed she had loved him her whole life, with no clear place where that started or finished. But in the end the Maiden's solace, the lighthouse herself, had offered him what she could not. After the hardship they had tried to face together but that had left her with nothing to give.

The tears came hotly but froze in her eyes. She told herself she'd known worse than this, but in that silent moment of captive weeping it didn't feel as if she had.

There was no point explaining it to those people indoors. How were they to see the most basic complaint she had, the hardest, most bitter complaint she harbored against her husband and that she never

found the words to talk to him about because his silence would leave
her more gagged than ever. That she hadn't been the only one who
looked elsewhere. There had been another woman. A love she couldn't
come close to, or hope to match up against. Who had taken Arthur
away from her, whom he thought about when they were together and
longed for whenever they touched.

34

JENNY

—Carol says I'm out of milk. That's going to be a problem for the children's bedtime but I'm not going out to get it, no, I'm not. I'm not leaving this house till Bill comes home. I'm not leaving till he comes back and we see it's all been a mistake because he'll come home any minute now, I'm telling you, and I have to be here, waiting for him.

The interrogation wasn't as she had imagined from police dramas on television. They weren't at a police station, for starters. They were in her home, Masters, carrying now the faint smell of tea and sausage rolls. All morning Jenny had watched strangers come into the cottage, the normal lines that separated private from public—her front door, the threshold to her bedroom—briskly overstepped. The investigators were pitying but thought it acceptable to eat at a time like this, and somehow acceptable to bring crinkly paper nests into her house, flecked with pastry and wedges of hot meat.

—We appreciate you talking to us, Jenny.

The baby started crying. In the hall, her sister flitted past to collect him. The front door opened. She startled: it was Bill. No, it wasn't.

—I don't mind talking so long as you don't keep talking as if he's gone. As if he's dead. He's not dead. It's just we've got to wait a bit longer. That's all.

Paper streamers drooped from the living room ceiling, weary after holding their smile since the twelfth. The angel on top of the tree closed one eye, unwilling to look. They had argued about the angel because he hadn't wanted an angel, he'd wanted a star, and she had gone at him since all he did was criticize her, whatever she did, however hard she tried, and couldn't he just let her have what she liked? He knew how much Christmas meant to her. Jenny decorated every year whether Bill was at home or not. On Christmas morning she would picture him on the Maiden with the cards and presents she had packed back in November, ready for him to open. The children shouted carols from the table in the garden, loud as they could so he could hear. If the wind was right, maybe he did.

—Where do you think Bill is, Jenny?

The man's voice was gentle, as if he were about to do something to her that hurt.

—I think he's out there right now, safe and warm on a boat.

—The first twenty-four hours after a report of missing persons are critical. We're now at ninety-six. . . .

—He's alive.

—You believe your husband and the men he was with escaped the tower?

—Yes. Something got on there with them and took them away.

—Such as the person mentioned in Mike Senner's report?

The woman had a round face and heavy eyelids, with a posture that was somehow both alert and bored, like an owl in a petting zoo, unimpressed by passersby.

—The place has a bad atmosphere. Bill said it a lot.

—Between the three of them?

—No. Just in itself. Like bad things have gone on there.

—Things Bill did? Or one of the others?

Jenny swallowed. Her throat hurt. Everyone assumed Mike Senner was lying, and maybe he was. Mike was known for telling tales as a way of getting attention for himself, and good sense told her no one could land on a tower without Trident's say-so. But he had seemed so sure. He promised he'd been the last to see them. He said Bill told him they'd had a man on there with them. Wasn't that important? Didn't it matter?

If she admitted she believed Mike's account, they'd put a cross in her box. They'd go through her stores, her bins. Her household-cleaning receipts.

—That's not what I mean. Things get stuck. Trapped. There isn't enough room on a lighthouse. Everything's cooped up.

—Are we talking about ghosts?

—Not a sheet with eyes cut out. Just what I said, an atmosphere, a bad atmosphere. Some lighthouses have it in them. Look at Smalls.

—What about Smalls?

She'd heard the story from Bill about what happened at Smalls Light-house, off the coast of Wales, last century. In those days the stations went two-handed, only a pair of keepers on them at a time, and a few weeks in, one of them died in an accident. Everyone knew those two didn't get on, so the one left behind grew worried he'd get done for murder if he got rid of the body. So he decided to sit it out and wait for all the time to go until the relief. The thing was, after a while, he couldn't stand the smell. All he could do was build a coffin to hang off the lantern, but as soon as there was a gale it blew right open, and the rotting corpse was there with his arms hanging all over the place. Every time the wind gusted, the dead man's arm hit the top of the tower.

Bill said it must have looked as if the man were beckoning. The dead one saying to the living one, *Come on*, beckoning him to join him. It started to get inside his head. Made him lose his mind. Ships passed off in the distance; they saw this man waving; they didn't think anything was wrong, so they never came. At the end of it, the living keeper wound up worse than the dead one. He'd had to listen to that rapping sound all day and night, tapping on the window, asking to be let in. By the time he came ashore he was a wreck, plagued by nightmares and the haunting whistle of the wind.

The owl sat straighter, but still with that blank, placid expression.

—That's an interesting story.

—That's all this is to you, isn't it? A story.

Doubtless Jenny looked mad, her hair unbrushed since Saturday, same clothes as yesterday, and anyway the shirt was Bill's. It smelled of him. Of bark and sweat.

—Helen next door says they drowned.

—She would. She's a liar. You'll find out.

—A liar?

—It's criminal her saying that. She's the PK's wife. She ought to have more loyalty, making it sound like they didn't know what they were doing. When Bill gets back, he'll be pleased I kept my trust in him and didn't say it was down to the fact he couldn't do his job.

—Helen led us to believe it's a supportive atmosphere in the cottages.

—It was.

—Was?

—Are you going to repeat every bloody thing I say?

—There were two stopped clocks on the tower, Jenny. Both were stopped at quarter to nine. Did that time have any special significance to Bill?

—No.

—To any of you?

—No.

—You don't know? Or it didn't?

—I don't know. Both. Either.

—Helen suggested the batteries had gone.

—Had they?

The woman had the courtesy to look self-conscious.

—Unfortunately, we weren't able to verify this. Both batteries were in place but there's a chance their points were reversed. The search crew Trident sent removed the batteries and replaced them. Then they couldn't be certain.

She had a flash of Bill flailing in the waves. He couldn't swim.

—Something was on that lighthouse with them. And before you say that's mad, it's not half as mad as saying two perfectly good clocks conked out at the same minute on the same day.

—The alternative would be that one of the keepers stopped the clocks.

—Why would they do that?

There was a knock at the door. An assistant brought in two cups of brown liquid that resembled the thin gravy they served at the carvery in Mortehaven. Jenny had a memory of Bill before they were married, taking her for dinner there in his best suit.

The smell of the coffee made her feel sick.

—I need to go to the bathroom.

Afterward, in the hall, she met Carol, who offered her the baby to hold, but she didn't want him. She didn't want to be touched by anyone except Bill.

When she went back into the living room, the stage was still set.

For the rest of their lives, this would be Christmas—the inspectors, the sausage rolls, the paper bells, and the balding tree. Hannah and Julia were at a friend's house, but she couldn't leave them there forever and soon she'd have to explain. Seven and two, they'd understand the bones of it: that they might never see their father again. Hannah might have a recollection of him, but Julia probably wouldn't. The baby wouldn't have anything.

He's coming back.

If she thought it enough times, it might turn out to be true.

What if it didn't? She would have to survive each day, knowing what she'd done. It served her right. She deserved her loss.

—We're considering whether the men could have planned their disappearance.

—That's ridiculous. Bill would never do it to me.

—Would Arthur do it to Helen?

—That depends.

—On what?

—I don't know what goes on in their marriage, do I?

The man drank his coffee. He wrote on his pad.

—Did your husband ever talk about Vincent Bourne?

—Bill didn't like talking about the tower when he was ashore.

—It might bother some people, that Vincent had been in prison.

—There're worse things than stealing. It's hardly as if he hurt anyone.

The man watched her for a moment. Then he exchanged glances with the woman, who traced a nail the color of prepackaged ham around the rim of her cup.

—Did you ever meet the Supernumerary, Jenny?

She had met him once, coming ashore in Mortehaven, after he'd traded places with Frank. Early twenties, lanky, round shoulders. He'd had a cigarette in his mouth, hardly visible beneath a deluxe mustache. She'd been able to smell his moth-eaten guernsey, musty, smoky, a damp, ancient smell she'd come to associate with the tower, because Bill smelled of it whenever he came back and it took days of her washing and sachets of potpourri in his shirt drawer to get him smelling of home again.

—You're right that Mr. Bourne served time over the years for petty theft. However, his last spell in prison was for a rather more serious offense.

—What?

—I'm afraid we can't disclose that. Such a detail could raise speculation and risk hampering the inquiry.

—A detail? I'd hardly call Vince being banged up for a crime that put Bill in danger a detail. What was it? Tell me. I'm his wife. I've a right to know.

—We can't surmise that Mr. Bourne's crime had anything to do with the disappearance, or that he put anyone at risk.

—But it's possible?

The pair looked sorry for her. Sorry, she thought, for more than just the circumstances. They conferred for a moment, then told her.

She took a few moments to process what they had said, and it was like reaching the end of a TV program and realizing you had watched it all wrong. The truth about Vincent Bourne rippled through her like a flag on the back of a ship, a lone stark flare of red.

She wasn't the only one with a secret.

35

PEARL

—I'll have you know it nearly killed me getting down here, a woman my age in the state I'm in. They've put me on blood thinners now for me heart but all they do is make me dizzy and freezing bloody cold all the time; look at me, I'm shaking! Hands like a bloody ghost, you can see right through 'em. That's the warfarin, that is. I'd rather be having another stroke at this rate.

—Would you like a drink, Mrs. Morrell?

—Not unless you've a cherry brandy, I'll have one o' those. And it ain't Mrs., it's Miz. S'pose you think a woman like me'd have a husband, don't you?

—I hadn't really thought about it.

—Well, I did once. We had a big fancy wedding an' all. Then he went and buggered off, di'n't he, went out to buy a pint o' milk one morning and never bloody came back. You hear stories like that. In my case it's true. Di'n't even give me a peck on the cheek before he left. D'you think I should keep my wedding ring on after that? Not bloody likely. Leaving me t' look after the baby, five months old and screaming murder at me all day and night, no, thank you very much.

Thought I saw him at a petrol station in '68, filling his car up with some tart in the front. Can I smoke?

The man passed her an ashtray, one of those posh glass ones to be expected in an establishment like this. Pearl had never stayed anywhere like the Princess Regent, with its gigantic bed and feather pillows and en suite bog, and the breakfasts . . . eggs and bacon, kippers and pancakes, it made a change from her usual crumpet and fags while staring out the window of her high-rise at the traffic lumping past on the A406.

—We appreciate you making the journey, Ms. Morrell.

—You're paying for me t' stay in this gaff till we're done, right?

—Trident House wishes to look after relatives at this difficult time.

—So you keep saying. I wouldn't want t' be in their shoes. Can't say I'm surprised about any of it, t' be honest. That boy was always set to come a cropper. He was trouble all his life and he'd carry on being trouble till the end of it. Now you're sitting there sweating when there's no big mystery the way I see it. Everyone's talking about this mystery but there ain't one. When I got that call, I thought, Ah, here we go.

—How's that?

—I saw it coming. Maybe not like this, I'll grant you it's a clever way of doing it. But I saw it coming.

—What, exactly?

—Ain't that your job to find out? I di'n't know nothing about it. Di'n't even know he'd joined the bleeding light'ouse service. When he got out the nick, he never called or bloody came round, the ungrateful sod; I di'n't even know he was out. It was only cos of the fact of Erica knowing this bird he started seeing. That's how we knew.

—He has a girlfriend?

—Stranger things.

—What's her name?

—Erica'll tell you. Erica's my daughter. She wanted to come but I told her no. I'm the adult in charge. I'm responsible for that reprobate whether I like it or not.

—What did you think about Vincent working on the lighthouses?

—Shocked they took him on, after what he did. But then I worked out he must've lied about it. Vinny was always a good liar.

—Trident thought his history made him a suitable candidate for the work.

—Ha! Now I've heard it all. Di'n't they mind what he got found guilty of? Di'n't that put 'em off? It bloody should've. Don't they care who they put on these light'ouses and the sorry sods that get lumbered with him? I feel for those men, I do. My nephew's the reason they're gone. An' it costs me a lot t' say that, that he's my nephew, cos if I had a choice I'd say he was nothing whatsoever t' do with me, not my flesh and blood. But if you'd asked me a year ago where I saw him winding up, I'd tell you something like this.

—Do you believe Vincent hurt the others?

— 'Course. He knew what was what. Picked it up on the streets, then the slammer finished the job.

—How would you describe your nephew? In your own words.

—Who else's bloody words am I going to use? Nightmare since the day he was born. My sister couldn't deal with him: she's in her grave now. He drove her to it.

—How old was Vincent when his mother died?

—Thirteen. See here, before you go looking sorry for him, life don't always come up smelling of roses. Quicker he learned that the better— 'specially when it was down to him. He had the devil in him, that boy. I said to Pam the second I clapped eyes on him, That baby's not all there, Pamela. He had a real wrong look in his eye, he did. When he grew out of being a baby and started being a toddler, he used to beat her up. Smacked into her. Gave her bruises and black eyes. Headbutted her when she went to pick him up, or he kicked an' hit her, and he never ate anything she put in front of him and he never slept neither, just spent all night shouting so she never got a wink o' sleep. Pam lost her head. He got put in and out of care—how old was he then, two, three? Up on his hind legs anyway, by the time they took him away. Services came and it shook Pam, it did, but she was in no fit state. She never wanted him in the first place and that makes it harder. At least with Erica I'd wanted her, that is to say at least I was all right with having a baby. With Vinny she coped with it for a bit, but she couldn't carry on. Not with the demon in him.

—When you say "in and out" of care, do you mean he came back to her?

—A few times. It weren't just Pam that couldn't deal with 'im, it were those foster families and all; they'd keep sending him back cos he ruined their lives too. And I'd be thinking, Give the poor girl a rest! She said she don't want him, bloody well leave her alone. It just made her worse.

—Worse?

—With the drugs. She overdosed in the end. Fairly sure she meant to. I can't say I blame her. It weren't Pamela's fault; it were his. His and his dad's.

—Where's his father now?

—Buggered if I know. Or care.

—He didn't help to bring up his son?

—That's a joke if ever I heard one. I never clapped eyes on that dirty fucking rat and let me tell you he can thank his lucky stars for that. I'd strangle him. I'd wring his bloody neck like a Christmas turkey, then I'd stuff him up his arse. Pam only met him the once. She di'n't agree to Vinny coming about, if you see what I mean.

—I'm not sure I do.

—He was some bloke in an alley one night who stuck it in her even though she di'n't want it. Get it now?

—I'm sorry.

—Why? It's nothing t' do with you.

The woman asking the questions sat back. They had obviously thought, You do the old bird, go on, you'll have your feminine ways about you. She'll be softer with you.

Now the man leaned in, interlacing his fingers on the table.

—Why did you take on Vincent after she died?

—Sisters stick together. Last talk I had with Pam, she made me promise. She said, "Pearl, you've got to swear to me you'll look after him." That's why I reckon she meant to top herself. You'd think with having two kids they'd have got me a better place t' live, wouldn't you? T' be fair that were part of it; I thought if I said yes to having Vinny, I'd get a better house. Turns out doing a saintly deed ain't what it used to be.

—When was his first arrest?

—Now you're asking. Would've been fourteen, fifteen? Hot-rodding cars, that sort o' thing. Vinny got warnings off the bill but what was I to do; I di'n't control him. Not being funny but I was pleased when he got sent down. Borstal were a good fit cos he weren't any good at living in the normal world but he di'n't get on with the fosters neither. It must've felt right to him too—he went back enough.

—How long was he in the borstal?

—Few months each time. 'Cept the last time. That were just over a year, and by the way I thought he got off lightly for that. Rita's Glen, he got six years just cos he never finished putting in some fancy bathroom in some rich punters' house up on the Heath. You'd think they could afford to get someone else in, wouldn't you, living all the way up there in a mansion? Without having t' make a song and dance about it.

—Was he ever violent toward you?

—Glen?

—Vincent.

—Wouldn't bloody dare.

—So, you never saw evidence of violence from Vincent yourself?

—Di'n't have to. I saw Pam's bruises, di'n't I?

—If Vincent harmed the men he was with—

—If he killed 'em, you mean?

—If he had, then what would he have done?

—I haven't a clue, mate. All I know's Vinny had a nickname in prison. Houdini. You've heard of him, the escaper? They called him Hairy Houdini cos of that mustache, horrible thing he fancied himself in. Some women like it but all that scruff round the chops, it looks downright disgusting t' me. When I saw my husband at that petrol station he had a great big beard hanging off his chin you could've kept a bowl o' cornflakes in and I looked at that tart in the front seat and I thought, You can bloody well have him, love.

The man frowned. Pearl lit another Rothmans.

—Houdini's after how he planned his escapes. For a boy without an education, his brain's all right. Makes me think his dad could've been anyone—we thought he was one thing but maybe he weren't, maybe he were posh, went to one o' those big posh schools and had a big posh house and just went after a bit o' rough one night and Pam were the lucky one. D'you know what it comes down to? Arrogance. Like father like bloody son. Vinny used to say anything you're good at is half talent and half believing you're the best and convincing others that you are. It's a con. He's a con man. He could talk his way out of anything. He could've escaped the light'ouse. He'd know just how t' do it. How t' make it look to other people, just how he wanted it t' look. How to get us thinking the wrong thing. I don't think Vinny's dead for a moment.

—Then where is he?

—Beats me. It's between them three t' know and that's it. But Vinny had people who could've helped him do it and cover it up, and make it seem like one thing when it was another.

The man smiled, as if what she'd said had satisfied him.

—Take that bloke that was on there with 'em. The mechanic.

The smile dropped.

—There wasn't a mechanic.

—That fisherman that went out there said there was.

—Mike Senner's account is flawed and therefore not a line of inquiry.

—Says who?

—Trident House. Every investigator we've got working on this.

—Bloody hell, you lot 'aven't a clue, 'ave you?

—It's the law of reason, Ms. Morrell. There isn't any such thing as an unauthorized landing on the Maiden Rock Lighthouse—especially in adverse weather. The Institution knows everything that happens on their towers.

—They don't know what happened on this one, do they?

—We're unprepared to waste resources on an unreliable witness.

—What if he's right?

—No mechanic was sent. No boat left the harbor. No boatman did the job. No one saw this individual, in Mortehaven or anywhere else.

—Don't ask me for answers, mate. You're the ones s'posed to have those. I don't s'pose it matters anyway, seeing as all it does is proves my point. That mechanic or whoever he was, he had t' be one o' Vinny's lot. An' if my heart were in better shape that sorry bleedin' tyke of a nephew might get a piece of it. Bloody weird business, ain't it. Erica said t' me before I came down here, she said Vinny had one hope in his life and that was t' make a clean break from all the people that knew him and start over, where there weren't those same faces lurking round the next corner. Vinny said he'd make his getaway one of these days. And what do you know? The little sod only went and did it.

IX

.

1972

36

ARTHUR

Machines

Helen,

*I saw him today. You think I never tell you things. Your face,
right now, reading this. That's why I don't.*

*I remind myself, sometimes, of my father. Shocked by bombs and
blasts. When I look in the mirror, I see a dead man. Shouts in the
night. My head shot to pieces.*

THIRTY-EIGHT DAYS ON THE TOWER

The fog's still on, a cloth stuffed into a mouth. It's sometime after five
when Vince gets up.

"Who's this?" says Vince.

Sid says, "Don't ye know, matey, they didn't send me out here for
shits and giggles." Vince is weaker than I've seen him; I tell him to eat

but he says he can't, he'll only chuck it back up. I slice bread anyway and we're out of butter so I use a knob of the crystallized fat we got off a beef joint three weeks ago.

Bill smokes and smokes. He's got his drill on the table and a shell he's given up on. The drill bit is thin and incisive.

This afternoon I found him searching in the bedroom, rooting through the trousers I borrowed and put back, pulling out the pockets.

"What are you looking for?"

"Nothing."

He shoved the trousers back in his cubby and pushed past me down the stairs.

Is that how he'd appear if I discovered them together? Red-faced, red-handed.

Vince sinks into a chair. "What day is it?"

I don't know what day it is. Only that it was two moons ago that I saw your boat: the vessel with the torn sail and the waving hand. You're coming for me. That's why I called off the help. I didn't want them interfering, sending someone out here who'd frighten you away.

Sid blows out a stream of smoke. He eyes Vince coldly, unblinking, reptilian. "Ye've got a look like a lad I know," he says. "Not got family up north, 'ave ye?"

"No," says Vince, picking at the bread.

"P'haps it's somewhere else I know ye from."

Vince shivers and sweats. "I can't see," he says. "I can't hardly see your faces."

"Eat," I tell him. "Then go back to bed."

"I need a bucket."

"I'll bring one up."

"To throw up in."

"I know."

✳

Suppertime. The stranger watches me over his plate, his eyes silver blue, a thin crust of ice on the windscreen in January.

Sid came the sunrise after I saw your boat. Two things arriving at the same time, unrelated but related—there's a book about that, *The Collision of Entities*. I read it in the lantern on a perfect spring day when the dawn refracted through the lenses so radiant that the light turned to purple and green, orange and pink, a psychedelic kaleidoscope. It might take days, years, millennia: a shout from the stars received eons later on the ground. I haven't told anyone about you. You're shy, you have to trust me. Did you trust me? I let you down.

I want to tell you I'm sorry.

"Who's chef?" asks Sid.

I put my knife and fork together, line up the ends. "Me."

"Ye could do wi' gettin' some more air in your batter. Toad's a bit flat."

"The toad's the sausage."

"No, it ain't. The toad's the batter."

"You make a hole in the batter, then put the sausage in."

"Those sausages look like holes. They're the holes; that's why it's called it."

"It's out of a fucking can," cuts in Bill. "Call it what you want."

Bill collects his plate to take up to the lantern, to keep the fog gun firing. His mouth is pinched. Maybe he's caught what Vince has got. I have the thought we all get it and by morning we're dead.

Sid eats more. I hear his tongue on the yellow batter. When Bill's gone, somebody says, "He's afraid of me." Did Sid say that, or did I?

"It's food poisoning." The stranger wipes his fingers on a sheet of kitchen roll. "Yer other man. Gone and eaten what he shouldn't."

"What?"

"The chocs were meant for Bill. Only he didn't 'ave 'em."

He smiles, and an idea slips into place. Silky and quick, like an otter off a riverbank.

"Ye can work it out," says Sid. "But ye've worked it all out already, old-timer, 'aven't ye? Fine mind like yours. It'll be a shame when they don't need keepers like ye no more. What'll ye do then, eh? Thirty years is a long time for a man with nothing to live for 'cept his pretty wife. Bet ye wonder from time to time what ye'd do without her."

To look at him is to stand on the edge. To walk into a room I'm not meant to be in. I can't unsee what my eyes show me. The gloom is on us, inside us, the cloth stuffed tighter.

"Who are you?"

The silence is studded by booms from above, the fog gun's lonely call, like whales moaning to each other through folds of black water. Questions echoed with no answer.

"I'll be gone in the morning, pal. Don't worry yerself about it." Then he turns to the wall clock and says, "Quarter t' nine. That's me t' bed."

"Quarter to nine," I repeat.

"That's me time to go to sleep and that's me time to wake up." He leans in. Those teeth. "Always has been, always will be. Day in, day out, end o' the day, start o' the day. That way I don't even have to think about it."

When I get up to the midnight lantern, Bill's inside with his thumb on the plunger. His head is slumped forward on his chest. He doesn't hear me coming. I can get right up behind him, close enough to see the pink strip of skin behind his ears that Helen's fingertips have touched. I want to ask him how he thought he could get away with it.

Blood fills me; it fills my organs, my heart, my veins, a bag full of blood.

"Bill."

He startles; the detonator blasts, involuntarily. BURRRRRRRRR.

"Shit. What?"

"You were asleep."

"Sorry."

"You're no fucking good to me if you're asleep on your watch."

I could grab him now. But there's you.

"What time is it?"

He stands. Nearly falls over. He's useless, a mole clambering out of the ground.

"Something wrong? You're awfully pale, Bill."

He won't look at me straight, an exception no ordinary person would think to see, but when you're a keeper with another keeper you haven't any choice but to see.

"Just tired."

"Never mind, eh. You'll be away soon. You'll be getting ashore before the rest of us and you'll be looking forward to that, won't you, mate. Tell Helen I'll be with her soon, will you? Tell her that for me."

I see him consider saying it then, almost open his mouth to say it; unspeakable words that could so easily be spoken.

"Come on, Arthur," he says, and I can't tell what he's asking of me.

"Fuck off downstairs."

He does as he's told. I flick out my cigarette.

THIRTY-NINE DAYS ON THE TOWER

At two a.m. I check the light, examine her burner, reload the charges, record the visibility and wind direction, which I'm certain is east-southeasterly but I use the compass card to be sure. Straight after I joined the service, I liked getting back to old ways and the skills worth having. We learned proper jobs like how to hang a door or sew a button on, how to bake bread, fix electrics, cook a meal, or light a fire. All worth knowing, but those men ashore wouldn't be able to do half of it, the sewing and cooking parts anyway. Then there was the instruction to do with the illumination, how it worked and how to mend it if something went wrong. It all struck me as helpful and useful—there was no vanity to it, nothing self-seeking, nothing materialistic or extraneous. I felt I could make a good fist out of living if I ever had to do it on my own. Helen's never been one to think she was put here to look after me, it's against her nature to think a woman's in the least bit responsible for that, but all the same I'm not sure she likes it—that I don't need her in any practical way.

I wish she knew the other ways I needed her.

Invisible ways. Important ways.

I could have told her all these years, but I never did. Why didn't I? If she were here, I'd be able to tell her things I could never tell her ashore. Sorry, and it will all work out, and if only we could go back to the start.

I worry about the day we won't need keepers anymore. Who am I without the lights, without this world, without my wife? When automation comes, we'll die out. I'm hearing about it happening already, up and down the country they're getting ready for it—progress, they say, and Godrevy's done it that way since the war. Soon, and I don't like to think about when, there'll be a machine doing my job. That machine won't need the tower like I do; it won't love it like I do. The technology can turn the light on and sound the fog gun, but it can't look after the lighthouse, and lighthouses need looking after, the materials of them, the souls of them. The tower will be empty, mourning the companionship and brotherliness of decades past, the kitchen cigarettes, the gatherings round the telly, the friendship and confidence that once prospered in them, and man won't ever have this place to be again.

×

Later, much later, sometime after my watch, deep night tipping into gloaming dawn. In the bedroom, I misjudge the distance between the door and the weight tube, knocking it with my hip. Vince is snoring. He's too long for his bunk so his feet skew off the end, twitching occasionally, like the wing of an Outer Hebridean tern, injured on a beach and trying to take flight. I press my palm to his forehead. The snoring stops, momentarily. Vince opens an eye, a liquid glimmer like a seal's.

Through the window, miles away, the sea dries up and the land hulks on.

There's a light flickering there, or is it on the water?

When they built these towers, they made sure our bedrooms faced the coast. A lighthouse keeper retires to his bed feeling his beacon settle on home, and they want your beacon there, they don't want you getting ideas about the sea beneath you, quieter and deeper than it's safe to know. When a keeper's in his bed that's when his memories grow bigger than he is, and he needs the land, to be sure it's there, the way a child listens for his father's footsteps in the middle of the night.

We're all tied to the land, ever since we were tongue-rough shapes creeping out of the water and our flippers first slapped against sand and our gills gasped for air.

The light ashore twitches coyly, then all of a sudden it's brighter, sparking, wanting, and I know it's you. I know you're there and talking to me. I understand what you're telling me. What I must do.

I smell your hair and feel the soft shape of the back of your neck, and eventually, eventually, that's how I fall asleep, with your light behind my eyes.

37

BILL

The Briefcase

I was seven when I found out I killed her. My brother kicked a football at my head and said, "Don't be a crybaby, Billy-boy; murderers can't cry." When I asked the old man what that meant, he looked up from his plate of fried eggs and told me I might as well know, I was grown up enough now; it was my being born that had slaughtered her.

The word brought to mind sheep's eyes rolling, shrieks in a gas chamber, blood spattered on an abattoir wall. I'd had my suspicions before the football. The looks I got from teachers and the parents of my friends, of pity and disgust. The whispers about the incident, what a poor boy I was, how kind she'd been, too kind to have deserved that wasteful end. A waste: nothing good to have come of it. The foot-high photograph that sat on the breakfront in the hall at home, like a shrine. It was never explained to me why my mother wasn't here. I was expected, still, to love her, and to feel sorry, even if I didn't know why, and to think twice before I let myself laugh or be happy because this came at a cost too high to say out loud. The suggestion that the wrong one had been lost. I hadn't been worth the trade.

That was the only picture I had of my mother. It was how she stayed in my mind, over the years, frozen in a gently smiling pose. I had never seen what she looked like angry, or sad, or hysterical at a joke—just that gracious, patient face gazing out at me when I came in from school or having been beaten up by my brothers.

Nobody else forgave me. Only her.

The moment I met Helen Black, she reminded me of that image. But this time I could talk to her, touch her skin; I could hold her hand.

I wanted to tell her about all she had missed, my father and his punishments, how he used to come into my room with his belt in his hands and sit on my bed, and how she might have saved me if she'd been there, glowing in the landing light. About the cousin who lived in Dorset, and the sea I hated but knew was my destiny. About having to make up for the fact of my living by doing what was asked of me, always, without question. And that's what brought me to the lighthouses, to a life I can't escape.

FIFTY-FIVE DAYS ON THE TOWER

When I wake in the morning, the bedroom is quiet. Weak light leaches through a crack in the curtain. The room is empty.

I check above me. The mechanic's bunk is made like no one slept in it. Vince has gone. I have a panicked feeling, as if a very long time has passed while I've been sleeping, and everyone's died, or left me behind.

Three days until I'm ashore. She won't have to lie to him now, or to me, or to herself. Not now Arthur knows the truth.

'Course he knows, ye idiot.

Arthur found the chain I stole from Admiral one afternoon when Jenny was in town. If anyone asked, I'd dropped into her cottage to fix a shelf. I hadn't intended to take anything, just wanted to be able to smell her awhile—her scarves, her perfume, her nightclothes. The necklace was gone from where I kept it, in the pair of trousers I was wearing when she kissed me. The same pair he borrowed without asking.

That's a man with nothing to lose.

Maybe I always meant Arthur to discover it. He'd bring it on himself, then.

I crouch to my hollow, hunting for smokes. Inside, at the back, my hand touches a brittle paper bag. For a moment, I'm puzzled. Then the penny drops. They're the chocolates my wife sent. It seems so long that I've been here. I pull them out: they smell floral and deep, but changed from how they did three weeks ago.

I think about eating one. To be honest with her, for the last time: Yes, I tried them. They were very nice, thank you.

Instead I go down to the kitchen and put them in the bin.

✴

Arthur is at the Formica with a book.

"Fog's cleared," I say, standing at the sink, careful to keep my back to him. "Where's Vince?"

"Upstairs."

The drinking water tastes of salt and seaweed. "Sid?"

Arthur says he left already; he must have got on an early boat. I turn off the tap. It carries on dripping. "Who was on the winch?" I ask.

"Not me."

"Vince, then."

"No."

This is all the PK is going to say. The Arthur of old would have pushed it: about Sid's arrival in solid mist, about how he behaved and the things he said. Instead no words come, and this blackout forms the last understanding he and I will ever have.

✳

Vince has got the weather log open in front of him. I think he's going to ask me about Sid, and I haven't decided yet what I'll say, how far I'll go, but I don't need to worry because his attention is elsewhere.

"You should look at this, Bill."

The lantern lenses blink. I step closer.

"Come here," he says. "See."

I peer over his shoulder to the pages on the desk.

"I thought this has got to be last year's," says Vince, unsteadily. "That's what I thought when I saw it. This can't be right. There's some mistake's been made. It's an old log; the PK must've got mixed up. But this is now, Bill. It's this month."

He shows me a jumble of letters and numbers, scrawled in the PK's black pen, loops and forms that dwindle to spider scratches, so hard in places he's torn the page: *Broken and tumbling. Chaotic. Spindrift. Violent storm turning to hurricane . . .*

"Force ten, eleven, twelve," says Vince. "We've never had a fucking twelve. This isn't real. None of it happened."

It's then I see the bag. It's sitting on the first step of the short flight leading up to the illumination: small, square, not something you'd notice right away, and Vince hasn't yet. It's not a kit bag like you'd expect a mechanic to have, but a briefcase. Sleek, compact: shiny as a cat when it comes in out of the rain.

"Bill," says Vince, "what do we do?"

The bag's the same color as Sid. That indescribable color.

This is our understanding. Arthur knows it and so do I.

That the mechanic isn't a mechanic, after all. That no ordinary person flees a tower on his own, leaving no trace of himself. Just as a silver man who steps out of a hedge in front of a Sunbeam-Talbot in 1951, one of him after another.

"What the fuck, man?" Vince closes the log. "Don't you care about this?"

I think about my brother's fag stash in the cabinet at home. Smoking in the porch, in the shadows, waiting for them to come back, the muggy-metal smell of the rain.

Run.

"What's that?" he asks, turning to see what I'm looking at.

I go to the briefcase, kneel down, click the latches, and am surprised when they open.

"Bill—" His tone is urgent. "What's in it? Let me see."

I look. I can't.

"Nothing," I say, snapping it shut. "It's empty."

Sometimes at home Jenny catches a spider under a glass. Because she doesn't like spiders, she does it quickly, as if she can't think about it or see it, just covers it, catches it, takes it away. I pick up the briefcase like this, without thinking about it, and take it out to the gallery and lob it up and over the rail and far out to sea.

38

VINCE

Tender

My first day on the training, I heard he was the best. Arthur Black, they said, now he's the fellow you want. Normally PKs weren't talked about. Notoriety wasn't a good thing. Take the PK in charge at Skerries, who spent his time there stark naked, presumably cos he could, cos his wife didn't allow him to at home. The man would perform every job with nothing on, from changing the mantle to washing the floors, and only when he was chef did he make himself wear a pinny. Everybody dreaded his cooking and any occasion you had to follow him up the stairs. But to know someone's name for the right reasons, that was rare. The day I started with Arthur Black, with his quiet pride and good heart and sensible head, I knew I'd never find a better one.

Going back days and days when all we've had is fog—but that's not what he wrote.

Arthur isn't who he used to be. Not the same person.

Something's happened. I don't know what.

My PK's gone strange. Stranger. What I read in that record doesn't make sense. I've turned it all the ways I can think of, but it always ends up the same.

Arthur's old. He got it wrong.

It isn't anything worse than that and I won't let my head suspect otherwise.

TWENTY DAYS ON THE TOWER

The sea's a watercolor painting, shot through with lemon-colored light. On my watch, but it's not the ocean I'm watching, it's the shore. Patrol the distant landline through my binoculars, eye out for Eddie's man cos I bet he'll come back, he will, whatever his real name is. He'll be reporting to the boss by now; they'll be working out the best way to do it, sketching it like any professional would. The boat setting out from the quayside, a dot swelling to a thumbprint, coming in fast, today, tomorrow . . .

Knock-knock.

I know who.

Try to take my mind off it in the making and mending. My shirts stink and my socks need a stitch, but I quite like the fixing, don't mind it too much: the activity takes me into a calm sort of place where I'm thinking about what I'm doing, and now I've stopped feeling rough, now I feel half human again, there's a real clean pleasure in being here to do it.

I check the binoculars.

When I met Michelle I thought, That's what'll happen. Erica'll tell her what I did and that'll be the end of it. Erica'll let me get close, then she'll snatch it away, cos that was the way of it growing up, every family they'd expect me to feel something for but after six or eight you just can't do it no more. Then you get told you're cold and strange and no one wants you; there's something the matter with you.

But Erica didn't tell. And now I can believe in our lives in the cottages for the first time, Michelle and me, a future for us. Sometimes I think she's like the lighthouses and that's why I got drawn to her in the first place, or why I got drawn to them: out in the dark, swilling about, then all of a sudden there's a fire burning brighter than any you've seen, and you've no choice but to go toward it and hope it takes you in.

I won't let that light go out. Not for Eddie. Not for anyone.

Down in the kitchen, I snake my arm into the cranny under the sink. It's just about brick sized: if you've a narrow wrist like mine, you can curve your arm round the wall inside. For a second I panic, thinking Eddie's man found it—but no, it's there.

I draw out the pistol and check it's loaded.

And when I think on what was in that weather log, in case I'm wrong and Bill's right, I know there's only one thing for it. Myself. Just me. I'll look after my interests.

Things turn rotten after a while on a tower. That's what they said to me at the depot, Watch out for the towers, they can turn you loopy, and I'm sorry for the PK and Bill if Sid comes back, if he brings Eddie with him. I'm sorry for that, I am.

✳

Late in the afternoon, the Trident tender comes to fill up the water storage tanks. Some of the rock stations have ways of filtering rain, and we get enough of that out here to keep us going for months, but being so remote and with little space we have to get the fresh pumped in. The boat's called *Spirit of Ynys*, whatever that means; Arthur said it's to do with a Welsh wizard, but who knows, boats get called all sorts.

"Mike, that you?" calls Bill from the set-off.

"Hullo, Bill. Anything you want to get ashore?"

"Not apart from me."

"You'll not be long off now, mate," says the fisherman. "How many days?"

"Three."

"Best keep your fingers crossed. Forecast says we're in for a storm. Meant to be a big one."

"We had Sid out fixing the generator," says Bill, suddenly. "D'you know him?"

"Who's Sid?"

"Big bloke. Stayed a couple of nights."

Mike Senner shakes his head. "Ashore they said your PK called it off."

"When?"

"Whenever it was your generator was broke." Mike puts his hand across his forehead, squinting up at the set-off. "I'll tell 'em to look into it."

"They definitely didn't send anyone?"

I say, "Leave it, Bill."

"No one's taken a boat out here in ages," puts in Mike. "You couldn't, what with the weather. If there'd been a man cracked enough to try, we'd know about it."

"No one's seen him ashore?"

" 'Fraid not."

Bill's shook. But I know. Eddie's got men practiced in the art of not being seen.

"I'll put it to them," says Mike, "if that makes you feel better. But I don't think they'll believe it, Bill. That you had someone on here without them knowing. They'll say, 'No soul could do that, Mike, you old dog; you know no living soul could do that.'"

X

.

1992

39

16 Myrtle Rise
West Hill
Bath

Rabbit's Foot Press
Tandem Publishers
110 Bridge Street
London

August 26, 1992

Dear Sirs,

I am currently assisting your author Dan Sharp in his study
of the Maiden Rock Vanishing. I understand the novels he has
published with you are written under a pseudonym and would be
grateful if you could please tell me his real name.

I look forward to hearing from you.

Yours faithfully,
Helen Black

40

HELEN

She got there early and could have gone in and waited for him. Instead, she stayed outside, despite the rain, and watched the entrance to the café from the other side of the road. After a while, he appeared—he was early too, but just by a minute—with his hair wet, beads clinging to his peacoat. His walk, the shape of his head, was so familiar: why hadn't she noticed it before? She couldn't believe she had missed it. Michelle had been right. When Dan Sharp embarked on the project, he'd told the papers it was nostalgia for the event plus an affection for the sea that had spurred him. Helen didn't doubt this, but he hadn't been honest about the rest.

She decided, after he'd gone inside, that she would leave him to get dry and organize his notes. She was ready, now, for the last. Now she knew who he was.

She had told him everything except this, the most important thing—and even then, she hadn't lied about it, she just hadn't revealed the full picture.

Before, she had felt a disconnect. How could he understand? He of pirate kidnaps and ocean jeopardy. But she recognized him now, as someone like her.

In the end, she couldn't bear the idea that he would hear it from somebody else: that he would put it in his book using another person's words when she had spent decades finding words that were in some way acceptable to her. It was relevant to the story. It was relevant to Arthur and who he was, and what he might have done.

She put up the hood of her coat and crossed the road.

41

HELEN

I t's nice to sit down. The bus dropped me miles off—my fault, you'd think I'd be able to tell them apart by now, but I can never remember which ones come all the way in and which ones don't. Yes, all right. A pot of tea, please.

I'll begin at the beginning; it's as good a place as any. Only memory doesn't work like that, does it? It's lots of little bursts of moments all popping up in a funny order. You can recall the oddest things, such as the couple we rented the summerhouse off. It always stuck with me that the man who owned it refused to work on Mondays. He never had and he never would; he'd tell them this at job interviews—the fact he didn't like to work on Mondays—because he didn't want to have that Sunday-night feeling, you know, when you're getting ready to go back to work and things seem, how should I put it? Off-kilter. I think the bigger the trauma that happens to you, the more your mind grasps on to frivolous things. It makes it more manageable. In a way, I owe a lot to that man who didn't work on Mondays.

Our son's name was Tommy. So, of course, the summerhouse wasn't where it began. It began six years before, when I found out I was pregnant. It was a shock, at first. I don't mind admitting the idea of it took some getting used to. It wasn't that I didn't want a child. It was just that I didn't see having a child as the be-all and end-all of everything: I was quite comfortable with myself without having to be a mother.

Before Tommy died, I didn't mind thinking that his conception had been an accident, but now I can't say it. It makes me feel as if I made his death happen by imagining he wasn't meant to be. He was *always* meant to be, and that's why the surprise I got when I discovered I was carrying him seems a miracle to me now. We hadn't planned him, but he was never an accident.

Arthur and I didn't know how we'd manage, or what kind of parents we'd be, but nobody knows those things. All you can do is go into it and do your best.

Tommy was a lovely baby. I was no expert in what was normal for babies in those days, but compared with what Jenny went on to deal with next door he was a delight. He slept for me and he ate well, he was crawling at seven months and walking at fifteen, and, goodness, it's sad what you forget. You think you'll memorize every tiny thing because every tiny bit about it consumes you—what they eat, the noises they make, the balled-up fists and flapping arms, the wispy hair at the back of the neck and the soft, rounded shoulders at bath time . . . But you don't. You can't. Every week your child gets replaced by a new one, a bigger, more advanced one, and I don't think it's possible to retain all the personalities faithfully. It's like knowing ten different people in the space of two years. But we had something, Tommy and I: we liked each other. We were friends. Right from when he was a newborn, he had a smile that was just for me.

You look sad. You don't have children? Well, that'll make it easier. It's easier for me to talk to you about it too. With parents you feel contagious, as if they're looking at you and worrying that this specific, unthinkable misfortune is going to infect them as well. Or you get the sense they're hearing your story but not really listening to it, because they're too busy thinking, Thank God it wasn't us.

When people ask me if I have children, it's up to me what I say. Sometimes I say no, which is technically the truth: no, I do not have a child. Other times I say yes, I had a son, but he died. And do you know what I wish they'd ask me? His name. I wish they'd ask me his name. But they shake their heads and say, I'm sorry, that must be awful, and I nod and say, Yes, yes, it was, it is.

Hardly anyone asks me his name. In death, he's anonymous. He can't have been a real child. He can't have been Tommy, because that means it could happen to any of us and none of us is immune.

I do consider myself a mother, yes: a mother who loses her baby as soon as it's born, or before it's born, is still a mother. The mothers like me, the ones who've lost a child, always ask me his name. That's how you can tell. For a long time after Tommy died, I hid from people— no one could understand the frame of mind I was in—but then I joined a bereavement group and it did bring me comfort. Grief can be incredibly lonely. Before you know it, you've gone inside yourself and it's not so much as you can't get back, it's that you don't want to.

Those mothers brought me back. I wish I could say it was Arthur who did that, but it wasn't. Those of us in the group used to call the children "the gang," and we'd celebrate their birthdays, not in a morbid way, just to acknowledge it. That was all I wanted: acknowledgment. Arthur never talked about Tommy. After the funeral, I don't think his name ever passed my husband's lips. He didn't want to see photographs or share memories. Whereas I needed those things to keep Tommy with me. I couldn't pretend he'd never happened.

I did pretend with you, yes. Aren't you going to ask why? Maybe there are things you've pretended about with me, because that's what people do. It's easier than being what we are, all the things we can't escape. You'll know that it's very forceful, sorrow. I cried and cried and thought I would never stop. For weeks I lay in the dark in bed, shivering and thinking I could hear his voice, a little whisper: *"Mummy."* That went on for months. Grief got me behind the legs. It still does, but now I sense it coming so I stay on my feet. Early on it caught me, a kick to the knees. I'd smell Tommy's clothes and it didn't seem real he'd gone. How could his smell still be there when he wasn't? All his things waiting for him, but he was never coming back. You can understand why I kept it to myself.

Arthur returned to the Maiden straight after Tommy died. I thought we were going to leave the service and put each other first, but we didn't. When he was off on the light, I'd be alone in the cottage, cutting crusts off toast by mistake and buying milk for bedtime that no one was going to drink. The bottles stayed in the fridge for days until I peeled their tops away and the stench of cheese came out, so I poured them down the sink.

Arthur and I grew further apart. I had never got on with the tower, but I despised her then. Whenever I saw her, I'd think what a monster she was, rearing up out of the sea. I was craving his comfort, but instead he gave it to her, or she to him, and that sounds doolally but that's how it felt. I knew Tommy's death had prompted it, but possibly he'd had it in him all along—this distance. Arthur told me that no man in his right mind would want to be a lighthouse keeper. I remembered that a lot in those days.

I knew he'd loved Tommy, so much. That was why he hadn't dealt with it. Well, faced it, perhaps that's better. Looked it in the eye, as you must do with these things, or they'll chase you around the house for the rest of your life and kick you behind the knees.

Many times, I wished I never had to see my husband again. So, when they disappeared, I feared I had made it happen, by wishing it. Then I wouldn't have to be part of the lighthouse service any longer. I could move away from the sea. I wouldn't have to sit in our kitchen, in Admiral, listening to Arthur sorting his rocks or his pencil scratching the crossword puzzle and not understanding why he couldn't just put his arms around me and tell me he thought about our son as much as I did.

Now I understand that Tommy wanted his father back. He needed Arthur more than I did, and that's right, that's how it should be. It was the sea that took Arthur, because that's the place we lost our boy. Sometimes I consider the sea to be like a great big tongue, licking up the people around me, and if I get too close to it, it'll lick me up too and swallow me down to the bottom. That's why I live here.

Tommy had just turned five. The summerhouse was a lovely place; it didn't deserve it. The people who let us stay, the man who didn't work on Mondays, didn't deserve it. Things happen in life and they hit you out of the blue, on an unremarkable Thursday when you're getting out of the bath. There isn't any warning. Those things you spend time worrying about never happen. At least not in the way you think.

Our boy was looking forward to his first holiday with a father he hardly got to spend time with. By that point Tommy was getting interested in Arthur's job, the fact his daddy came and went and took a boat to get back to the lighthouse; the stories he'd return with about storms and smugglers that I assumed were for the most part made up, but maybe they weren't. Tommy missed him when he was away. Arthur never wrote to me; he wrote sometimes to Tommy, but those letters were only picked up in fair weather when there was a boatman who felt like it. He used to tell Tommy that when the Maiden light came on after sunset that was his way of saying good night. When Arthur was off on the tower, we'd talk about what he was doing, and I invented as much for myself as for Tommy. Children have a wonderful way of seeing the world. He used to say his daddy was the sun after the sun had gone to bed, and all these years later, I still think that's the best description I've heard.

He drowned. It was a beautiful morning, the summer of the Queen's coronation. I thought I'd have a bath after breakfast. The bath was claw-footed, and very deep, and I'd been soaking in it long enough for the water to cool when I heard Arthur shouting from downstairs. When I came out, he was standing by the door with his hands by his sides, but the palms were facing up to the ceiling. He had absolutely no color in his face. It took me a few seconds to register he was wet all over.

"Where's Tommy?" But Arthur just kept looking at me, and it was like throwing a bucket of water at a stupid person to wake them up, only they don't wake up.

"I lost him," he said.

"What?" I said. "Where?" For a second we could have been talking about the car keys.

"The sea," he said.

"Where in the sea?"

"The sea," he said.

Tommy couldn't swim. Not without his floats. That's what I was searching for when I went out and scanned that horrible water; I was looking for the red-and-yellow floats that Tommy wore around his little arms. I knew I'd be able to spot them. But I didn't expect to see them sitting there in the porch, unused, with the waterproofs we'd brought down and hadn't yet needed.

Gone. No, Arthur hadn't said gone. *Lost.*

I had the irrational thought that it could still be fine; Tommy would come up the beach any moment, the current having delivered him to shore. But since when did the sea do anything like that for me?

I don't know what happened after that. At some point we must have called for help because the people arrived and the ambulance, and it was me they wrapped in a blanket even though I wasn't cold.

It was two days before his body washed up. Tiny, blue, his skin mottled, in the green bathing trunks he'd chosen at the supermarket four days before. Arthur said he would go to identify him, but I had to see for myself. He didn't look dead, just sleeping. When I kissed his head it felt quite normal, a bit cool, that's all. It struck me that his soul had left his body and the two weren't holding hands anymore. The body was a body and the soul had gone. Some say that's a comfort, but it wasn't for me. I worried the body would be lonely without the soul, no light inside it, nothing to keep it warm. I didn't want Tommy buried because of this loneliness. It possessed me. I couldn't get rid of the idea he was cold and alone in the morgue, in his casket, finally in the ground. I know to this day that if we'd buried him, I'd still be having sleepless nights that his bones were lonely in the earth. We had him cremated. I didn't want anything left.

They'd gone paddling. Not deep, Arthur said, that's why he didn't take the floats. Tommy was up to his tummy button in the water, that's what Arthur kept saying, and I wished he wouldn't because it only made me think about Tommy as a baby, the point that had tied him to me, all those months when I'd kept him safe and *twenty bloody minutes* I was in that bath. Arthur had left him to get his camera. Only a few paces away, up in the porch. Always a curious boy, Tommy must have stepped farther out, a step or two, and gone under. The currents were notorious. He stumbled, floundered, and then he drowned. That's how I have it in my head. As a quick, painless thing. By the time Arthur came back with his camera, it was too late.

Blame was a beast I had to shake off. If I let it get the better of me, I'd have killed Arthur without a second thought. I'd have smothered him in his sleep. But he didn't need me to tell him it had been his fault. I don't know how a person ever gets over that because the sadness is bad enough without the guilt, and I know he felt guilty and that was the root of it. Why he couldn't look at me or touch me; why he wanted the lighthouse instead.

Of course, it's occurred to me that he wanted to go with Tommy. Be with him again. That everything my husband felt built up and up inside him and then it exploded. I can't say how he'd have done it and I can't think of him doing it—not to Bill and Vince, not to himself, I can't, but I do believe that any person is capable of any act, if the circumstances are right. If the moment is there. If they never show their full hand. The fact is, it isn't normal for a man to be stuck on a tower lighthouse. Trident won't admit that they shouldn't have been making men do that at all, any man, ever, because it isn't a natural state to be in and it takes its toll in the end.

I wasn't ready, when we met, to talk about the clocks. But I can talk about them now. Eight forty-five is the time Tommy died. Both those clocks on the Maiden were stopped at eight forty-five. I didn't believe it when I heard. I still think there's a chance it's not true. One might easily have caught at five or ten minutes on, or behind, in which case it's nothing but an unlucky coincidence. But people like patterns, don't they, and it's a compelling detail. I never forgot it, though. It's always in my mind.

What if Arthur was responsible? What if, what if, what if.

Countless paths not taken. What if I had never met him? What if he had never said hello to me in the queue at Paddington? What if we had never joined the service? What if we had never been on holiday, or the summerhouse had never been built, or the man had decided to work on Mondays and earned more and ended up buying not here but abroad, a little cottage on a Tuscan hillside? What if I'd never taken that bath?

I sometimes think that if I had the chance to say this to Jenny Walker, explain who I am, she might understand. My slip with Bill. My one mistake. Or else there is no excuse.

It's more than Bill, yes, probably it is. I even agreed to Michelle going down to Cornwall to put my side across, but that was a silly idea, and besides it has to come from me or no one. But I believe that if I can mend things with Jenny, if I can make it right with her, then there's some good to come of it.

You see, there are words I should have said, and wish I had. To Arthur, and to Tommy—but there's no going back to them. It's too late.

It's not too late for the others. There are some lights that can still be lit.

42

JENNY

For a long time after she had finished speaking, they sat next to each other on the bedspread. Hannah was quiet. She held a rigid, unfriendly sort of pose, straight backed, her hands on her knees. Jenny studied the quilt with implausible keenness; peach florals, it was one of hers from ages ago, softened and pilled by dozens of washes.

Downstairs, the front door closed, the last of the party guests dispatched. Greg had come up to see where they were; Hannah told him to make her excuses.

She turned to her mother and said, "You're telling me you tried to . . . ?"

Jenny wiped her nose on her sleeve.

"I don't know what I was trying to do, love. I never wanted to hurt him. You have to believe me. I only wanted him to . . ."

"What?"

"Be my husband again."

Through the open window, a lawn mower started up next door. An everyday sound, sharper now. The old world before Jenny revealed her secret, and the new.

"That's the thing about children," said Hannah. "You think you're being clever in keeping things from them, but you can't. Keep things. You can't keep anything."

Jenny didn't take her eyes off the embroidery. She'd lain under it many times with Bill, the children clambering in, those precious mornings.

"What do you mean?"

"That I knew. Somewhere, I did, deep down. I remember you standing there in the kitchen. Dad was about to go off. You were crying, not talking to him. I could smell bleach. There were those cases for the chocolates, the label on the bottle. I didn't understand what it meant. I thought I'd made it up. You were my mother. You'd never do that. Then this happens, and you're telling me I was right."

Hannah went quiet. Jenny made herself look up.

"Do you remember him?" she asked. "You always said you did."

"Yes. I remember he used to kiss me good night. Every night he was home, when he thought I was asleep. He came in and brushed my cheek with his hand. I remember sitting on his knee for a story, before bed. What he smelled like. Creocote and smoke. We used to go outside to look for the moon, when the sky was clear, when the sun went down. I thought of his lighthouse like that. Like the moon."

Jenny had never felt so ashamed.

"When you're seven," said Hannah, "it feels like life's just made up of moments. Pieces of the picture with nothing to connect them. It's not until later you can join the dots."

"Now you can," said Jenny.

Hannah shook her head. Outside, in the road, children rode past on bikes. Their shouts reached a loudening, then were lost in the distance.

"When you told me about Dad being unfaithful," Hannah admitted, "that should have been a shock as well. But it wasn't, Mum. I already knew. We went to Helen's that time. You and me standing in her sitting room. Dad's seashell was on the shelf, behind the photo frame. It wasn't like the ones he did for you; it was meant for a lover, not a wife. You could see how she'd tried to hide it, but she hadn't done it properly. I'd have recognized his anywhere, even on the beach with millions more."

The pink stitching had turned to liquid, swimming in Jenny's vision.

"You squeezed my hand so hard when we walked home," said Hannah. "Beans on toast for tea. Only you burned the bread; you scraped it off in the sink."

"Yes."

Hannah faced her; her eyes were wet. "Why didn't you say anything to me?"

"How could I?"

"Not then. Later. When you said about his affair."

"And have you be horrified at me?"

"I'm not horrified."

"You should be."

Jenny saw her daughter in a new way, then, as a woman, not her child, not anyone's child. Concern scored between her brow, like slits in a mince pie. Readiness to understand, which had never come easily to Jenny. To listen and reserve judgment.

"I know how much you loved him," said Hannah. "And how much he hurt you by doing what he did. It doesn't make it right, Mum. It wasn't right; it'll never be. But . . ." She felt for the words. "I suppose there isn't any way of ending that. Just 'but.' There's always another way of seeing things, isn't there? There's always more to it."

"What must you think of me?" said Jenny.

"That you were angry and sad."

"I'm sorry. I'm just so sorry, love."

"Was he?"

"What?"

"Sorry."

"I don't know," said Jenny. "There was a lot I didn't know about Bill."

Hannah passed her a box of Kleenex. Their fingers touched.

"I thought you'd hate me," said Jenny.

"I don't hate you."

"If I'd known that was the last time I'd see him . . ."

"Don't." Hannah wrapped Jenny's hand in her own. "You were a good wife."

She reached over and hugged her. It was the nicest hug of Jenny's life, warm and tight and strong as tree roots, and nicer than any that Bill had ever given her.

✖

Motorways made her nervous. She preferred the country roads, only they took twice as long. She'd heard it was safer on the motorway, if you believed the statistics, but she couldn't see how that could be what with how fast everything happened. All it took was a split second and that was her through the windscreen. Jenny had nightmares about this arrangement: bonfire of limbs on the hard shoulder; blood on shattered glass. Occasionally she saw herself in the wreckage; other times it was people she knew. Or else it was Bill—the scene of a fatal crash she happened across, only to recognize his face and that's where he'd been, after all these years, living another life, driving another car, on his way to another home filled with another family, and he looked regretfully up at her as she realized all this, and she held his hand while he died.

"I'll drive, if you want," said Hannah, picking through a bag of Jelly Babies for the green ones, which she fished out and put in the storage slot under the hand brake.

"Don't do that," said Jenny. "They'll stick and go furry."

"This is it! Junction six."

Jenny indicated out of the slow lane. A lorry's horn blared.

"What did I do?"

"You're on the hard shoulder. There's the slip road. Here. There. God! *Mum*."

Half an hour later, they pulled into the Birmingham Spire of Light Psychic Convention. Crystals and cards, rainbows and angels, a man with a Mohawk promising to discover her animal spirit guide: 50p only. Jenny normally hid the trip, lied that she was off to the pools. Now, she didn't need to pretend—about that or anything else. She had wasted too much time pretending, when she hadn't needed to pretend at all.

"You're sure about this?" said Jenny, knowing it wasn't Hannah's sort of thing. Still, she'd said she was keen to come along if it meant she could meet Dan Sharp. They would give him an hour, they'd agreed, till eleven, when Wendy was doing a channel.

"Yes," said Hannah. She unclipped her belt and unexpectedly leaned over to kiss her mother on the cheek. "I might've had my ideas about him—but if the last few weeks have taught me anything, it's that there's more than one side to every story."

43

JENNY

I've come every year since Bill went. I was into it before, a bit, but I never traveled up to anything like this; I didn't have the time and it didn't matter much to me then. It matters now because it's something along these lines that'll get me back in touch with him. They do a good show if you're not going to get snooty about it. Wendy's my favorite, Wendy Albertine; her guide puts her in touch with the other side, and if she finds someone for you, she'll call out your name. I keep waiting for it to be me.

After you first came to visit, I went and had my fortune read. The medium said then I was going to get taken advantage of and I thought, Well, I bet I know who that'll be. But then Julia dropped by and asked to borrow a fiver and later on I saw she'd taken twice that out of my purse, so that could've been it. I *knew* Hannah would roll her eyes at that. Come on, love—it's not as if you haven't done worse.

Each to their own, that's all I'll say. Go through what I have and you don't care what folk think. I identify with the people here. They've lost a loved one, like I have, but they also know that person might still be out there for them. I hope in the course of us knowing each other, you've opened your mind a bit. Like Hannah said just now in the car, it's important to be able to change your perspective about things.

Helen would never be seen dead at a convention like this. Ha, get it? She isn't interested in what's extra in life. She takes what's in front of her. Anyone would think after her son died, she'd need it. Plenty come because of children they've lost. They're the ones that get you. When there's a child and they come back for Mummy or Daddy, we're all sobbing by the end of it. I always keep an ear out for Tommy. If Wendy were to tell us one day Tommy was here, I'd put my hand up for him. It makes me sad to think of this little one on the other side and there's no one there, no one's coming.

If he did come through, no, I wouldn't tell Helen. I never knew when we were living at the cottages if she took against me because of my three. Because she only had one, didn't she, and he drowned. I felt bad for her, I'd be heartless if I didn't, but she might've done herself a favor if she'd confided in me. Maybe she just didn't think of me like that, as a friend she could talk to. I never asked either, which was awkward, but what was I meant to do? It might be making her feel bad when she doesn't want to think about it.

Helen never forgave Arthur. I know that much. I can't say if I would or I wouldn't, with Bill, if he'd been responsible for that. But it always annoyed me how Bill thought of their marriage as perfect. He'd say how good it was that the Blacks didn't have to live in each other's pockets all the time, you know, do everything together and know each other's business like a man and wife do. When we moved to Masters, I asked Helen how she coped with so many years of Arthur being off, and she told me it was in their natures; they liked being together, but they also liked being on their own, and it was really like two lives happening next to each other rather than one joined together. I thought it was all to do with Tommy. Didn't our husbands get enough independence on the tower? They had all the time in the world to themselves on there.

Anyway, it turned out Helen did need someone, because she went after Bill. I'm not saying there aren't shades of gray in it, what with the boy and what that did to her. I can't think about it, to be honest; I can't get my head around losing a child.

But I still don't understand why Bill did it. The man who'd married me, who I thought loved me for all the reasons I'm me and not her. Helen wasn't one of us. She wasn't a Trident wife in the traditional sense. Whether it was up at St. Bees or down at Bull Point, we were cut from the same cloth—wives and homemakers, recipe books on the shelves, Victoria sponge baking and tea on the table at six. We mucked in together. We never went behind each other's backs and we didn't have tea with each other's husbands. Frank's wife, Betty, was more up my street, a good honest Bolton girl, no airs and graces, and her boys and my girls often played together. I saw Helen was jealous of that. I'm not proud of it, but I admit I enjoyed it—that she was jealous. There was a lot she had that I didn't, and this was one thing I'd won at.

I should have spoken to Arthur about the affair when he was ashore. Hannah says I should've, and I wish I had. Now they're gone, it's too late.

It makes me wonder about my mum. How I could have one last try with her. Find out if she's still around, ring her up, send her a note. See, I'm protecting myself if I do that. It's selfish, in a way. I want to know I've done everything I can. I know better than anyone how it feels to have that choice taken away from you.

If I'd talked to Arthur, we could have decided on a better course of action. Because it was only a silly thing, a silly idea I had to pay back some of what they'd made me feel. What can I say but that I wasn't thinking straight?

I didn't ever bring it up with Arthur because I suppose I was nervous of him. Hannah was too. It's because the PK never made himself known to us. He didn't come over or say hello or act friendly at any time. I never could work him out.

Looking back, he did seem unbalanced to me. One of those who never says boo to a goose, then one day the building goes up in flames and the neighbors go, "Oh, but he was the quiet one, wasn't he? He wouldn't have done anything like that."

What? Hannah thinks I've got too many fantasies. I do make things up in my head, then I think about them so much they start to turn real.

But it's always the quiet ones, isn't it? Especially when they're pushed. Helen pushed him. She pushed him with the guilt, then she pushed him with her lies. Arthur was the sort to keep it cooped up inside and not say a word and then one day, *pow!*

The fact is, if I found out, then he might have found out too. If Arthur did hurt Bill, I suppose I can . . . I mean I suppose I can understand it.

Oh dear, is that the time? We've got to get in for Wendy so we can get a good seat. I didn't travel all this way to have to sneak in the back.

All right! Hannah made me promise. I don't want to, but she'll be in a huff with me all afternoon if I don't. Here goes, then. Helen used to write me letters, but she hasn't in a while. Hang on, love, I'm getting there. Give me a chance.

Is everything OK with her? With Helen. That's what Hannah

wanted me to ask. Because you've been talking to her, haven't you? So you'll know. If there's been anything that's meant she's had to stop writing her letters. Not that I care. It's not important. It just crossed my mind, then Hannah made me ask.

Good. That's good. Satisfied? I *told* you.

Now, can we get on with our day? If we sit up at the front at Wendy's, there's more chance of a name coming through for us. They can sense you there and that makes them find you more easily. The communication is better.

44

MICHELLE

Tonight, when she made steak and kidney for Roger, he would ask about her day and she'd fib that she had done nothing much, ironed the girls' school uniforms, sewed name tags on PE kits, pulled the weeds out of the veg bed. She would leave out the fact of coming to Clearwater Shopping Center and drifting down the aisles at Woolworths, gazing at neon confectionery wrappers and checking her watch every minute and a half.

Part of her had known she'd end up meeting him. Her conversation with Helen started it. *It matters, doesn't it? To say what he was really like.* Then those transcripts. What Pearl had claimed—unfair things that made Vinny into someone he wasn't. Vinny wasn't here to defend or prove himself. Michelle was.

She was tired of being afraid. Of Trident House, of Eddie Evans, of the truth.

The writer was standing beneath the clock in the atrium. She identified him from the black-and-white headshot on his book jacket. He had an agitated, restless demeanor, waiting to be approached but he didn't know by whom: she could have been any of the women rushing past on their lunch hour.

Hesitating in Boots, Michelle wondered what ideas he had about her. Her idea of him had been wrong. She'd had him down as a Roger type, sharp suit, oiled hair, golf at the weekend, cuff links and cognac. The writer's clothes didn't fit well, not because he couldn't afford better, she suspected, but because he didn't care much about clothes, and his shoes looked like they'd been worn every day of his life. If he was any type it was her younger brother's, who was living back in Leytonstone with her dad and working in the local Betfred while he saved up enough money for a haircut.

She disliked this shopping center intensely. Mainly it was the foyer part, with its chichi café selling overpriced grilled sandwiches, and the gigantic clock from which, on the hour, a plastic frog emerged from the cuckoo's window and croaked the time.

She waited for it to finish its cycle before going over.

"I'm Michelle," she said.

Dan Sharp smiled and shook her hand, and seemed relieved, she thought, that she had come.

45

MICHELLE

There they are. Bloody depressing, isn't it, keeping birds in cages. It's the worst of the worst. Normally I'd never stop at this store 'cause I can't stand the squawking. Either that or them sitting there all miserable. Here you go: £3.99 to take it home with you and the cage'll be ten times as much. There was this girl at school who kept birds in cages. Her mum's flat smelled rank, of cat food and droppings. She had a cockatiel called Spike and a budgie called Ross. Ross was the dominant one; he was in charge.

Do you like birds? I think it's best if you like them to just let them be, out in the trees and things. I used to think how nice it'd be to let Spike and Ross free. Open the door and say, Go on, get on with it then. I'm not sure they could fly, to be fair: might've just flopped down on the carpet. Maybe they weren't sad anyway. That was just me.

All right then, you wanted to meet; you're the one who's been asking for it, so I'll let you have it like it is. I've got nothing to hide. Vinny didn't either. It's been years since I read those interviews and to answer your question about why I'm here, why I changed my mind, it's 'cause of them. I can't let Pearl's lies have the last of it. No matter how many times I tell myself it doesn't matter what you put in your book, I can't let Pearl be the person representing him to you. She didn't know him. I did.

People've made their minds up about Vinny. He was the criminal, so he must've done it. They can't say what he actually did, but who minds about the details when you've got someone to pin it on? Those other two, Arthur and Bill, Trident'd have you believe they never set a foot wrong—but scratch the surface and the dirt comes out. Vinny's dirt was there for anyone to see. He had nothing to hide.

Trident knows you're writing a book. They're nice enough on the surface, but they've got to be worried 'cause now they're getting in touch with me saying that if I speak to you, they'll make me pay. They'll stop my compensation, which I never thought I'd get in the first place 'cause Vinny and me weren't married, but they want to keep me quiet so they kept it coming. Roger, my husband, he's happy to take it. He can't stand any mention of Vin but he's fine with taking the money. I bet Helen and Jenny have had letters as well. But I s'pose the time comes you get too long in the tooth to let people scare you off.

Trident have kept their distance, making out it was nothing to do with them. They wouldn't want people knowing they had an enemy of Vinny's in their ranks. It was bad enough having one criminal on the books. If people saw the connection between Vinny and this man, it'd drag the Institution right back into it again.

I can't tell you what happened. But what I think happened, that's another thing.

It was the person Mike Senner told them about. The mechanic. I've never accepted how Trident did away with that. Even Helen said it was rubbish 'cause of Mike's character, he was a local loop, and yeah, maybe he was, but even if a crackpot gave that kind of information, I'd still want to follow it up, wouldn't you?

Fact is, it didn't suit Trident to give time to anything Mike Senner said 'cause that made a mockery of their operation. And it does sound impossible, when you know about tower landings—that this bloke went out there without them knowing.

Only it *must* have been possible. This so-called mechanic wanted payback on Vinny and sure enough he got it. But I'm jumping ahead, aren't I. Shall we sit down?

Pearl had her mind made up about Vinny from the start. I get that she was standing up for her sister 'cause of how Vinny came to be, but to make a child believe that no one wanted him? To tell him he's just like his rapist dad, then lock him up and batter him whenever he gave her lip? You ask then why he wound up in prison. Well, Vinny didn't see a point in anything else. Nobody showed him there *was* anything else. You give back what life gives you and what can I say but life gave him shit.

Except for the lights. The lights gave him hope and there's no sense thinking he'd chuck that away. If Pearl was here, she'd say, "Remember what he did the last time? Someone who does that's got it in him to do anything." But she'd be wrong. Just like she was wrong saying he'd beaten Pamela up and spat on her when he was little. Vinny wasn't even with his mum most of the time she was alive, and the way I see it he might've whacked her by accident like all babies do, like my babies did, when they're learning to sit in a high chair or have their nappy changed, or have a bottle or go to sleep or whatever. It's garbage to say he meant it. Pam's bruises came from the needle.

Vinny did have a mean streak, yes. He must have, to do what he did. It wasn't meanness in a petty way, as in saying something to hurt your feelings, but properly, like if he wanted to hurt you, then you were probably going to get hurt. You didn't want to get on his wrong side. But I have to tell you he was loyal too. Once he liked you, he'd never doubt you. That's how I know he'd been loyal to Trident, 'cause they were loyal to him. It was that job that made the difference to him.

Do you know about the White Rook? Real name Eddie Evans. Erica told me how it was, back round where they lived. She said it was Eddie and Vinny that ruled the roost. They were always up against each other, out to pick the other one off—who was on whose turf, who had what girl, who'd nicked off with what, and the crap thing is no one remembers what any of it was about 'cause it was all so bloody pointless. But when Eddie went after Vinny's best friend, that was when the situation changed. Erica said he smashed Reg up so badly that Vin had to go over there to sort it out. They only meant to warn Eddie off. They didn't know he had a little girl. How were they to know that?

After Vinny got the job with Trident, he heard the news Eddie was working there. Vinny hadn't seen him since that night, when the last thing Eddie'd said to him was that one day he'd get his revenge for what they'd done.

I told the investigators. And they talked to Eddie—at least they said they did—and Eddie said he couldn't help. He hadn't clapped eyes on Vinny in ages and that was for the best. He said that was a distant time in his life anyway and he was a new man by then. And how would he have got on there and done what they were suggesting, and made all three keepers disappear from inside a tower that's hardly wider than this bench we're sitting on? But it got me thinking then and it still does now. Just 'cause Eddie didn't get his own hands dirty doesn't mean someone else didn't do it for him.

Trident kept to it that they'd never sent a mechanic to the tower. There was never anyone else on there but those three. They replayed the radio transmission, to prove it—Arthur asking them to send a mechanic, then taking it back, saying, It's all right, call it off, it's fixed after all. But Arthur didn't say who fixed it or how. Trident just assumed, like they assumed everything else, that it was him or Bill or Vinny. I can tell you now Vinny wouldn't have a bloody clue what he was doing with fixing anything, let alone a diesel generator. He could hardly change a light bulb.

It's 'cause no one else saw this mechanic. Trident's lot reckoned there had to have been *someone* who'd witnessed him, 'specially 'cause this man sounded so unusual looking. They couldn't find any trace of the boatman either.

But that's what Eddie's men are. Ghosts. He could've had his pick out of any of the individuals that worked for him, but it was Sid he chose. Sid was told to kill all three and get rid of the bodies, then make himself scarce. And that's exactly what he did.

It got forgotten about with the other speculation. There was plenty of that at the time, so it was hard to know what to hold on to. Rumors flying everywhere, people saying crazy stuff, and after a while you didn't know what to believe. Take the length of rope missing from the storeroom. Trident denied that, of course they did, even though one of their investigators came out years down the line saying it was true. I know that could fit with a wave coming and washing them away, like Helen thinks, and the rope got thrown in to help. . . . Maybe. I think this Sid bloke strangled them with it.

I've told you already how it was and how Vinny was in the thick of it. And when Eddie went for Reg that was it; Vinny got mad; he said they were going round to show him what for. The dog was never meant to come into it. It was wrong place, wrong time. They just decided on it last minute, a spur-of-the-moment thing, and it was a bad thing to do; they only meant to break into Eddie's flat and they didn't know his six-year-old daughter was there. But then she came out in the hallway in her pajamas and started crying and that woke Eddie up. Someone was like, "Shut her up, shut her up," and then Eddie found her and thought the worst, so he pulled a knife and it all went down.

Eddie put a knife in Reg and killed him. Reg died in Vinny's arms. Vinny must've lost his head 'cause this had been his idea and now what; they hadn't known about the girl and that was his fault too. He freaked out. They all did. Then they heard the dog outside, tied to its kennel. I bet Eddie wished he hadn't tied it up that night of all nights— a German shepherd; Vinny said it had a rotten nose and bits of its fur were missing. It wasn't his idea to set fire to it, it was one of the others', but no one's thinking and there was blood all over and Reg was dead, so they did it. They strung Eddie up and made his girl watch her dog getting burned. Eddie watched her watching the dog.

It had been Vinny's decision to go, even if it wasn't his decision to do what they did, and he might've been a lot of things, but he wasn't a coward. He took the hit with the police—he had nothing to lose, no family to look after, he already had a record, so it might as well have been him. Like I said, if he was loyal to you, he was loyal. At the end of the day it was a dog; he got a couple of years, then out. But there's something in the fire, right? And in making the girl watch. Yes, there's something in that.

People can say what they want about Vinny and maybe he did have a bad side. Don't we all? If we're pushed hard enough, if something makes us lose our heads, all I'm saying is, don't we all?

After Reg died, Vinny wanted out. That was the last time. He wanted to be better and he knew he could be. I knew it too.

Here. Vinny included this poem with the last letter he sent. You can make of it what you will. When Trident asked me if I'd had anything from him during that time, I said I hadn't. I knew I'd never see it again otherwise. But the more years pass, the more I doubt that Vinny even wrote it. He was into his poetry; he loved words. He thought the poems made him look soft—but how good is it that a man with no education can put things down on paper like that?

The thing is, this isn't the kind of thing he wrote. I can't explain. It just isn't, if you knew him. He sent me love poems from time to time, but you're not getting your hands on those. This one's different. He said he talked to the PK a lot about poetry. I think Arthur was the one who wrote it, got Vinny to put it down, I don't know. That's just what I think.

Vinny always knew his past would trip him up. He thought that whatever he did and however fast he did it that past would always be there, waiting for him. And it did, that's the saddest bit of it. It did wait for him. That he'd had that time on the lights at sea, thinking he could be free. It's like a bird in a bloody cage, isn't it, it's fine while it's in the cage but then as soon as you let it out it sees what it's been missing. It sees it wasn't ever meant for this, and its wings don't work after all.

46

[Address withheld]

September 10, 1992

Dear Mr. Sharp,

Thank you for your letters dated June 12 and July 30. It's taken me some time to reply, for which I apologize. My work under Trident House at the time of the Maiden Rock Vanishing is a source of some difficulty to me: the matter has long weighed on my conscience and this has both deterred my response to you and finally encouraged it. The secrets kept in the Inner Circle cannot remain secrets forever.

Yes, the Institution does know what happened to the keepers. It's only between a few of them and I shouldn't imagine it will ever be widely noted. Whatever your book settles on will become a theory like any other, with neither corroboration nor confirmation from the people who can give it. I can offer you answers, but only in the strictest confidence.

In those days we didn't talk about the disappearance. I was employed by one of the Elder Fellows and was encouraged, to put it mildly, to turn a blind eye and deaf ear to all I saw and heard. It could never be acknowledged. Even after I terminated my engagement with Trident House, I still don't like to see a lighthouse anymore.

Trident have a version of what happened based on the evidence they shared with the public. To all intents and purposes, they blamed it on the Supernumerary Assistant Keeper and that remains to this day the party line. They would never admit the truth. That it wasn't anything on the outside that did it, but rather the nature of the work itself.

There was more than what the families were told. Work Trident did afterward, under the radar—fingerprinting, psychological evaluations, and the crucial discovery of the weather log. Those things threw up a different perpetrator. One keeper had touched all those items last. That same keeper completed the logbook erroneously and was appraised by experts as harboring a personality disorder in line with post-traumatic stress and depression. They believe he killed the others in a fit of temper.

Trident have never wanted to reveal this because they valued Arthur Black. He was well regarded, a badge of honor for the Institution in showing how they looked after people for life. Principal Keepers are golden to Trident: the Fellows won't appoint a man to PK unless they hold him in the highest regard. To admit he was to blame is a shameful reflection on what's thought of today as a romantic way of life.

Investigators had two theories about why Arthur did it. One was concerned with the SAK: that Vincent Bourne had hidden money on the tower; Arthur discovered it, planned to steal it, rid himself of the other two, then make his escape. Does that sound far-fetched? Perhaps, but no more than the myriad other guesses hazarded down the years. *The second was talk that Bill Walker had been engaged in a love affair with Arthur's wife, Helen. You don't need to look far for a motivation in that.*

I've never been convinced of either of these, though. I think the lighthouse life simply got the better of Arthur. I couldn't do that job. Could you?

I hope the above proves helpful to your research, and I trust you to preserve my anonymity in this matter.

> *Sincerely,*
> *[Signature]*

47

The Signal

I met a man beside the sea,
He was looking out and he said to me,
Can you see it; can you see it true?
And I saw it—a black fire burning blue.
My heart is lost, he said to me,
It's lost out there upon the sea,
Will you find it; will you bring it back?
I cannot go for what I lack.
The more I swam, the keener the light,
The more it called, a fire upright,
But when I turned and saw the shore
The man I'd met was there no more.
I found his heart and in it slipped,
The brine was rising; the tidal tip,
It tipped and fell and drew me on
To where the keeper's soul had gone;
There you are, the blazing flame
It was you all along—I know your name,
The light, the light, it burns for us;
His ghost, and mine, dissolved in dust.

XI

.

1972

THE KEEPERS OF THE
DEEP-SEA LIGHT

48

He went to visit the birds on Friday, every Friday, before the sun came up. He climbed the hill, it was difficult in the dark, and unlatched the gate. The sound of the gate as it unlatched—*click*—was like a match being struck, and that's how the sun knew when to come up. The sun would say, Arthur's here, he's lit the candle: it's time.

It was a hostile path if you didn't know it well. Divots and grooves lay in wait; tufts of overgrown grass, bleached and dried during the long hot summer, scratched his bare legs. He'd sooner have worn trousers, but it was time and motion, his father said; he had to be dressed for school.

When he got there, Mrs. McDermott would make an example of him: "The state of you, Arthur Black; you look as though you've been dragged through a hedge backward." Sometimes in the rush down to the primary his laces unraveled, he tripped and scuffed his knee, or a tree branch snagged his blazer. There'd be a splash of bird shit on his shoe. The children called him Bird Boy. He didn't mind. Being high above the sea, the gulls cooing and warbling in the soft shadows of the rafters, was all he desired, the kind of contentment that sat in his hand like a paperweight.

At lunch, when the other boys were flicking custard at one another and slipping baked beans up their noses, Arthur thought of the birds. On the sports field when Rodney Carver thrust into him with a rugby ball and hissed, "Go on then, you scrawny-arsed girl," he'd have visions of their wings diving down from the hillside, a cloud descending on Rodney and the despotic PE teacher, whose pale, freckled, hairless legs visited Arthur in dreams like the left-behind pork rind of his mother's Sunday roast.

With the birds he wasn't lonely. Sometimes he sketched them, watching their bodies shuffle awkwardly over each other, feathers shivering, pellets of crap splashing on wood. The smell was of deep, unused cupboards and the faint tang of meat paste.

When his father had first shown him the coop—"Come on, tuppence, do you want to see something clever?"—Arthur had staggered with him up the hill. "They get better," he'd said, "then they fly away." Nobody knew why the birds fell from the sky. Arthur found them outside the front door or among the yew berries in the garden, their wings slapping the ground. His father woke him in the night: "Look, lad, quiet now, gently now, see . . ." The twilight mystery of his father's cupped palms and the quivering body inside: its heart thrumming, exquisitely vulnerable and soft.

Loneliness hardened in Arthur's stomach. At home each room was silent except for the ticking of a mantel clock. His mother drifted about half asleep while her husband tinkered with watches in a back room, slowly growing myopic. He couldn't recall what his father had been like before the war—lighter in the shoulders, softer in his smile; now his old claws scratched, leaving blood on the bedsheets. The house woke at four in the morning to a sharp cry, like a chair being scraped from a table.

Frequently he could feel his loneliness: he could locate it with his fingers and if he pushed too hard, it hurt. If he ate quickly, it hurt. He drank a lot of water, to flush it out, but it never came. He kept expecting to see it after he'd visited the lavatory. Small and blue. Afraid. He did not know what he would do with it. He did not know what he would do without it.

The sun arrived as a smelted line, fierce orange, throwing kindling across the sea. Arthur detected the lighthouse from here, a yellow eye peeling soundlessly open.

At school he learned about the tower. He found it incredible that men lived on there, a family of three, and this seemed to him the answer, for he'd never be lonely again, then, with two others who couldn't get off. While the boys in class put up their hands to answer questions about shipwrecks and the engineer Stevensons, melancholy sanded a nook in his heart. The lighthouse reached for him in a way that was indescribable, yearning, as if it were sad and it needed him.

He learned about sailors drowning on tooth-sharp rocks, swaying masts by the hunter's moon, the metallic chime of a death bell, vomit spraying, shit stinking, merchants' bellows as their stocks sank and those on land waited for riches to drift into shore. He read *Treasure Island* and thought it marvelous that a storyteller and a lighthouse builder could be part of the same family. He learned about the men who erected the sea towers, how a lot of them died, how they worked on half-sunk slabs miles from land, blown sideways by crosswinds, their hands salt splintered, fixing blocks to watch them wash away, or, once finished, to witness years of toil topple on a high sea. Nobody ever admired their work because nobody ever went there.

On his eleventh birthday, he saw the white bird. It was larger than the rest. It flew in off the sea, as pure as snow, and looked at him with a pinkish eye.

Later, he asked his father, who said, A dove? Arthur said, No, not a dove. What then? I don't know. His father went to look. When he came back, he told Arthur that there was no white bird, what a bloody imagination, you don't get birds like that out here. But I saw it. 'Course you did. Now go get me my matches, there's a good lad.

49

I explained to you about light and how it works. How it isn't just a question of light and dark, there are spaces in between, and those spaces, the shape and size of them, matter more. Your mother wasn't listening. She stood at the sink, her hands in the washing-up, limp on the surface in their rubber gloves like daffodils with the heads hanging off.

Night drew in and we went outside. I kept you warm in my coat; the crown of your head, your hair freshly washed, gleamed in the moonlight. I put the palm of my hand across it to see how neatly those two shapes fitted. Parts of the body slot together when two bodies belong, a chin for a hand, the crook of an elbow a home for a head.

We went to the shore where we could hear the waves and jostling shingle. I passed you the torch. My coat was big on you, the sleeves covering your fingers. We rolled up one of the sleeves and the wrist that protruded was like a bone discovered in soil, shocking white. The torchlight cut a path through the sea, bright close to shore, then conceding defeat as it chased the night further than was safe to go.

The character of the Maiden is fixed. Its beam is constant. I showed you how to keep the torch still and steady, shining it back, as the Maiden did for those ships at sea.

"The keepers will be able to see your light," I said. "Just as you can see *theirs." You said it was funny to think that your light could be seen miles away, but that was the thing about light, I said, you don't need a lot of it. The other way round, a sliver of dark in a sunny garden, you'd never spot it, the light's stronger and quicker and the eye goes looking for it. If you think of the world like that, it doesn't seem as bad a place.*

We switched the light off and with it the sea.

On again and the sea returned.

The moon was waning gibbous, a mint half sucked. The night seemed gentle to me then, with you by my side. First, we made the light periods short and the dark periods long, on for three seconds, off for nine, that was called a flashing. Then if you reversed it and made the light last longer than the dark, that was called occulting.

You enjoyed those words and repeated them. I told you some people say "occulting" with the emphasis on the "occ" and others say it with the emphasis on the "ult." If I were out on the tower now, I said, I'd be able to see your light, sending out a signal from here on land, fixed then flashing, then occulting, then fixed.

I'd know it was you from every single thing about it, I'd just know it was your light, I would. You made being ashore good. There wasn't much else about it, but you.

Arthur woke with a start, the black night close. Thick wafts of dream floated dumbly to the surface. Only it wasn't night, it was morning. Eight thirty. It was the curtain that made it dark. He drew it and saw Bill in the bunk opposite. Christmas Eve.

He held his hands in front of him, palms turned upward, as if in offering for his life, something loaf sized, a newborn baby. Memories or inventions, he could no longer tell them apart. When he shut his eyes, visions of Tommy remained. Hazel eyes. An outstretched hand. Where did his boy go in these halfway hours?

Frequently, when alone, he heard it. A tap of footsteps. A rustle in a dark corner. A scrape down deep in the store when the others were asleep, but when Arthur reached it, he could only stand there confused, like an elderly man at a bus shelter.

◼

Vince was at the window, looking back to shore.

"What are you waiting for?"

"Nothing."

Arthur judged how the young man's size and strength compared with his own, the long legs, the wide back, but there must be a weak point, if nothing more than the element of surprise. He put the television on; there was a piece on the one o'clock news about Ghaffar Khan. When Arthur moved, when he talked, it was as though in the strangle of a deep sleep. He felt inexpressibly heavy and withdrawn.

"What'd you be doing at home?" asked Vince.

"Wrapping presents. *Carols from King's*. It isn't what it used to be."

"No. 'Course not. Sorry. I was forgetting."

"I don't expect you to remember."

"But I should."

"I'd rather you didn't. Anything else on?"

"Some Davy Crockett pile o' shite. Tea?"

"I'm going fishing."

"Fishing?" said Vince. "It's freezing."

"Christmas tradition," Arthur said. Not that it was or ever would be.

The point was not to catch anything, the point was to sit and look. Ripples lapped beneath the dog steps. A chill darted into his coat. Shapes curled out of the mist, distorted and divided. He could feel the thing looking back at him now, intently, invisibly. It could come at him from anywhere, across the water or down from the sky. He didn't know when that would be.

The sea smoldered, gray wisps playing over the surface. Looking up, he saw the tower was decapitated at the kitchen, with the fog gun sounding in the cloud.

Arthur heard a patter behind him, of lightly running footsteps, as in a game of hide-and-seek. *Patpatpatpatpat.*

He turned. Nobody there.

He was imagining too much these days.

The footsteps came again. *Patpatpatpatpat.*

A tinkle of laughter: a child.

Arthur put down his line and followed the curve of the set-off, right the way round until he was back where he started. The laughter skipped in and out of the mist, muted one second, then ringing the next. A giggle.

Wait, he said, light-headed. Round and round. The fishing line dissolved and so did the door, nothing to mark where the circle was complete, and it occurred to Arthur that a circle had no start or finish, of course it didn't, it just went on forever. One hand on the tower, the other in front, thinking at any moment he'd touch it.

What? A shirt collar. An elbow. Skin.

Wait, he said. Wait.

He stopped and listened, so the footsteps could catch up with him. Unsure which of them was running to find and which to escape. He advanced, the steps seeming by now too fast altogether, too fast to be contained on the warp of the set-off, too fast not to have come up on him already and rushed straight past. He tripped and fell and caught hold of an eyebolt, legs thrown and dangling over the sea. The gun blasted, high above. No one would hear him.

He felt for the safety line and dragged himself up.

Laughter pealed, tantalizingly near.

Hey!

A dry cough. A cat with a hair ball.

Hey!

Arthur blinked.

He hauled himself to sitting and held the fishing rod. Immediately there was a tug: a youngster pulling a lock of hair. It tugged again, jerking him forward.

The line was taut. He drove his weight against it; it was heavy, and grew heavier with every wrench, the line stretched to snapping, but now he was bringing it up, and for a second it felt as though he were winning because there it was, a shape floating to the surface of an uncertain, mist-bathed sea, just as his dream had that morning, a shape horribly familiar to him and yet unknown. It was a shark, after all—but the dreadfulness of it was distorted by the mist and of course it was not a shark, and he wished to drop his line but a grim compulsion made this impossible, rooting him to the spot only to sit and see, as he had come out here to do, his eyes flinching from the sight but retained by the force of malign curiosity.

I've caught not a fish but my boy.

I've hooked him in his cheek.

The line broke. The boy took it with him, down, and disappeared in the murk: the surface parted and came together without comment and all that was left was the mirror madness of the father's desperation, looking down, his face twisted and strange.

50

The *Spirit of Ynys* had brought a turkey crown from the mainland and a bottle of red wine, which did along with tinned vegetables and a jug of Bisto gravy. No Christmas pudding, instead a can of spotted dick. Bill was cook. He chain-smoked over the pans.

Arthur pushed his food away. The more he watched Bill through the curling smoke, the louder it got: the sound of fingernails on plaster. Sometimes the scratching sounded very close to him, as if it could be on him or inside him.

"Can you hear that?"

"Hear what?" said Vince.

Afterward, in the living room, Vince found an *Old Grey Whistle Test*. Four men in a band called Focus, one on a keyboard singing in a high-pitched voice. At the end they sang "Merry Christmas and a Happy New Year."

They watched the Queen's Speech. Twenty-five years married to Philip; Britain about to join the European Economic Community; the Troubles in Northern Ireland. Patience and tolerance were more vital now than ever, she said, in families as well as nations.

Arthur judged his nation of three. Private thoughts infected him.

He wondered that it was possible to be so full of something that was not apparent to other people.

*

The others claimed the forecast was wrong. There was no storm on the way: Bill was going to be fine for his relief. Arthur's head hurt. It had hurt for a week. It was hard to remember things he had done and things he had said. Not being able to worried him.

The mist had lifted. Through his binoculars, he saw land in the distance, boats, smudges of houses. He thought his wife could be staring back; they'd be signaling to each other without ever knowing.

He hoped Helen was happy; he hoped she found happiness.

It hadn't been fair to marry her. He shouldn't have married anyone.

He went down to the kitchen, because if he was away it might come, then. It might come when his back was turned, as it had in the fog, when he wasn't paying attention, just as he hadn't been paying attention on the day he'd lost his boy.

Arthur filled a cup with water, then ascended to the bedroom, where Bill and Vince were sleeping. He stood for a minute, maybe longer, in the doorway. He held the water like someone who had been asked to bring it but who hovered, uncertain, until invited to come forward.

The pain in his head was sharp. Piano keys played in the wrong order.

Hey!

Footsteps ran up the staircase.

Patpatpatpatpat.

When he got up to the lantern, it was only a bird. A shearwater, wings on glass. It had found its way in through an open window. He let it fly about for a bit, hurting itself. Then he opened the door to the gallery and went back downstairs.

✖

Darkness fell after four. The moon was so huge he could see its craters. A full moon: a bad omen. There was a connection between those cosmic things—the moon, the tides, the winds—that amounted to an equation, the closest man could witness to the signature of God. Arthur could not believe that a human had been there; a human foot with blisters and bunions and toenails in need of cutting had felt the moon's surface beneath and it was real, as real as the dust. Before science they believed that stars were holes in the floor of heaven.

The wind stirred. A keeper he had worked with on the Longships used to say the stays out here wouldn't be as bad if you knew you could rely on your relief. If you could get ashore when you were meant to, that'd make it better. You could look forward to it without it getting moved at the last minute and messing around with you.

Arthur had invited the weather. The storm he'd inscribed in the log, writing it every day, summoning it into being by sheer force of will.

Later, when they found the journal, they would say that he had lost his mind. He was frail, unable, defective; he'd be better off abandoning the service. Better off at home with a wife who didn't love him and every time he looked at her, he would see the face of their dead child and of the man she had betrayed him for.

Arthur had prided himself on his thirty years' service. When he'd been given Principal Keeper, his noblest award, he'd pledged to wear the regimentals every day. Clean-shaven, shoes shined, it was a matter of dignity, his long-service stripes. People said, "It can't do you any good, Arthur, doing that job, it can't do you any good after Tommy; you should be with Helen, that's where you should be, at home, with her," but the light was the only place he had left. Being here had saved his soul, but his head was gone away now, he knew, as if he'd left the house with it still hanging on the key hook.

※

Do you remember walking over the fallow field? I held your hand, soft and damp. We watched the swallows dive and soar. Sunset light. I loved you.

※

His reflection in the mirror was alarming. The pouches under his eyes had grown hard. His expression was not his own. His beard had grown full without him noticing, and the noises in his head grew louder by the hour.

Outside, in the dark, he drew the sea toward him.

The wind blew a warning, up, up; from the bottom boulder rising a black and twisted thing, waiting always, ready now.

51

Arthur woke cleanly, like a swimmer breaking the surface. The wind was deafening. Around and everywhere the sea thrashed, sucking and slapping the granite, sending up whorls of spray. With the shutters closed the air inside was fetid and stifling, deathly cold, stinging the nostrils. His head felt clear, his thoughts transparent.

Boxing Day. Bill wasn't going anywhere.

Arthur heard it again. He moved out of bed and went downstairs, down around the sweating inner wall, down into the weather, down into the sea.

His wife never understood why he continued to abide the water— but he saw no point in hating the place where their son had gone. For her, the sea had killed Tommy, his body brought back and burned, the ashes kept in a box. Arthur didn't think a boy should be kept in a box, a five-year-old who in life had never been still for a minute. Instead he was here, in the ocean, where he would wash from north to south, from east to west. He would shimmer in the morning sun and dance circles in the twilight.

Helen said, How can you stand it, I don't know how you can bloody *stand* it, and he never knew how to reply. To reply that this was where Tommy was, that he felt him here, would have hurt her. So he said nothing. And she turned in bed, and Arthur thought of the neighbor lights he would see on middle watch, their reassuring company, reminding him that another man had his eyes open somewhere not far away.

If he'd said: *When I'm there, our son's not alone. He waits for me when I'm ashore, with you; he wants me back, his daddy.* If he'd said that, she would have hit him, because Tommy was hers more than his. She didn't know how Tommy's death cry haunted him. It would never leave him. It was crusted in the stars and molten in the water; the dancing fire at dusk and the instant at dawn when he pinched the wick to black.

Arthur put a hand on the banister. When he took it away it left a misty print, shrinking and vanishing.

Nothing survived. Nothing was permanent. All was lost in the depths.

The entrance door, when he reached it, was as cold as his rocks. There was hardly an instant between feeling the marks and knowing their origin. Fingernails on the locking bar. Trying to get out or trying to get in.

52

The storm worsened. White lather spumed on top of mounting waves. The wind dashed and bawled. Thunder ground across the flashing vault.

Arthur climbed the stairs to the lantern. The walls dripped condensation. He expected to find it too, on his own skin, as if there were no space between his body and the building that contained it, but when he touched his cheek it was dry and warm.

Vince's watch ended. His began. He loaded the charges and the detonator tore into the cyclone, shouting a warning that was split by the wind. Waves toppled, crests broke, spindrift flew from the chaotic surface. Bolts of light cracked the churning dark, the sea black, the heavens black, the ocean heaping and foaming. His tower trembled against the onslaught, foam exploding from her base to her lamp.

Arthur closed his eyes and imagined falling forward. The thought of drowning did not frighten him.

A dart of lightning shot into the sea.

For an instant, the waves illuminated. Arthur thought he saw the boat. He couldn't be sure until there was another clap and there it was: a flailing vessel.

Tiny. Wooden. A torn sail.

He heaved open the door to the gallery, blown back by wind and rain, and threw himself against the rail. It was a simple craft, a rowing boat, lifted and smashed on the swell.

Stay clear!

His words were snatched by the gale. A burst of radiance and the boat reappeared. The oarsman came into sight and what he'd believed before he now knew.

Down the stairs, gripping the rail, his feet unable to keep up with his need to meet that sailor face-to-face. But before he had a chance to reach it, three floors down he heard the entrance door bang.

Patpatpatpatpat.

Coming toward him, up, up, childish laughter.

Hey!

Arthur turned on his heel. He lost the footsteps somewhere past the living room and it was only later, much later, that he went back down to look and saw the marks left there, not shoes but a bare sole, a little violin, and five dots for toes.

53

By Friday the wind was dead, the rain soft now but constant. Bill radioed the mainland.

"Can you get someone out?" His lips were scabrous, the skin around his fingernails torn. Sixty-one days on the tower.

"Not possible, Bill, it's heavy back here."

Arthur stood behind him, observing from the doorway.

Bill turned. A gloss of sweat shone on his brow, in spite of the cold.

"All right," he said. "Let's do it tomorrow."

"Right you are, Bill, we'll get someone out for you in the morning."

Arthur thought, He thinks I've got it in me to hurt him.

He would have every reason, he knew, to hurt Bill. But then he thought of the rowing boat. The small head piloting it and the hand lifted in hello.

I see you.

Arthur wasn't made of that and never had been. He could make a fist but not use it, however much he might like to.

Bill paused in the transmission. One day. One night. One more.

"OK," he said, and there was another beat, a longer one, during which he hung his head and closed his eyes. The line pipped. "Over and out."

54

A rthur, wake up. Wake up."
      He opened his eyes. The bedroom was a wormhole in outer space, soft blue interior, scattered with stars. Bill stood next to his bunk. Even in the gloom, because of the gloom, he saw his mate's worried face, the sockets deep and the glint of his irises.

"Wake up," said Bill again.

"What is it?"

Bill's voice was hoarse. Hardly a whisper.

"Something's happened."

"What?"

"He's gone."

"Bill."

"Vince. He's gone. Just now. He's gone."

Arthur peered at those ink-bright eyes.

"Bill," he said, "you're dreaming."

"I'm not."

"You're not making sense."

"Are you?"

"Bill—"

"Are you awake?"

"Sit down. You're walking in your sleep."

"He's dead," said Bill. "Vince. He's gone. Just now."

"I'll get him."

"I saw."

"I'll get him. I'll show you."

"I couldn't," said Bill. "I tried."

"Wait."

"We were outside. It came from nowhere."

"Sit down, Bill."

"It came from nowhere."

"Sit down."

"Vince was shouting. I couldn't—"

"I'll get him."

"I tried. But the sea."

"It can't—"

"He's gone. The sea. He's gone."

Arthur heard the soothing wind and the gentle surge of the water. He could not hear music from a cassette player, or smell cigarette smoke.

His feet met the floor; he pulled on his trousers and sweater. He knew it was too late, but that was the thing: what happened on his tower was his cross to bear.

Behind him, in the pit of the bedroom, Bill lifted an object from the cupboard. There was a sliver of time in which Arthur turned his head and realized what that was, and a series of thoughts ran through his mind, one after the other. He thought of his father leading him up the grass-knotted hill, the soft ferns against his bare legs, the warble and shuffle of the gulls in the rafters. He thought of the sea glowing yellow at sunrise, of nebulous clouds tinged with pink. He thought of the

first lighthouse he had been stationed on at Start Point, and the keepers there, older than him, with their throaty laughs and sour-smelling
pipes, climbing the iron staircase and grinding their fags out with the
hard pads of their thumbs. He thought of Helen on their wedding day,
of kissing her; her telling him they were going to have a baby and the
joy he'd felt when she had. He thought of Tommy, always his, the
light that never lowered. He thought of the thousands of times he had
put a candle on the sea and the many sailors who'd steered their ships
by it. He thought how sorry he was for what happened to them, his
wife, his friend, now and in the past, and for never being able to make
it up to her.

He thought what a shame it was for it to end this way, in loss and
confusion, because he had made mistakes and he wasn't the man he'd
been. Arthur had liked loneliness, but in the end, loneliness hadn't
liked him; it had done things to him that took parts of him away and
it wasn't enough to be on this island, after all. There was an instant in
which he realized what object Bill had picked up, what Bill intended to
do with it, before he opened the door and the bar of sedimentary rock
collided with the back of his head.

55

Bill hadn't meant for Vince to drown. But once Vince had drowned, the rest seemed straightforward.

Jenny always told him that he never stood up for himself. His father had said the same. Bill would have liked to stand up to his father. He'd have liked to put his hands around the old bastard's throat—his hands or his belt, the old bastard's belt—and squeeze.

He lifted the PK's body from the bedroom and dragged it downstairs. It was heavy; he had to switch to hauling him over his shoulder and carrying him that way, like a soldier in the trenches, saving another man's life.

He had never seen Arthur's feet. The nails were cut short, the toes smattered with hair. Poor fool hadn't had time to put his socks on.

In the hall at home, above the shrine of his mother, there'd been a ship's clock with *Carpe Diem* stamped across the top. Bill thought of her smile, her admiring eyes.

Helen's smile. Helen's eyes.

He reached the kitchen. Threw his burden to the table. Blood smeared across the laminate top, trickling from a now indistinguishable place—the smash in the PK's nose, his split eye and temple, but those injuries were lost amid the mess of blood and bone. Bill saw he had done more than was necessary, but he'd had to make sure.

Adrenaline made him strong. His heart beat wildly; his breath was ragged, stimulated, the oxygen fresh. His hands before him were stained the color of iodine. It impressed him how effectively his mind was working, how sharp were his thoughts. In the morning, the relief boat would come. Bill would explain. No one could blame him for these tragedies, and no one could hold him accountable for what he did later, once Jenny had calmed, once it was deemed acceptable to go after a dead man's wife.

How could his marriage be expected to survive? How could he be expected to return unchanged? There would be no expectations. For the first time: none.

Bill wiped the PK's hands and then his own. He cased his own fingers in gloves, then lifted the clock from the wall and set it ahead, to eight forty-five, the time of the son's demise. Helen had told him that on the settee at Masters, when she'd turned up one day asking for Jenny. Jenny had been out, so Bill had made tea and listened while she talked and cried. She told him everything, right down to the detail. Eight forty-five in the morning. In the end, to kiss her was the only kind thing.

Arthur was leaving his signature. It was as close to an admission as they'd get.

Bill put the batteries back the wrong way round. He pressed Arthur's fingertips to the places he had touched. Then he climbed two floors to the living room, where he changed the clock there, switched the points, and took it back down for the same.

Now he stood over Arthur's body, thinking what to do with it. It was hard to believe this was the man who'd made Bill feel so small. The master PK: felled like a tree.

Wiping the table relaxed him. Bill cleaned its top, its sides, its underside, the chair, and the marks on the floor. He didn't hurry; he took his time. He rinsed the blood down the sink and then he cleaned the sink, and then he balled the cloth into a fist and threw it out the window into the sea. Next he lifted two plates from the dresser, stepping over the PK in order to do so, and two sets of cutlery from the drawer. Again, he knelt to brush Arthur's hands over these items before setting them all on the table, with two cups, salt and pepper, and a nearly-done tube of mustard.

The jar of sausages was a conceit. Arthur told him once that sausages had been Tommy's favorite. Bill didn't need to incorporate the detail, but he did because it made him feel diligent. Attentive. All the things a good lighthouse keeper should be.

With the kitchen stage set, he made tea in the PK's mug and took it up to the living room, where he sat in the PK's chair and thought about the PK's wife.

Helen deserved happiness. She would be happy after this. Bill vowed to spend the rest of his days chasing down her happiness, and when he found it, he'd nail it to the bed where they made love every night and he'd never let her go.

How deep would Vince be now? How far down? Bill had the faint concern the SAK's body would wash up, but it didn't really matter if it did. He had his story. They'd have no reason to disbelieve it. Arthur had lost his senses, killed his Supernumerary, and meant to kill Bill too. There had been no other way but for Bill to defend himself.

He was sorry, he'd tell them, for the old-timer, he was; he'd liked Arthur, and it had been a shock, what he'd turned into and what he'd become.

56

Vincent Bourne ought to have died many times before he did. He ought to have died when he was born, due to the umbilical cord getting wrapped around his neck and the midwife who delivered him not noticing until he was blue. When he was four and living with the Richardsons, he'd walked out into the road in front of a car and the car had swerved at the last minute. At fifteen he'd fallen off a twenty-foot wall, breaking his arm.

All these episodes in his life adding up to the eventual payback: his number called on this particular date at that particular time.

He'd been smoking on the set-off when it caught him. Not a boat with Eddie Evans or a mechanic with an alias. None of the things he had convinced himself of.

The air was crisp. The sea pitched on, rinsing the boulders and rocks. Today, the world felt good.

He allowed himself to believe it was over. That, perhaps, there was no one out to get him. Nothing to be afraid of. The future lay ahead. Michelle wouldn't care what he'd done; she knew him; she wasn't going anywhere. Relief and lightness touched his soul. Happiness, he supposed.

Bill came down, looking carsick. Vince offered a fag, but the Assistant said no.

"I should give up," Bill said.

Vince lifted an eyebrow. "That'll be the day."

What happened was simple—insultingly simple for a moment that took a man's life. Vince flicked the butt and it landed on the set-off instead of in the water. He went to the edge to scuff it in, when very quickly the sea foamed up, as sudden as boiling milk in a pan. The tower seemed to sink, momentarily, like a dunked biscuit; then it came up again and the sea fell away. Vince fell with it, smacking his elbow, then his head. He thought, Shit, and tried to hold on, but there was nothing to hold on to. His head was leaking blood, making it difficult to see or concentrate. The water sucked him down over the concrete, and when the concrete was lost there were only the waves.

His muscles seized. His ears rang. The tower was gone: how could it be that he'd just been standing there, and now it was beyond reach?

All he could think of was Michelle. Her mouth, her arms, how it felt to go into them and rest his face in the soft, sweet hollow of her neck.

He lost the strength in his legs and the sea was pushing him farther out.

Bill was shouting. Vince shouted back, but he didn't know what he was shouting, if they were words he was using or a different noise he had never made before.

57

B ill drank his tea, sitting in the PK's chair. It wasn't that he had disliked Vince. Liking had nothing to do with it. It had simply been too good a chance to pass up, so he hadn't. Vince's death was an exit sign. A way out. A parachute in a nosedive.

What he'd told Arthur was true. He *had* tried. When he had seen Vince in the waves, he'd thrown a rope across the water. It had been a weak throw, admittedly—too far for the Supernumerary to be able to catch it. Then it had dawned on him that he didn't have to throw very well. Not if he didn't want to.

Vince had fought awhile and it was then that Bill had decided, as coolly and evenly as he decided to get rid of one of his shells. When he knew it was one he could do without. He dropped the rope into the sea, and stood, impassive, watching his comrade drown.

❋

Tomorrow the men who came would say, Yes, we see it now, oh hell, what an unfortunate business. But Trident House would choose to keep it quiet. They would award Bill a prize for his bravery, promoting him quickly to another light.

Months on, he would leave the service and take Helen with him. He would marry her. They would move away from the sea.

Possibly he would tell her the truth, one day. Possibly he wouldn't. It depended how upset she was; how pleased she was that he was the one who had lived.

58

A noise from downstairs made him startle.

Bill doubted whether he had heard it, but then it came again:

Patpatpatpatpat.

Far below, way below.

He took a hardback from the living room bookcase—*Prehistoric Man* by J. Augusta and another faded name. The PK would be addled; that ought to do it.

You're a stupid boy, he heard his father say. *Check, don't assume. I knew you'd cock this up.*

Bill went down to the bedroom, his back to the wall, round and down, but when he reached the kitchen Arthur was lying exactly where he'd left him.

Hey!

He turned. "Who's there?"

His voice echoed down the spiral.

"Who's there?"

Patpatpatpatpat.

He descended, the book held high, telling himself it was the wind. When he reached the entrance level, he felt reassured. The door was closed as it had been.

The only person on this tower was him.

Still, he checked the gunmetal and shook the bolts across as far as they would go, before securing the locking bar. He resolved not to open it again until there was somebody living on the other side.

⚜

Evening arrived, though it was close after four. The day swam beyond the horizon.

In spite of what happened, the light was put in as it always was.

Bill was the last man alive. Sometimes, on middle watch, he would pretend this was true. That everyone on the planet had perished. He would turn the transmitter off so he could no longer hear the ships talking to each other and he'd sit with his back to the shore lights.

The Maiden glowed steadily, a head torch in a mysterious cave. Bill had been caving once, at school, and recalled the tight passages and claustrophobia. They had been roped to each other's waists, slithering through oily warrens like babies about to be born. The caves had seemed organic, like intestines. All it took was for one of them to lose his head. He'd banged his shoulder, fear surging, thinking he could neither breathe nor move, before a shove from behind splurged him into an echoless chamber and the worst was in knowing the only way out was back the way they'd come.

⚜

Rigor set in and Arthur's corpse stiffened. Hauling it up four floors nearly finished him.

Next to Bill in the lantern, the Principal Keeper's body was a shadow bulk, mountains at dusk in winter. It was fitting to keep a companion for these last hours, before doing what had to be done. By the time morning came, Bill would be shaken but coherent. He had never been creative—*an unimaginative boy*—but this wouldn't take much elaboration.

First, he would show them the clocks. The meal for the dead son. Then he would show them the log. Years, Arthur had been living and dying out here on this rock, slowly losing his mind. It was bound to get to a bloke, after all. Couldn't put up with it, sick and tired of it, sick to death of it, the lights, the bloody lights.

Ashore, they would marvel at how Bill had survived.

What a tale it would be, and Bill Walker its hero; it would be passed down through generations like the tale of the keepers at Smalls.

⬛

Through the night he polished every surface, as if preparing the tower for burial. He scrubbed and scoured each step between the kitchen and the lantern, every inch that Arthur's body had touched. No mark or blemish escaped the scrutiny that only lighthouse keeping had taught him. Bill left no trace.

Downstairs, he worked swiftly; he did not like to linger long in that underbelly, soft with shadows and the mystical shapes of dinghy and rope. He did not like to think of the noises he had heard or the laughter, the whispers that circled, imagined, just imagined, a product of the task and the aloneness. He could not open that door.

From Arthur's cabinet, he collected the rocks. Many times, he had seen the PK lean over them. It seemed fitting that their weight should now carry him down.

Bill took a dozen and left the rest. Nestled among the ones he'd chosen was Helen's silver anchor. There it was, then. Arthur had claimed it back for himself. Bill smiled, fastening the chain around his neck.

59

Tonight, the light burned beautiful. Across the sea the Maiden lantern dispatched her beam, smoothing a path through which ships could pass without fear.

The air was crisp, stinging his lungs. It was difficult getting Arthur into the overcoat, the arms locked, his joints dense and awkward to manipulate. Bill rested the Principal Keeper on the gallery rail. He packed his four pockets with stones.

One push would be all it took. Bill thought of Helen at home, going to bed, unaware that in the morning her life would begin again.

He drove his weight against the man on the bar and leaned as hard as he could.

Hey!

Running footsteps, a child's laughter.

Patpatpatpatpat.

A jolt from behind. Bill grunted, knocked off balance. Footsteps came at him from every direction. Whispers. A whistle. Then another blow, shunting him forward.

Alarmed, Bill gripped Arthur's body. Horror stole his breath, and whether it was that alone that joined them or a thing he could not name, he had no time to think, for next the weight of the dead man dropped, and dragged him over the rail.

White wall sped past, ghostly, everlasting. Arthur's body fused to his, and together they smashed into the cold, liquid dark.

Briefly Bill lost consciousness; he sliced his leg and hit his head. His ears flooded with blood and terror and water. Over and over, he thought, No, this isn't it, pointlessly, over and over. Arthur's mass drew him down, while Bill rolled in a surfeit of fear, his legs thrashing and fighting, and the more he thrashed and fought, the more the sea engulfed him. Blood filled his nose and mouth; it seemed to fill his head.

In desperation, in shock and regret, he gripped the keeper who kept him. Arthur was Bill's guardian, the man he had always wanted to be.

In the dark, in the dim, from a distance the scuffle resembled a flock of gannets scrapping over fish entrails. Agitation on the surface, a few muffled cries. Nothing to hear but seals calling sadly for each other.

Through the mist of Bill's drowning, there came a boat, its captain leaning over, his hand outstretched.

In a glow it arrived, a lamp-bearing wanderer down a long tunnel. Its sail was windless and torn. The hand that came to them was small.

Arthur's touch left him and the cold bit him like an apple. The boat took Arthur in, warm, home; Bill clawed for it, but it had not come for him.

On the lighthouse gallery, a hundred feet up, the metal door blew closed. A white bird circled the top of the tower before heading out to sea.

XII

·

1992

END POINT

60

HELEN

After Christmas was done with, she traveled down to Cornwall for the anniversary.

It was an English afternoon, the sky the color of Tupperware and the sea mixed up in grays and browns. Rain fell steadily, soaking ditches that were thick and mucky from autumn's slip into winter, steeped in leaf mold and blackened wood. She'd brought the dog this time, who sniffed earnestly for foxholes. Drops spat on the shell of her umbrella. In the trees, abandoned doves' nests fell apart, shards of ghostly eggshell glimmering among the moss.

Helen felt her bones inside her these days, aware of them as she started up the hill toward Mortehaven Cemetery—interlocking, blunt white, her rib cage like something prehistoric. The dog stayed close to her side, sensing her need for company.

How much longer could she make this trip? This could be the last. Twenty years was an arbitrary milestone anyway. It wasn't as though her husband would decide, it's been long enough now, that's a good round number; I ought to go home.

But still she came, just in case.

In case what?

The thirtieth of December, every year, she had to set eyes on the Maiden Rock, her partner in this peculiar birthday. Perhaps it was akin to keeping a wild animal in her living room, opening the door on it each day to make sure it knew she was still there. To leave it only bolstered its spars and gave it more strength than it deserved.

She doubted Jenny would come. At the ten-year mark, Helen had seen her from a distance, standing with the children, looking out to sea. She had thought about going over, but in the end had lost her nerve. Michelle hadn't appeared for that one or any of them, she didn't see the point and she wouldn't today. She would call Helen next week with the excuse that her husband hadn't wanted her to make the trip.

As they arrived at the cemetery, the wind filled her umbrella. She could hear the Atlantic Ocean as it crashed and spumed against mussel-crusted rocks, chucking up gusts of salt.

Helen knew where she was going, a headstone close to her husband's memorial bench. The epitaph on the grave was stippled with lichen:

JORY FREDERICK MARTIN, B.1921
CROSSED THE BAR 1990, DEARLY MISSED

She stood for several minutes, until the rain stopped.

Yellow bruises tinged the clouds, the sunshine weak but willing. She put down her umbrella. Two years ago, then, Jory had died. Helen hadn't known. In the time since the vanishing, the boatman had dipped in and out of her mind. Even though they'd been close in age, she had always felt toward him a motherly sort of gratitude. She supposed it was that he had been the first on the scene. He'd called for the lost keepers: later, he'd mourned them. Jory had been the longed-for relief, the rescuer who hadn't been able to rescue, the shout in the wind that never found a reply.

The dog went off, following a scent between gravestones. She felt someone come up behind her, and was so confident in who this was that she could have greeted him without turning, but she wanted to see his face.

"Hello," she said. She felt suddenly glad to be with another person.

The writer was wearing a red anorak and jeans, and shoes that had soaked up the rain. He had a canvas bag over his shoulder. His expression was chastened, a little apprehensive, as it dawned on him that she knew. It made sense to her now why he wasn't suited and polished. He was a boatman's son, had grown up tangled in nets.

"Why didn't you tell me?" she asked.

Dan Martin held a stone in his hand, smooth and pearlescent, with a white band across it, as fine as a cotton thread. He placed it on his father's grave.

"Dad thought for a long time it was his fault," he said. "That he should have done more for them. Got there quicker. Defied the weather. He couldn't have, but still."

"You should have told me."

"I thought you might blame him too."

"It never crossed my mind."

He put his hands in his pockets. "I'm sorry, Helen. I wanted you to talk to me without knowing who I was. Without changing what you told me or how you told it. As if I had nothing to do with it. I thought that would make it easier for you."

A moment passed between them so warm and close that she had to glance away, remembering all he knew about her that no one else did.

"I should have been honest," he admitted. "How did you find out?"

"You're not the only one interested in the truth."

He returned her smile.

"I couldn't pursue the story while Dad was alive. Entertained him instead with books about guns and frigates. I think he'd be pleased, though. He'd have wanted to talk to you himself."

Helen searched the horizon for the Maiden Rock, disguised by mist but intermittently reflecting a shy gleam of light.

"Twenty years," she said. "It feels different this time."

"How?"

"I'm not sure. It might be me who feels different. All this talk, I'm glad it's come out. I don't know if Jenny feels the same, or Michelle— she told me she'd decided to meet you in the end. But it's a curious thing. It brings that time back, but it also pushes it further out. It makes me see how many years have passed and what's changed in my life. I'm not the woman I was. People think I should be looking back with sadness, and I do have sadness and I always will. But it's long ago. It doesn't hurt as much now."

Dan hesitated. "I always pressed my father to talk about it," he said. "But he never did. It's one of those things: nobody knows what words to use."

"Any are better than nothing."

"Yes."

"And you do."

"What?"

"You know the words to use."

He faced her. His low, straight brow; his seafarer's eyes. He was so like his father.

"It was always inside me to write about Arthur and the others," he said. "The day they disappeared was the day my life changed. My family changed too. Dad never got over it. Neither did I. When I grew up, I tried to get a grip on the sea by putting it in my stories, but I never managed it, because this was the one that kept asking to be told. Mortehaven was never the same after they vanished. No one knew about our town before. No one associated us with loss, or haunting. Children had happy childhoods, then they grew up and moved away and brought their own kids back on the holidays to see the boats, and the Maiden Rock, and go crabbing on the quay. Afterward, they didn't."

"You couldn't accept there being no answer," said Helen.

"No. I couldn't."

"But there isn't one."

He unzipped his bag. "It hasn't stopped me searching," he said. "Over the years, I've asked anyone who'll listen. I've given the riddle: three keepers go missing off a lighthouse, what do you think happened to them?"

"What do *you* think happened to them?"

He pulled out a block of pages encased in a plastic sleeve, tied twice with rubber bands, intersecting in a cross.

"This is it," he said. "Your book."

"Mine?"

"And you were right, by the way. It didn't end up being the project I thought it was going to be."

"You're disappointed."

"No," he told her. "The opposite."

He peeled off the bands.

"It's strange to think there's no one out there." He walked over the stones to the edge of the headland. "That they're all automated. No more keepers. No reliefs, no overdues. I got near her again awhile back. We had the weather for it, so I thought, All right, Dad, just for you. There's an odd feeling about it now. There must be around all lighthouses, but in particular the towers. It's in knowing they're deserted. All that stonework, all that way away, with no one living inside. It's an eerie atmosphere. You'd think it held on to something, wouldn't you? When I went out there, it seemed like it did. Like it might."

"That Arthur could be there on the set-off," said Helen, "waving at you."

"There are people who still think they'll come back."

"I hope you're not one of them."

"Why not?"

"It's unrealistic."

"The subject itself is unrealistic."

"Even so."

"To think that they lived?"

"To think that they'd turn up after all this time." Helen stood next to him. "Arthur's gone. He's not coming back. You say you need answers, but I don't. I'm not sure I ever did. I need acceptance. Peace. Hope. It's taken twenty years, but I'm close."

He passed her the book. "Here."

It was heavy. "That's a lot of work."

"Yes," said Dan, "it was. I finished it. I know more than I did before. But as for knowing what happened on that tower, Helen, I'll never be certain of that. I'm not foolish enough to think that I might. There are a hundred endings, maybe there are more."

Helen looked down at his soggy shoes, at the rain-spattered manuscript, and it was on the tip of her tongue to thank him. She had said sorry to Arthur and that she loved him. She always had, through the worst of it, right to the end. Even if he never heard it, it was out there now and that seemed the most important thing of all.

"The truth is theirs," Dan said. "And yours. It isn't mine, or anyone else's."

The ocean air was raw and clean in her chest, as new as an early morning.

"We're not sure of the truth, are we," she said. "Isn't that the point? Some mysteries just aren't meant to be known. I'm talking about Arthur and the others, of course I am. But I'm talking about the rest of it too. You know. The rest. Why we do it. Why we strike a match. Why we built any lighthouses in the first place and every other thing you think on a good day might save a life. We're not the ones who decide, but we wouldn't be human if we didn't set these attempts in place. Put in as many lights as we can, while we're here. Get them shining bright. Keep them shining when the dark comes in."

He watched her.

"Go on then," he said.

"What?"

"You write the ending."

He took a sheaf of pages and threw them into the air.

"What are you doing?"

Papers soared recklessly against the wind, scores of them in flight, bursting wings of white brilliance against sky and sea, drifting and scattering and dancing down to the water.

Helen laughed in shocked exhilaration as she followed his lead, flinging sheet after sheet extravagantly, like lottery winners showered by banknote confetti.

She watched the pages disperse, gently rocking on the waves in every direction.

"Thank you, Helen."

The dog came back to her. Dan folded his bag and set off up the path.

As he reached the cemetery gate, Helen turned to see two figures standing beneath the yew. She would know them anywhere, like members of her family.

The writer stopped, to check she'd seen.

She dared to step closer, worried the women would disappear if she did.

But the nearer she drew, the clearer the vision became. Michelle's arm was linked through Jenny's, her expression soft and optimistic. Jenny looked the same as she always had. She hadn't grown old. People didn't, when you grew old beside them.

After a moment, Jenny raised her hand in hello.

Helen did the same.

Before she went to meet them, she turned to take one last look at the Maiden. The lighthouse was only the faintest line from here, a gray spike on a milk-green sea. The wind carried in; perhaps it had touched her face first, salt water on both, drying in the fledgling sun.

She knew the tower was empty, but her heart thought different. It always would. She could picture the Principal Keeper as clearly as if she were there; he was climbing the stairs, his face lifted to the light. Up to the lantern without touching the rail; further and further he traveled from the point of his dark descent, until all that was left, all that filled him, was a star almost done with its twinkling.

ACKNOWLEDGMENTS

I owe a debt of gratitude and admiration to the book *Lighthouse* by oral historian Tony Parker, whose interviews with lighthouse keepers and their families illuminated the way I wished to set about this novel and the telling of this tale. Parker's portrayal of a vanished way of life makes understood not just the occupation of lighthouse keeping but also the wisdom and humanity of those who dedicated their lives to the service.

Some of the anecdotes and experiences of life on a sea tower are based on recollections belonging to real keepers. For this insight into the hearts and minds of that community, I have the following memoirs and anthologies to credit: *Ceaseless Vigil* by William John Lewis, *It Was Fun While It Lasted* by A. J. Lane, *Stargazing* by Peter Hill, and the keepers' voices in *The Lighthouses of Trinity House* by Richard Woodman and Jane Wilson. I drew further inspiration from *The Lighthouse Stevensons* by Bella Bathurst, *Lighthouse Construction and Illumination* by Thomas Stevenson, *Henry Winstanley and the Eddystone Lighthouse* by Adam Hart-Davis, *Eddystone: The Finger of Light* by Mike Palmer, the *Lore* podcast episode "Rope and Railing" by Aaron Mahnke, and the poem "Flannan Isle" by Wilfrid Wilson Gibson.

Thanks to my brilliant editors Francesca Main, Andrea Schulz, and Iris Tupholme for their insight, intuition, and improvements to the manuscript; and to Sophie Jonathan for steering it so ably, and with such cleverness and kindness, out to sea. To the teams at Picador in the UK, Viking in the US, and HarperCollins in Canada for their enthusiasm and expertise, in particular Jeremy Trevathan, Camilla Elworthy, Katie Bowden, Katie Tooke, Laura Carr, Roshani Moorjani, Claire Gatzen, Nicholas Blake, Lindsay Nash, Carolyn Coleburn, Molly Fessenden, Lindsay Prevette, Kate Stark, Nidhi Pugalia, Sona Vogel, Bel Banta, Amanda Inman, Meighan Cavanaugh, Claire Vacarro, Tricia Conley, Sharon Gonzalez, Nayon Cho, Jason Ramirez, and Julia McDowell.

To my agent Madeleine Milburn and all at MMLA, especially Anna Hogarty, Liane-Louise Smith, Georgina Simmonds, and Giles Milburn. Maddy, you've known this story for as long as we've known each other. Much like the lighthouses when they were a glimmer in a Stevenson's eye, many drafts were built and fell, but we got our lantern shining in the end.

Mimi Etherington, Rosie Walsh, and Kate Reardon, thank you: I hope you know what for. I'm grateful to Kate Wilde, Vanessa Neuling, Caroline Hogg, Chloe Setter, Melissa Lesage, Jennifer Hayes, Joanna Croot, Emily Plosker, Chioma Okereke, Laura Balfour, Sarah Thomas, Jo Robaczynski, and Lucy Clarke for their friendship and support. Love to my sister Victoria, my nephew Jack, and my parents, Ian and Katharine, to whom this book is dedicated.

Thank you, Mark, for encouraging me toward my beloved lighthouse, in life and imagination. But most of all, to Charlotte and Eleanor, who are forever my brightest lights.